Gail Hamilt

A New Atmosphere

Gail Hamilton

A New Atmosphere

1st Edition | ISBN: 978-3-75232-806-6

Place of Publication: Frankfurt am Main, Germany

Year of Publication: 2020

Outlook Verlag GmbH, Germany.

A

NEW ATMOSPHERE

BY

GAIL HAMILTON

I.

VITIATED atmosphere is fatal to healthy development. One may be ever so wise, learned, rich, and beautiful, but if the air he breathes is saturated with fever, pestilence, or any noxious vapor, nothing will avail him. The subtile malaria creeps into his inmost frame, looks out from his languid eye, settles in his sallow cheek, droops in his tottering step, and laughs to scorn all his learning and gold and grandeur. He must rid himself of the malaria, or the malaria will rid itself of him.

There are many evils in the world, deep-seated and deleterious. I rejoice to see noble men and women working at the overthrow of these old Dagons; but the processes are many and long. Grievances are suffered which can be redressed only by the repeal of old and the enactment of new laws. Health suffers from ignorance which scientific discoveries, patient observation, and correct reasoning must dispel. Religion suffers from a narrowness and shallowness which broader and deeper culture must remove. Heaven send the laws, the science, and the culture, for these ills are indeed sore and of long continuance; but we need not wait upon the slow steps of law and science. Every man and woman can begin at this moment a renovation. Behind all law and all literature, the very air we breathe, the moral atmosphere not of books and benches only, but of kitchen and keeping-room, is impure and unwholesome. The interests of humanity demand a purification.

What I am going to say may have been said before; but if so, the present condition of things shows that it has been said to too little purpose. I have myself glanced at it askance, but I have never looked it square in the face. I have spoken ships bound to my port, but not freighted with my cargo. Success to them all! There is sea-room for every keel, and use for all their treasures. I am so far from claiming to be original, that I rather marvel there is any necessity for my being at all. The truths which I design to illustrate lie so on the surface that I should suppose they would commend themselves to the most casual notice. I can account for the obscurity which seems to enshroud them only by supposing that the days of Eli have reached down to us, and that there is no open vision. Therefore the truth needs to be repeated and repeated, in different forms and tones, if it is to be made effectual to the pulling down of strongholds. I will do my part of the reiteration. If I can state no new truths, I will at least help to ring the old truths into the ears of this generation till every unjust judge shall moan in bitterness of soul, "Though I fear not God nor regard man, yet, because these women trouble me, I will avenge them, lest by their continual coming they weary me."

In pursuance of my plan, it will be necessary for me sometimes to recur more than once to the same topic; but the repetition involved will be more apparent than real. It will be such repetition as the multiplication-table displays, whose first column gives you two times four, its third four times two, its fourth four times five, and so on to the end. You have the same figures, but in different combinations. I shall bring forward the same facts, but they will be presented under different lights, and will bear upon different conclusions.

I shall also, without hesitation, discuss topics on which I have spoken at former times, but without perceiving all their relations. No architect would reject stones which were necessary to the symmetry of his building because he had previously used them for other purposes.

I shall touch upon many and diverse themes; but nothing will be irrelevant. An atmosphere embraces the whole globe, and nothing human is foreign to it.

One person may not succeed in dispelling all the miasms of the earth, but if he can only cleanse one little corner of it, if he can but send through the murky air one cool, bracing, healthy gale, he will do much better than to sit under his vine, scared by the greatness of the evil and the dignity of those who support it.

II.

HE laws and customs regarding the education of girls and the employment of women may be wrong and difficult of righting; but a more elemental wrong, and one that lies within reach of every parent, is the coarse, mercenary, and revolting tone of sentiment in which girls are brought up and in which women live, entirely apart from their technical education and employment. I refer now to the refined and educated, as well as, and indeed more than, to the rude and illiterate, for it is their altitude which determines the level of all below. This tone of sentiment is such as to diminish girls' self-respect, mar their purity, and dwarf their being. They inhale, they imbibe, they are steeped in the idea, that the great business of their life is marriage, and if they fail to secure that they will become utterly bankrupt and pitiable. Naturally this idea becomes their ruling motive; all their course is bent to its guidance; and from this idea and this course of action spring crime, and sorrow, and disaster, "in thick array of depth immeasurable."

In this and in many other instances you will doubtless think that I overstate the truth. Looking into an empty bucket, you would say the air is colorless; looking into the depths of the atmosphere, you see that it is blue. I am not writing about a bucket, but about the atmosphere.

Viewing the circumstances which form women,

together with the women who are formed by them, one is filled with astonishment at the indwelling dignity and divinity of the womanly nature; and the thought can but arise, if a flower so fair can spring from a soil so badly tilled, what graceful and glorious growths might we not see did art but combine with nature to produce the conditions of the highest development! We lament heathendom, but much of our spirit is essentially heathenish. Little girls see in their geographies pictures of Circassian fathers selling their daughters to Turkish husbands, and they think it very inhuman and pagan. But, little girls, your fathers will traffic in you without scruple. Matters will not be managed in quite so business-like a fashion, but such a pressure will be brought to bear upon you that you will have very little more spontaneity than the Circassian slave who looks so pitiful in the geography book. At home you will hear yourself talked about, talked at, and talked to, in such a manner that you will have no choice left but to marry. It is expected and assumed. I do not mean girls who are to snatch their unhappy fathers from exposure and disgrace by a rich and hated marriage. Such things belong to ballads. We are dealing now with life. I have seen girls,—respectable, well-educated, daughters of Christian families, of families who think they believe that man's chief end is to glorify God and enjoy him forever, who profess to make the Bible their rule of faith and practice, to eschew the pomps and vanities of this world, and consecrate themselves to the Lord,—who are yet trained to think and talk of marriage in a manner utterly commercial and frivolous. Allusions to and conversations on the subject are of such a nature that they cannot remain unmarried without shame. They are taught, not in direct terms at so much a lesson, like music or German, but indirectly, and with a thoroughness which no music-master can equal, that, if a woman is not married, it is because she is not attractive, that to be unattractive to men is the most dismal and dreadful misfortune, and that for an unmarried woman earth has no honor and no happiness, but only toleration and a mitigated or unmitigated contempt.

What is the burden of the song that is sung to girls and women? Are they counselled to be active, self-helpful, self-reliant, alert, ingenious, energetic, aggressive? Are they strengthened to find out a path for themselves, and to walk in it unashamed? Are they braced and toned up to solve for themselves the problems of life, to bear its ills undaunted and meet its happinesses unbewildered? Go to! Such a thing was never heard of. It is woman's rights! It is strong-minded! It is discontented with your sphere! It is masculine! Milton and St. Paul to the rescue!

"For contemplation he, and valor formed,

For softness she, and sweet attractive grace."

So "she" is urged to cultivate sweet attractive grace by acquainting herself with housework, by learning to sew, and starch, and make bread, to be economical and housewifely, and so a helpmeet to the husband who is assumed for her. This is the true way to be attractive, she is informed. "Men admire you in the ball-room," say the mentors and mentoresses, "but they choose a wife from the home-circle." Marriage is simply a reward of merit. Do not be extravagant, or careless, or bold, or rude, for so you will scare away suitors. Be prudent, and tidy, and simple, and gentle, and timid, and you will be surrounded by them, and that is heaven, and secure a husband, which is the heaven of heavens. A flood of stories and anecdotes deluges us with proof. Arthur falls in love with beautiful, romantic, poetic, accomplished Leonie, till she faints one day, and he rushes into her room for a smelling-bottle, and finds no hartshorn, but much confusion and dust, while plain Molly's room is neat and tidy, and overflows with hartshorn; whereupon he falls out of love with Leonie, in with Molly, and virtue and vice have their reward. Or Charles pays a morning visit, and is entertained sumptuously in the parlor by Anabel, and Arabel, and Claribel, and Isabel, in silk, while Cinderella stays in the kitchen in calico and linen collar. But Charles catches a glimpse of Cinderella behind the door, and loves and marries the humble, grateful girl, to the disappointment and deep disgust of her flounced and jewelled sisters. Or Jane at the tea-table cuts the cheese-rind too thick, and handsome young Leonard infers that she will be extravagant; Harriet pares it too thin, and that stands for niggardliness; but Mary hits the golden mean, and is rewarded with and by handsome young Leonard. Or a broomstick lies in the way, over which Clara, Anna, Laura, and the rest step unheeding or indifferent, and only Lucy picks it up and replaces it, which Harry, standing by, makes a note of, and Lucy is paid with the honor of being Harry's wife. Moral: Go you and do likewise, and verily you shall have your reward, or at least you stand a much better chance of having it than if you do differently. "Be good, and you will be married," is the essence of the lesson.

Laying aside now all question of the dignity and delicacy of such proceedings, assuming for the time that it is the proper course, let us notice whether it is followed out to its conclusions. Not in the least. Having done its best to transpose the feminine raw material into the orthodox texture and pattern of "good wives," society lays it on the shelf to run its own risk of finding a purchaser. It neither provides husbands for the "good wives" which it has made, nor suffers them to go and look up husbands for themselves. If a girl is ready to enter service, she can enroll her name at the intelligence office. If she is prepared to teach, she sends to the "Committee." If she desires to be a saleswoman, she applies at the different shops; but your "good wife" candidate must wait patiently,—not the grand old theological "waiting in the use of means," but the Micawber waiting for something to turn up. She has learned the bread-making and the clear-starching; she is mistress of domestic economy; she is familiar with all the little details of puddings and preserves; she is ripe for wifehood and green for all else, and now she wants an arena for the exercise of her skill. But she would better pull her tongue out at once than say so. People may talk to girls at pleasure of the fair domestic realm where they will be queen, of the glory of such a kingdom, and the unsatisfying emptiness of any and every other; but no crime is more fatal to a girl's reputation and prospects than the suspicion of husband-hunting. That fate, that career, that glory, which has been constantly mapped out to her as the very Land of Promise, the goal of her ambition, the culmination of her happiness, is the one fate, the one career, the one glory, which she must not lift an eyelash to secure. Let a girl, the very same girl whom you have been pushing through a course of the received proper training, be supposed to set but so much as a feather on her hat, a smile on her lips, a tone in her voice, to attract the admiration which she has been constantly taught is the guerdon of all the virtues,—and her reputation sinks at once to zero. "Trying to get a husband," whether couched in the decorous phrase of polite society, or in the uncompromising language of more primitive circles, is the death-warrant of a girl's good name. She must sedulously prepare herself for a position to which she must be totally indifferent. She must learn all domestic accomplishments, but she must take no measures, she must exhibit no symptoms of a desire to secure a domestic situation. You bid her make ready the wedding-garments and the marriage feast, and then sit quietly waiting till the bridegroom cometh, her small hands folded, her meek eyelashes drooping, no throb of impatience or discontent or anxiety in her heart, no reaching out for any career at home or abroad, except a meek ministration in her father's house, or a mild village benevolence. But will Nature set aside her laws at your behest? Is it of any use for you to lay down your yardstick and say, "Thus far shalt thou go, and no farther"? Do you not see the inevitable result is a course of falsehood?

Is this a strong statement, a libel upon the female sex? But you read novel after novel in which the larger number of women—all, perhaps, except the heroine—are represented as artful, sly, deceitful, managing; and generally the main object of their artifice is to secure a husband for themselves or for their daughters: yet you do not at once cry out in indignant protest against such misrepresentation. On the contrary, you follow the plot with lively interest, think the author has a very clear insight into human nature, and especially excels in the delineation of female character!

Hear what one of your own writers says: "If all the world were paper, all the sea ink, all the plants and trees pens, and every man a writer,—yet were they not able, with all labor and cunning, to set down all the craft and deceits of women."

If my statement is a libel, it is less a libel than statements and implications under which people have hitherto rested with a wonderful degree of equanimity. It would be marvellous if it were a libel. A girl receives such training that it is wellnigh impossible for her to be sincere. You cannot give her whole life for six or a dozen years one direction, and then set her face suddenly towards another quarter, banishing from her mind every remembrance of past lessons, and every thought of her portrayed future. But unless such an erasure is made, or seems to be made, she knows that she forfeits good opinion, and stands in great danger of losing the one prize which has been placed before her, and which she may hope, but must not be detected in hoping, to win. Consequently she learns to dissemble. It is her only resource. Duplicity passes into her blood, and she learns to conceal and deny what you have taught her it is improper to feel, but what you have also made it impossible for her not to feel. I only wonder that any uprightness is left among women. That there are women upon whose garments the smell of fire has not passed,—that there are women whose robes of whiteness have but a faint tinge of flame,—is not because the fagots have not been piled around them and the torch applied.

This is one result of the famous, the infamous "good wife" doctrines.

Another, less fatal but sufficiently evil and more vexatious, is the injury that is inflicted upon natural and healthful association. Men and women are not allowed to look upon each other as rational beings; every woman is a wife in the grub, every man is a possible husband in the chrysalis state. If young people enjoy each other's conversation, and make opportunities to secure it, there are dozens of gossips, male and female, who proceed to forecast "a match." Intelligent interchange of opinion and sentiments between a man and a woman for the mere delight in it, with no design upon each other's name or fortune, is a thing of which a large majority of civilized Americans have no conception. Such a commodity never had a place in their inventory. A man and a woman find each other agreeable, they cultivate each other's society, and anon, East, West, South, and North goes the report that they are "engaged." It is easy to see what a check this gives to an intercourse that would be in the highest degree beneficial to both sexes; beneficial, by giving to each a more accurate knowledge of the other, and by improving what in each is good, and diminishing what is bad.

One of three things should be done: cease to urge a girl on to marriage by every terror threatened and every allurement displayed; by making it the reward of all her exertion, the arena of all her accomplishment, the condition of all her development; or take measures to provide her with a suitable husband, so that she shall not be left for an indefinite time in uncertainty and doubt, settling, perhaps, at length into frivolity, waste, and despair; or cease to condemn her for taking matters into her own hand, and furnishing herself an opportunity for the exercise of those powers whose cultivation you have strenuously urged, and for whose employment you have made no provision. "Get a husband!" Why should she not get a husband? What should you think of a boy who had been fitted by long training for the duties and responsibilities of a clergyman, or a lawyer, or a statesman, and should then make no attempt to become a clergyman, a lawyer, or a statesman? What would you think of a father who should train his son for any especial office, and should then forbid his son, upon pain of universal derision, to do anything to secure an induction into office?

I am loath to linger here, but I descend into the valley of shadows to show that, even on your own ground, you are a wicked and slothful servant.

Whom do I mean by "you"? I mean ninety-nine out of every hundred of the men who will read this, and, in a modified degree, all the women whom they have drilled to acquiescence in their decisions.

This baleful teaching goes still further. It not only drives girls into deception: it drives them into uncongenial marriages. It forces them to degradation. It does not permit them to view marriage in its natural and proper light. By perpetually assuming it as their destiny, even before they have any knowledge either of marriage or destiny, you so force their inclinations that they come to prefer marrying an indifferent person to not marrying at all,—or even to running the risk of not marrying at all. Instead of letting their minds take a healthful turn, branching off in such directions as nature chooses, you dwarf them in every direction but one, and in that you stimulate. If society were equally divided; if for every girl there were a man exactly adapted to her, and the two might by your words be induced to meet and marry, your talk might be harmless, and possibly beneficial; but as the world is, at least this part of it, there is no such arrangement, and no remote possibility of such an arrangement. The material does not exist, even suppose the sagacity to discern and dispose of it did. The number of women is much larger than the number of men. In New England, at least, it is a dangerous thing for a woman to set her heart on marrying for a living. When, therefore, you make marriage indispensable, you institute an indiscriminate scramble. Since in theory every girl must marry, and there are few to choose from, she must take such as she can get, and be thankful. She would like this, that, or the other quality, but it will not do to dally. The chance of a better husband is very remote; numbers are worse off than she, inasmuch as they have none at all; the contingency of going unsupplied is not to be thought of, and accordingly she takes up with what comes to hand. The few who are endowed with unusual charms of mind or person may exercise a limited choice, but the common run of girls must make a common run of it. If one who is so attractive as to have many admirers remains long unmarried, she is abundantly admonished of her danger. She is duly informed that she will one day grow old, and will certainly not always have such opportunities as she now enjoys. Her attractiveness is her stock in trade, which she must invest while the market is brisk. Great will be her loss if she does not. If without special attractions, a girl's position is still more embarrassing. Dependent in her father's house, with no career open to her, no arena for her action, what is to become of her? Anything is better than a dependence which, her own heart tells her, is not long grateful to her father. He may not be unkind or miserly toward her; he may not—and he may, for such things are done—taunt her with her want of success in making a match; he may even be generous and chivalric towards her; but she is conscious that he is disappointed. He may not acknowledge it even to himself, but she knows that she is not fulfilling his wishes, not meeting his ideal. Her support is somewhat a burden, her enforced presence somewhat a shame. He rejoiced in her infancy, childhood, and youth, but he did not expect to have her on his hands all her life. He would gladly spend twice as much on her dowry as he gives for her allowance. She has a *sense* of all this, and, rather than remain in this state of pupilage, a woman in character, a child in position, she marries the first man that holds out the golden spectre,—I meant sceptre, but perhaps the first will do just as well. I am speaking of the masses. I know that there are exceptions. In spite of circumstances, there are women so strong,—strong-minded if you like, but so symmetrical that you see no peculiar strength or sweetness, only "a perfect woman,"—so strong, that public opinion and private opinion, all the blare and blarney of lecture-room and female-school orators, all the thinly disguised paganism of church-worldlings, beat against them and leave them unmoved as Gibraltar by the summer ripples of its southern sea. You see them yourself, perhaps; but so beautiful, so gentle and lovely, that you do not discern the granite which underlies beauty and grace, and which alone redeems beauty and grace from the charge of gaud, and makes their value; and in your low Dutch dialect you "wonder she doesn't get married."

There are fathers and mothers, though these are rarer, who joy in their children with a rational and Christian joy; who believe in God and righteousness, immortality and human destiny; whose daughters are polished stones, not in the palaces of earthly pride, vanity, and ambition, but in the temple of the living God. Such parents and such children are few, but they are enough to reveal possibilities. The higher the few can reach, the higher the many shall rise. But these are the strong, and the strong can take care of themselves. I have nothing to say for them. I speak for those who are not strong,—for the good and true-hearted, who feel themselves overborne by external pressure, and swept along into a hateful and hated vortex,—for those who wish to lead an upright Christian life, but who need a helping hand. Still more, and saddest of all, I speak for those on whom the blight has so long rested that they have lost the sense of uprightness; they feel no wrong, and aspire to nothing higher. More than this, I speak for those whose opening lives are yet untouched, for whom warning and caution may not be too late. It is these —the weak, the plastic, the impressible—whom your earth-born morality is corrupting, whose possibilities of happiness and self-respect your enervating woman's-sphere-ism is destroying. Women may be weak, yet even in weakness is strength, but you have trodden down strength. You trample under foot all sensibility, all delicacy, all dignity. A woman can preserve her integrity only so far as she repels and represses your miserable didactics;—by word and look, if the power be given her; by a silent indignation of protest, if that is her only resource.

I know well, judging from past experience, that there will not be wanting those who will think I am depreciating and deprecating marriage. But it would be extremely foolish to set one's self against marriage, for it would be holding out a straw to dam a river. I not only do not hold out the straw, I do not even wish to dam the river. But I would prevent it from being banked up here and banked up there, and narrowed, twisted, and tortured, till it bursts all bounds, natural and acquired, and rushes wildly over the country, destroying villages, inundating harvests, sweeping away lives, and becoming a terror and a fate instead of the beneficence it was meant to be.

I depreciate marriage? I magnify it! It is you that depreciate, by debasing it. You lower it to the level of the market. You degrade it to a question of political and domestic economy. You look upon it as an arrangement. I believe it to be a sacrament. You subordinate it to ways and means. I see in it the type of mortal and immortal union. You make it but the cradle of mankind. I make it also the crown. All that is tender, grand, and ennobling finds there its home, its source and sustenance, its inspiration, and its exceeding great reward.

But by as much as marriage is sacred, by so much is he a blasphemer who travesties it; and he thrice and four times blasphemous who leads others to do so. No sin is so dwelt on in the Bible with a stern, reiterated fixedness of divine abhorrence as the sin of Jeroboam, the son of Nebat, who made Israel to sin. They who barter their children for a string of beads, or a talent of gold, are no more pagan than they who, by accumulated indirections, lead them to barter themselves. I do not undertake the defence of all "woman's rights," but with whatever strength God has given me I will do battle for woman's right to be pure. "Cæsar's wife should be above suspicion," said haughty Cæsar, and the world applauds; but every woman is czarina by divine right. No wretched outcast, wandering through the darkness of the great city,

"With hell in her heart

And death in her hand,

Daring the doom of the unknown land,"

but has lost a crown. For her who, through weakness or despair, has forfeited her birthright, the world has no pardon. I do not say that ye should pray for it to be otherwise. But a deeper sin, a tenfold more gross and revolting violation of God's law written on the human heart,—giving force to the law written

17

erewhile on the tables of stone,—does she commit who, in the holy name of love, under the holy forms of marriage, burns incense to false gods. Where love may walk white-robed and stainless, brushing the morning dews from the grass, only to descend again in fresher and fragrant showers, pride or prudence or ambition can but bring the deepest profanation: roses spring in his pathway; behind them is the desert.

Marriage contracted to subserve material ends, however innocent those ends may be in themselves, is legalized prostitution; as much more vilifying, as mischief framed by a law is more destructive than mischief wrought in spite of law. To such vice the world is lenient, scarcely recognizing it as vice; but the soul bears its marks of wounds forever and forever.

Marriage is a result, not a cause. In God's great economy it may have its separate and important work; but from a human point of view, it is conclusion and not premise. It cannot be made the premise without bringing fatal and disastrous conclusions. Whatever ends nature may design her institution to compass, be sure nature will work out.

III.

DO not design to sketch any Utopia for woman; but there are certain things which can be done in this world, in this country, in this generation, at this moment,—simple, practical, practicable measures, which can be accomplished without any change in laws, without any palpable revolution or disruption of society, but by which women shall be relieved of the indignity that is constantly put upon them, even by the society which considers itself, and which perhaps is, the most civilized and chivalric in the world.

First, every man who has daughters is either able to support them or he is not. If he is, he ought to do it in a way that shall make them feel as little trammelled as possible. He should so treat them, from first to last, that they shall feel that they are dear and pleasant to him, his delight and ornament. So far from wishing to be rid of them, he finds his balm and solace and zest of life in their society, their interests, and their ministrations. While he contemplates the contingency of their marriage, and makes what preparations such contingency may require, it should be well understood that he contemplates it only as a contingency; and that all his wishes and hopes will be best met by their happiness, whether it is to be promoted by a life away from him or with him. If they are so deficient in amiability, capability, or adaptability that his home cannot be comfortable with them in it,—that, so far from being a reason why he should be eager to part with them, is the strongest reason why he should earnestly endeavor to keep them with him. Almost without fail, their faults lie at his door; and it is just and right that, if any home is to be made miserable by them, it should be the one which has made them *miserific*. On the other hand, if they wish to go from his roof to follow paths of their own, he ought to aid and encourage them as far as lies in his power. It matters not that he is able and willing to supply their every want. He is *not* able, if they have immortal wants,—wants which the parental heart and purse cannot satisfy,—want of activity, want of a plan, want of some work which shall engage their young and eager energies. However liberal, kind, and fond he may be, in their father's house their position must be subordinate, and it may well happen that they shall wish to taste the sweets of an independent, self-helping, self-directing life. They wish to feel their own hands at the helm; they wish to know what responsibility and foresight and planning mean. They are drawn by a strong, inexplicable attraction in certain directions; and as he values not only their happiness, but their salvation,—their love for him, their health of body and mind,—he shall give them ample room and verge enough. He shall not abate one jot or tittle of fatherly affection. He shall not attempt to persuade them from their inclination till he finds persuasion of no avail, and then in a fit of angry petulance bid them go, and leave them to their own destruction. He shall give them such aid as can be made available. He shall surround them with his love, if not with his care. He shall, above all, show them that his arms are always open to them, if through weakness or weariness they faint by the way.

His sympathy and protection, and fatherly cherishing, shall be new every morning and fresh every evening. If they quickly tire in their new paths, they will come back to him with stronger love and faith. Their life abroad will have only endeared their happy home. The enlargement of their experience will have intensified their appreciation of their blessings. If their call was indeed from above, and their first feeble explorations opened for them a new world, through which they learn to walk with ever firmer tread, they will return from time to time to lay at his feet with unutterable gratitude the treasures which he enabled them to discover. He will know that he has contributed to the world's wealth, and his happy children will rise up and call him blessed.

But if they do not incline to such a life, he shall not force them, however strongly he may be persuaded of its propriety, wisdom, and dignity. Because they are obliged to grow under the whole superincumbent weight of society, he must not be severe if they attain but a partial growth. With boys the preponderance of influence is overwhelmingly on the side of an active, positive life. With girls, it is against it. If a boy does not do something in the world, he must show cause for it; a girl must show cause if she does. Therefore, if the father is not able, by precept and persuasion, to induce his daughters to embrace an active life, he must lay it to society, and do the next best thing by protecting them as far as possible from the resultant evils of their situation; not quite all to society either, for, as a general thing, if his own precept and example have been right, his children will be right; the influence of father and mother, by its nearness, intensity, and continuity, very often more than balances the superior bulk of society's influence. Parents say things which they ought to mean, and which they wish to be considered to mean, and which they suppose they do mean, but which they are really the farthest in the world from meaning, and then marvel that their children should disregard their instructions and go wrong; but such instructions are but as the dust in the balance. The ideal which they actually, though perhaps unconsciously, hold up to their children, is the model upon which the children form themselves. What they are, not what they say, is the paramount influence. So if a father heartily believes in womanly work, his daughters will hardly fail to be woman-workers.

If a father is not able to support his daughters in a manner compatible with comfort and refinement, he should see to it that they have some way opened in which they can do it, or help do it, for themselves, in a manner consistent with their dignity and self-respect. It is very rarely that a human being is born without possible power in some one direction. The field which is traversable to women is much more circumscribed than that which is traversed by men, yet I have somewhere read a statement that the number of employments in which women of the United States are actually engaged is, I think, greater than five hundred. If this is so, or anything nearly so, men surely have no need to "marry off" their daughters as an economical measure. Out of five hundred occupations, a woman can certainly choose one which, though not perhaps that which enlists her enthusiasm, is yet better than the debasement of herself which an indifferent marriage necessitates. It is better to be not wholly well-placed than to be wholly ill-placed. Indeed, there are many chances in favor of the assumption that she may find even a suitable employment. Literature and art are open to her on equal terms with men. Teaching is free to her, with the disadvantage of being miserably, shamefully, wickedly underpaid, both as regards the relative and intrinsic value of her work; but this is an arrangement which does not degrade her, only the men who employ her. Many mechanical employments she is at perfect liberty to acquire, and the greater delicacy of her organization gives her a solid advantage over her masculine competitors. In factories, in printing-offices, and in all manner of haberdashers' shops, she is quite at home; and this branch of trade she ought to monopolize, for surely a man is as much out of his sphere in holding up a piece of muslin at arm's length, and expatiating on its merits to a bevy of women, as a woman is in the pulpit or before the mast. Especially do private houses invite her over all the country. The whole land groans under inefficient domestic assistance; and if healthy, intelligent, well-behaved American girls would be willing to work in kitchens which they do not own one half as hard as most women work in kitchens which they do own, thousands of doors would fly open to them. There is a foolish pride and prejudice which rises up against "going out to service." But everybody in this world, who is not a cumberer of the ground, is out at service. If it is true service and well performed, one thing is as honorable as another. The highest plaudit mortal can hope to receive is, "Well done, good and faithful servant." It is the absence of moral dignity and character, not, as is often supposed, its presence, which causes this reluctance. A nobleman ennobles his work. A king among basket-makers is none the less a king. How women can be so enamored of the needle as to choose to make a pair of cotton drilling drawers, with buckles, button-holes, straps, and strings, for four and one sixth cents, or fine white cotton shirts with fine linen "bosoms" for sixteen cents apiece, rather than go into a handsome house in the next street to make the beds, and scour the knives, and iron the clothes for a dollar and a half a week,[1] besides board and rent, I do not understand. That so many are ready to brave the din of machinery, and the smells of a factory for ten hours a day, with only a great, dreary, unhomelike boarding-house to go to at night, while there are so very few, if any, who are willing to preside over a comfortable and plentiful kitchen, with at least a possibility of home comforts, pleasant association, and true appreciation, is equally inexplicable.

But enough has been said to show, that, if women have a desire, or are under the necessity, of getting an honest living, ways and means may be found; not so stimulating, not so lucrative, not so varied as might be desired, but honest and honorable. Girls, however, make the mistake of rushing pell-mell into school-houses, as if that were the only respectable path to independence. I heard a man the other day speaking about the High School of his native city. It was a good school,—he had nothing to say against its conduct,—it gave girls a good education; and yet he sometimes thought it did more harm than good. Every year a class was graduated, and they were all ladies and did not want to work, but must all teach, and there were no schools for so many; what could be done with them? It was an evil that seemed to be growing worse every year. The implied grievance was, that educated women were a drug in the market; and the implied remedy, that girls should be left more uncultivated that they might be turned to commoner uses. I pass over that accurate knowledge of things shown in the unconscious contrast between working and teaching,—over the gross utilitarianism implied in both grievance and redress,—simply remarking, that, if the excess of supply over demand would justify the breaking up of High Schools, the domestic education of this generation should be largely discontinued for the same reason, and that in fact there seems to be no real and adequate resource, except to manage with girl babies as you do with kittens, save the fifth and drown the rest,—to say that girls do very wrong in regarding teaching as the sole or the chief honorable employment. That occupation is the one for them to which a natural taste calls them, no matter what may be its rank in society. In fact, let it not be forgotten that society looks with a degree of disfavor on any remunerative employment for women. To be entirely beyond the reach of cavil, they must be consumers, and not producers; and since, to turn into producers will forfeit somewhat their caste, let them make capital out of the rural and remote adage, that one may as well be hung for a sheep as a lamb, and while they are about it, follow the thing that good is to them. If girls of wealth and standing, who also possess character and decision, would act upon their principles when they have them, and follow the lead of their tastes when their taste leads them into a milliner's shop, or a watch factory, or a tailor's room, they would do much more than satisfy their own consciences. They would do a service to their sex, and through their sex to the other, and so to the whole world, which would outweigh whatever small sacrifice it might cost them. For the world is so constituted that to him that hath shall be given. If he have power, he shall have still more. Those who are independent of the world's sufferance are tolerably sure to get it. Let a poor girl go to work, and it is nothing at all. She is obliged to do it, and society does not so much as turn a look upon her; but let a girl go out from her brown-stone five-story house, from the care and attendance of servants, to work for three or five hours a day, because she honestly believes that the accident of wealth does not relieve her from moral responsibility, and because, of all forms of labor practicable to her, that seems the one to which she is best adapted, and immediately there is a commotion. The brown-stone friends are shocked and scandalized, which is probably the best thing that could happen to them. Desperate cases can only be electrified back into life. But it is the first girl alone that will cause a shock. The second will make but a faint sensation. The third will be quite commonplace, and when things come to that pass, that if a woman wishes to do a thing she can do it, and that is the end of it, there is little more to be desired in that line.

I know a young lady, the only daughter of a distinguished family, with abundant means at her command, with parents whose great happiness it is to promote hers,—a young lady who has only to fancy what a nice thing it must be to live in a bird's-nest on a tree-top, and immediately the carpenters come and build her a bower in the tallest tree that overlooks the sea. This young lady has a strong inclination to surgery, a most perverted and unwomanly taste, of course; but so long as it is a womanly weakness to break one's arms, perhaps it is as well that some woman should be unwomanly enough to set them. At any rate, there was the taste; nobody put it there, and something must be done about it. Being the sensible daughter of sensible parents, who looked upon tastes as hints of powers, instead of disregarding this hint and devoting her life to her garden, making calls, and a forced and feeble piano-worship,—all very nice things, but not quite exhaustive of immortal capacities,—she set herself down to the study of surgery and medicine. It was no superficial and sensational whim. Year after year, month after month, week after week, showed no abatement of enthusiasm. On the contrary, her interest grew with her growing knowledge. She left without regret, without any weak regrets, her luxurious home for the secluded and severe student's life, and by patient and laborious application made herself master of the science. I look upon her almost as an apostle, though she is very far from taking on apostolic airs. She quietly pursues the even tenor of her way as if it were the beaten track. But in doing this she does ten thousand times more. She opens the path for a host of feet less strong than hers.

But one great obstacle in the way of woman's attaining strength is her lack of perseverance. Of the many pursuits possible to women, few are embraced to any great extent, because girls are said to be, and probably are, unwilling to bestow upon a trade or a profession the study and thought which are necessary to insure skill. But this is a result as well as a cause, and must be removed by the removal of the cause. Promotion and political preferment shine before a man as a reward for whatever eminence of character or intelligence he may attain. His business is a separate department, and dispenses its separate reward. The first of these is entirely, and the second partially, wanting to women. A female assistant in a high school, a woman of education, refinement, accomplishments, tact, and sense, receives six hundred dollars, and if she stays six hundred years she will receive no more. A male assistant, fresh from a college or a normal school, thoroughly unseasoned, without elegance of manners, or dignity of presence, or experience, teaching only temporarily, with a view to the pulpit, or the bar, or a professorship, receives a thousand dollars. His thousand is because he is a man. Her six hundred is because she is a woman. Her little finger may be worth more to the school than his whole body, but that goes for nothing. In a certain "college" I wot of, the "Professors" have a larger salary than the "Preceptresses," who perform double the amount of labor, and without any hope of promotion. Female assistants in a grammar school receive three or four hundred dollars where the male principal has ten or twelve hundred, and where the difference of salary bears no proportion to the difference of care and labor. No matter how assiduously they may devote themselves to their duties, nor how successful they may be in results, they have attained the maximum. Worse than this: since the increase of prices consequent upon the war, teachers' salaries have been increased; but where two hundred dollars have been added to the salary of the male principal, only twenty-five have been added to those of the female assistants: so that the man's salary is sixteen per cent higher, while the woman's is only six per cent higher. This is done in Massachusetts. One excuse is, that it does not cost a woman so much to live as it costs a man. It costs a woman just as much to live as it does a man. If men would be willing to practise the small economies that women practise, they could live at no greater expense. There are some things in which women have the advantage; there are others in which it lies with the man. A woman's calico gown does not cost so much as a man's broadcloth coat, but her dress, the wardrobe through, costs just as much as his. He can be decent on just as small a sum as she. Another excuse is, that men have a family to support. I suppose, then, that women never have families to support. No female teacher ever has a widowed mother or an invalid father to assist, or brothers and sisters to educate. No widow ever had recourse to the school-room to provide bread for her fatherless children. Or if such things ever happen, the authorities make adequate provision for it. The school committee, of course, before it assigns the salary inquires into these background facts, and acts accordingly. The rich girl has indeed but a small income from her teaching, but the poor girl is paid according to the number of people dependent upon her, and the unmarried man is confined to narrower fortunes.

You know that such a thing is never done. The men always receive the high salaries and the women always receive the low salaries; no one ever asks who does the work or who supports the families. It is only a feeble excuse to hide men's selfish greed. They are the lions, and they take the lion's share. They *can* give themselves plenty and women a pittance, and they do it, and they mean to do it, and they will do it. It matters not that the ten or twelve or fourteen hundred dollars divided among the man's family of himself, his wife, and his one or two or no children, gives to each, even to the little baby playing on the floor, as much money for support as the female teacher receives who devotes her whole time and strength to the school. It matters not that his children are growing up to be the staff of his declining years, while the unmarried female assistant has only her own self for reliance. Man is a thief and holds the bag, and if women do not like to teach for what they can get, so much the better. They will be all the more willing to become household drudges.

Again, read the following paragraph from a prominent newspaper printed in Massachusetts.

"The custom of employing ladies as clerks in the public departments at Washington is meeting with increased favor. It is said that, generally speaking, they write more correctly than the men, and as they receive much smaller salaries, the gain to the government is considerable."

Could six lines better express the wickedness of the relations which exist between man and woman under the "best government in the world"? The shabby chivalry of "ladies"; the matter-of-fact manner in which not only a wrong, but an absurdity, is mentioned, as if it were as evident as a syllogism, and had no more to do with morality than the multiplication-table; and then the neat little patriotico-economical chuckle at the end! Women do the work better than men, and receive much smaller salaries. A logical sequence, and an excellent example of the reasoning which is brought to bear on women. Especially dignified and commanding is the attitude assumed for our government. The Great Republic, stretching its arms across a continent, vexing every land for its treasures, and whitening every sea with its sails, yet stoops over a poor woman's pocket to take toll of the few pennies which her labor has fairly earned. "The wise *save* it call."

But there is a lower deep than this. The very same paper that so naively blazoned forth its own shame, made another brilliant essay at about the same time. I quote the paragraph from memory, but it is substantially correct.

"Miss Anna Dickinson demanded three [or six, or whatever it was] hundred dollars for two lectures delivered for the benefit of the Sanitary Fair in Chicago. Miss Charlotte Cushman gave eight thousand dollars, the entire proceeds of her theatrical tour, to the Sanitary Commission. Comment is unnecessary."

For all that, we will have a little comment. Here is one woman in a million rising by the sheer force of her God-given genius above the miserable necessities of women. She needs not to endure or to beg. She is sovereign in her own right and can dictate her own terms. Men cannot grind her face, for she is stronger than they. What do they do? They hold her up to odium because they cannot extort from her the money which they cannot prevent her from earning. Most women they can prevent from earning it. Most working-women they can keep down to what prices they choose to pay. But here is one to whom they cannot dole out pennies: "with one white arm-sweep" she gathers in a golden harvest. But they will at least force her Pactolian stream into a channel of their own choosing. Not at all.

"If she will, she will, you may depend on
't;

If she won't, she won't, and there's an end
on 't."

Nothing, therefore, is left to these high-minded gentry, but to stand at a distance and "make faces"!

Somebody assumed to excuse Miss Dickinson, by saying that she gave up other and far more lucrative engagements for this; but it was entirely a work of supererogation. Miss Dickinson needed no excuse. One might, indeed, think within himself that Miss Cushman has nearly closed her public career, and is already possessed of an independent fortune, while Miss Dickinson's life lies before her, and her fortune is still to be made. But all this is irrelevant. The whole paragraph is an impertinence. Why is any person to be mulcted at another's instance in any sum for any charity or any purpose whatever? What right has any newspaper to decide the direction or the amount of a citizen's benevolence? Had it concerned a man, it would have been impertinence; concerning a woman, it is something worse,—not because of her womanhood, but because of the injustice which is wrought upon her sex wherever there is the ability to be unjust.

These are very small things, but they are signs of great ones.

It may be inferred, therefore, that woman's indifference to excellence in work does not necessarily impugn either her character or calibre. Excellence is indeed good in itself, and desirable, without reference to the money it brings; yet money and promotion are a spur, and therefore they must be taken into the account when we are dealing with facts and not merely with theories.

Now, then, let women, disregarding senseless and wicked customs, make a point of making a point of something, and then let them lay aside every weight which social injustice or indifference hangs upon them, and the consequent sin of superficiality which so easily besets them, and make that point perfect. No matter that they are ill-paid and held down, let them assert themselves; let them work so well that their work shall assert itself, and pay and promotion will come—to woman, if not to themselves—as the inevitable result.

I do not mean that every woman should study medicine, or apprentice herself to a trade. Indeed, I consider it to be a wrong state of society in which there is any other necessity for her doing so than that which arises from her own inward promptings. It is very likely that she can find in her father's house abundant scope for the exercise of every faculty. She may have a leaning to home life, and to no other.

Because a girl remains at home, it by no means follows that she is accomplishing nothing. What I do mean is, that she shall not dawdle away her time simply because she is a girl; and that if, moved by her own instincts, which are from God, or impelled by circumstances, which are generally the fault of men, she enters the arena where men strive, she shall have no other disabilities than those which Nature lays upon her. Do not fail to note the distinction between choice and necessity in her adoption of a career. When a woman, of her own free will and delight, pursues a study or an occupation beyond the common female range, it is one thing. When she is obliged to earn her own living, and for that purpose goes out into the paths where men walk, it is another thing. In both cases she should work on equal terms with men; in the first, because the very strength of her purpose, overcoming the natural disinclinations of her sex, shows it to be of celestial origin, and therefore worthy of respect; in the second, because, if man fails to give to woman the support which is her due, the smallest step towards reparation is to allow her every advantage in the attempt to support herself. It is always a sorrowful, I think it is always an injurious thing, for a woman to be obliged to compete with men, that is, to earn money. She can do it only at the constant torture, or the constant sacrifice—perhaps both—of something higher than can be brought into the strife. But so much the more should she be freed from every unnecessary pain and hinderance. Moreover, evil as is the imperative assumption by woman of man's work, it combats a greater evil, and therefore also should her hands be upheld. The most persistent and kindly encouragement can never change, in the womanly heart, love of home into love of conquest and renown; but it can do much to soften the harshness of an uncongenial lot, and take somewhat from the bitterness of a cup that never can be sweet.

The mere fact of a daughter's services being needed at home is no reason why they shall be claimed after she has become of age, either through years, or maturity of character, when such service is distasteful to her, and other service is tasteful and possible. If, for instance, a girl has a strong desire to be a milliner, or a mantua-maker, or an artist, she should not be prevented because her mother wants her at home to help take care of the children and do the work. I suppose to many this will seem unnatural and undutiful. It is neither the one nor the other. There are remarkable notions afloat concerning nature and duty. If one may judge from popular ethics, the duty seems to lie chiefly on one side. Lions, we are told, would appear to the world in a very different light if lions wrote history; so filial and parental relations, discussed as they always are by the parental part of the community, have a different bearing from what they would if looked at from the children's point of view. In our eagerness to enforce the claims which parents have on children, we seem sometimes ready to forget the equally stringent claims which children have on parents. Much is said about the gratitude which parental care imposes upon the child; very little about the responsibility which his involuntary birth imposed upon himself.

Here is a daughter, an immortal being, accountable to God. Surely, when she has become a woman, she has a right to direct her life in the manner best adapted to bring out its abilities. No human being has a right to appropriate another human being's life,—even if they be mother and daughter. You say that she owes life itself to her parents. True, but in such a way that it confers an additional obligation on them to give her every opportunity to make the most of life, and not in such a way as to justify them in monopolizing it, nor in such a way as to render her accountable to them alone for its use. The person who gives life is under much stronger bonds than the person who receives life. Life is a momentous thing. It may be an eternal curse. It is almost certain to involve deep sorrow. Sin, disease, pain, are almost sure to follow in its wake. It is a Pandora's box whose best treasure is only a compensation. The happiest thing we know of it is, that it will one day come to an end: Psyche will rend off her disguises, and soar in her proper form. The uncertainty of the future is our solace against the certainty of the present. Surely, then, of all people in the world, those who impose this fearful burden are the very last who should add even a feather's weight to it, and the very first and foremost who should at any sacrifice of less important matters lighten it as far as possible. Filial unfaithfulness is a sin, but parental unfaithfulness is a chief of sins. The first violates relations which it finds. The second violates those which it makes. Almost invariably the second is the direct cause of the first. There may be extraordinary malformations: a child may be born with some organic incapacity for love, or gratitude, or virtue, as children are born blind or deaf. But, as a rule, parental love and wisdom result in filial love and duty growing stronger and stronger every day, and removing the possibility of sacrifice by making all service a pleasure. Because, where I knew the circumstances, I never saw an instance of filial misbehavior that could not be traced directly to parental mismanagement or neglect, I believe it is so where I do not know the circumstances. I am persuaded that Solomon had the spirit of truth when he declared, "Train up a child in the way he should go, and when he is old he will not depart from it." A son administers arsenic to his parents, and the world starts back in horror. I would not diminish its horror; but before you lavish all your execration on the son, find out whether the parents have not been administering poison, or suffered poison to be administered, to his mind and heart from his earliest infancy. Be shocked at that. I never saw or heard of a son born of virtuous parents, and wisely trained in the ways of virtue, who turned about and poisoned his parents after he had grown up. The eider-duck plucks the down from her own breast to warm the nest for her young, and I do not suppose an ungrateful or rebellious eider-duckling was ever heard of; but if the eider-duck plucks the down from the breasts of her young to line the nest for herself— what then?

If a daughter, out of love or a "sense of duty," chooses to sacrifice her inclinations,—by inclinations I do not mean the mere promptings of self-indulgence, but the voice of her soul calling her to a work in life,—I say not that she does not well. I only say that her mother has no right to demand such a sacrifice. It is an unjust exaction. It is a selfish building up of comfort on the ruins of another's happiness, possibly of character, since few things are so apt to warp the tone of mind and temper as a forced performance of unsuitable work. Before children are old enough to choose for themselves, their parents must choose for them,—even then with a wary care lest they mistake a prompting of nature for a whim, but every restraint that is put upon a child for any other purpose than his own benefit is a sin against a soul. What duty his love does not prompt, you shall not by the sheer brute force of your position require. His life is in his own hands, put there by you, and he must make it into a vessel of honor or dishonor. You shall not hold back his hand from working its own beautiful designs, that it may putty up the cracks in your time-worn vessel. You make great account of the care which you took of his helpless infancy; but he owes no especial gratitude for that. As may be inferred from what I have before said, it was a debt you owed him. Having endowed him with life, the least you could do was to help him make the best of it. It would have been cruel not to do it. You have only made things even in doing it,— and hardly that. Besides, such considerations are logically useless. You may fill a child's book, paper, and ears with his mother's anxiety and care for him. You may tell him how she has watched over him and toiled for him during his helpless infancy, and conjure him on that account to love and obey her. It will be a waste of breath. You might just as well conjugate a Latin verb to him. He will no more form an intelligent conception of a mother's love and care from your most forcible description, than he would from *amo, amas, amat*. He is not capable of such a conception. A child's love is an instinct. It gradually develops into a sentiment which permeates his whole being. The mother's love is also an instinct. She nurses her child just as instinctively as a hen gathers her chickens under her wings. There generally is something more than instinct, but there is instinct. But at no stage of a child's life is love a matter of reasoning. If it is within him, it cannot be argued out; if it is not, it cannot be argued in. Never a person loved because he was convinced he ought to love. He loves because he loves, and that is all that can be said about it.

I hope I shall not be considered as attempting to

weaken the cords between parents and children. On the contrary, I wish to strengthen them. But I wish to strengthen them by making them of that unseen, spiritual substance which alone is worthy of the relation,—proof against every external force, and drawing more and more closely with every opening year,—not of that gross and palpable outward material which chafes and irritates, and which will snap asunder the moment that young vigor spreads its wings.

IV.

NOTHER truth, which seems to have been forgotten, and which needs to be newly revealed to this generation, is, that though manhood and womanhood are two distinct things, the humanity which underlies them is one and indivisible. We are told that God made man male and female, but we are first told that God made man in his own image. There is no distinction. Woman is made in God's image just as much as man; and it is just as wicked to deface that image in her as in him. It is defaced when her powers are crippled, and her organs enfeebled, whether it be by turning her toes under till they touch the heels, and then bandaging them so, or whether that process be enacted on her mind. If a boy should stand god-like erect, in native honor clad, so should a girl. She may not be as tall, but she may be as straight. The palm cannot turn into an oak, and has not the smallest desire to turn into an oak; but there is no reason why it should not be the best kind of a palm,—and in the deserts of this world a fruitful palm cheereth the heart of both God and man.

Read, in the light of these facts, a "sonnet" and its accompanying comments, which I chanced to find while looking over a twelve-year-old number of a magazine which stands among the first in America.

"The learned 'science-women' of the day, the 'deep, deep-blue stockings' of the time, are fairly hit off in the ensuing satirical sonnet:—

'I idolize the LADIES! They are fairies,

That spiritualize this world of ours;

From heavenly hot-beds most delightful
flowers,

Or choice cream-cheeses from celestial
dairies,

But learning, in its barbarous seminaries,

Gives the dear creatures many wretched
hours,

And on their gossamer intellect sternly
showers

SCIENCE, with all its horrid accessaries.

Now, seriously, the only things, I think,

In which young ladies should instructed
be,

Are—stocking-mending,   love,   and
cookery!—

Accomplishments that very soon will
sink,

Since   Fluxions   now,   and   Sanscrit
conversation,

Always form part of female education!'

"Something good in the way of inculcation may
be educed from this rather biting sonnet. If woman
so far forgets her 'mission,' as it is common to term
it now-a-days, as to choose those accomplishments
whose only recommendation is that they are 'the
vogue,' in preference to acquisitions which will fit
her to be a better wife and mother, she becomes a
fair subject for the shafts of the satirical censor."

Leaving "gossamer intellects" to educe whatever of good in the way of inculcation may be found in this biting sonnet, and in the equally mordacious remarks of the mulierivorous commentator, let me refer to another paragraph in which popular opinion is crystallized. It is found in a book printed and published in London, and coming to me through several hands from the library of an English nobleman, but a book so atrocious in its sentiments, and so feeble in its expression, that I will not give the small impulse to its circulation which the mention of its name might impart: "In woman, weakness itself is the true charter of power; it is an absolute attraction, and by no means a defect; it is the mysterious tie between the sexes, a tie as irresistible as it is captivating, and begetting an influence peculiar to itself." This is the fancy sketch. One of our best writers has drawn the true portrait of such a woman: a woman "to be the idol of her school-boy son, to be remembered in his gray old age with a reverential tenderness as a glorified saint, but a woman also to drive that same son to desperation in actual life by her absorption in trifles, by her weak credulity,... by her inability to sympathize with his ambition, to enter into his difficulties, or to share in the faintest degree his aspirations."

"In short," proceeds the advocate of the oak-and-vine humanity, "*all independence is unfeminine*; the more dependent that sex becomes, the more will it be cherished."

Independence is unfeminine: what a pity that starvation and insanity are not unfeminine also! Independence is unfeminine, but what provision is made for dependence? Look about the world. How many men are there, dependence on whom would be agreeable to a sensitive woman? and what shall the women do who have nobody to be dependent on,— the women without husbands or fathers, and the women with drunken, thriftless, extravagant, miserly, feeble or incapable husbands or fathers? When every woman in the country is placed above the possibility of want, it will be time enough to talk about the sweets of dependence; but so long as women are liable, and are actually reduced to want, to shame, to ignominy, to starvation, and degradation and death, through the meanness, the misconduct, or the inability of their natural protectors, it will be well at least to connive at their efforts to help themselves. An independent woman may be a nuisance, but I think rather less so than an immoral woman, or an insane woman, or a dead woman in the bottom of a canal in Lowell, or a live woman making shirts for Milk Street merchants in Boston, at five cents apiece. O men, you who shut your eyes to the stern and awful facts of life, and rhapsodize over your fine-spun theories, what will you say when the Lord maketh inquisition for blood? In that great and terrible day that shall open the books of judgment, that shall wrest from the earth and the sea the secrets which are in them, when the dead women come forth from their suicidal graves, when they swarm up from under the river-bridges, when they pour out from the gateways of hell, will it seem to you then a wise and righteous thing that you branded independence as unfeminine?

Apart from the bearings of this doctrine, one word as to its facts. There are two kinds of dependence,— the one of love, the other of necessity. Each may comprise the other, and all is well. But each may exist without the other, and then half is ill. The first is a delight. The second is a dread. The first is a delight,—but no more to woman than to man, for though the matters in which they are dependent differ, the dependence itself is mutual, and mutually dear and precious. Nobody need enforce it by argument. It commends itself by its own inherent sweetness. But the second is an evil, and only an evil under the sun,—a state which no man and no woman of any spirit will for a moment willingly endure. Dependence is a joy only where it is a boon; otherwise it is a burning torture if there is any soul to feel.

But masculine deprecation of feminine independence is not entirely owing to a tender regard for the preservation unimpaired of feminine loveliness. Men think if women strike out in a career of their own, the matter of securing and disposing of a wife may not be quite the easy thing it is at present.

They now have things their own way. The world is all before them where to choose. They have only to walk leisurely on, and it is O whistle and I'll come to you, my lad. You think I put it too strongly: that is because you are looking into the bucket. I am speaking of the atmosphere. You have only to listen to the usual talk of usual people in villages and cities, and to the floating literature. You are not to take the intellectual in the one, nor the immortal in the other, for their rills spring from deeper sources, and represent the individual. It is the flitting, the ephemeral, the stories that Maggie Marigold and Kittie Katnip print in the county papers; it is the talk that Mrs. Smith and Mrs. Jones have about Nancy Briggs; it is the women in the novels who are not the heroines,—these give the best photograph of actual popular opinion, and these give you six women intriguing for one man. It is not surprising that at first sight men should think it a fine thing to have a whole bazaar of beauty to choose from, with the market so glutted that the goods will be sold at prices to suit the purchasers. It is not necessary to be very good or very great, to win the prize. There is no prize to be won. It is only pick and choose. But have men no misgivings? Is necessity the surest warrant of adaptation? Are men conscious that their assumption is, that they are so unattractive, and the marriage yoke so heavy, that women will not endure either unless they are left without any other resource? Is it pleasant to reflect that they cannot trust themselves to woo, but that girls must be reduced to the alternative of marriage or nothing? What pleasure can there be in a victory so easily gained? I know a man who says the reason why he married his wife was, because she was the only girl in the town whom he was not sure of beforehand. With nothing to do, women are as beggars by the wayside, holding up their feeble hands to the passer, and entreating, "We will eat our own bread and wear our own apparel: only let us be called by thy name to take away our reproach." Is this pleasant to think of? Does it flatter a man's self-love? Would it not be more agreeable for a husband to suppose that he is his wife's choice and not—Hobson's?

Let boarding-school anniversary orators and Mother's Magazine editors trust more in nature, and make themselves easy. Providence is never at a loss. There is not the slightest danger that marriage will fall into disuse through the absorption of female interests in other directions. If every girl in the world were independent, full mistress of herself, she would not be any more disinclined to marriage than she is now. She would not hang upon its skirts, dragging them into the mud, with such a helpless, desperate death-clutch as now. She would not be at the mercy of every schemer, every speculator, every unprincipled, unscrupulous manikin, who knows no better use for angels than to wash the dishes. She would not be such an article of traffic, such a beast of burden, such a tame, spiritless, long-suffering, sly little sycophant, as she too often is now. There is not one woman in a million who would not be married, if—I borrow a phrase from the popular, pestilent patois, but I transfigure it with its highest meaning— if she could get a chance. How do I know? Just as I know that the stars are now shining in the sky, though it is high noon. I never saw a star at midday, but I know it is the nature of stars to shine in the sky, and of the sky to hold its stars. Genius or fool, rich or poor, beauty or the beast, if marriage were what it should be, what God meant it to be, what even with the world's present possibilities it might be, it would be the Elysium, the sole complete Elysium, of woman, yes, and of man. Greatness, glory, usefulness, happiness, await her otherwise; but here alone all her powers, all her being, can find full play. No condition, no character even, can quite hide the gleam of the sacred fire; but on the household hearth it joins the warmth of earth to the hues of heaven. Brilliant, dazzling, vivid, a beacon and a blessing, her light may be, but only a happy home blends the prismatic rays into a soft serene whiteness, that floods the world with divine illumination. Without wifely and motherly love, a part of her nature must remain unclosed,—a spring shut up, a fountain sealed; but a thousand times better that it should remain unclosed than that it should be rudely rent open, or opened only to be defiled. A thousand times better that the vestal fire should burn forever on the inner shrine than that it should be brought out to boil the pot. But the pot must boil, you say, and so it must; but with oak-wood and shavings, not with beaten olive-oil.

This it is that I denounce,—not the use, but the abuse, of sacred things. I want girls to be saved from sacrilege. I do not want them to lay open their lives to spoliation. I want every woman to fill her heart with hopes and plans and purposes; and if a man will marry her, let him be so strong as to break down all barriers, check the whole flood-tide of her life, and sweep it around himself. If a woman is worth having, she is worth winning. Jacob served seven years for Rachel and seven more, and they seemed unto him but a few days for the love he had to her. Shiver and scatter the wan, weak attachments that dare to call themselves *love*. Scorn for this frothy, green whey that stands for the wine of life! Better that girls should be pirated away as the rough-handed Romans won their Sabine wives, than that a man should have but to touch the tree with his cane as he walks through the orchard, and down comes the ready-ripe fruit. In Von Fink's fiery wooing of Lenore, I hear the right trumpet-ring: "With rifle and bullet I have bought your stormy heart." I would have a woman marry, not because it is the only thing that offers, but because a magnificence sweeps by, in whose glorious sun her pale stars faint and fade. Her soul shall be filled and fired with the heavenly radiance. All her dross shall be consumed, and all her gold refined. She shall go to her marriage-feast as Zenobia went to Rome, crowned with flowers, but bound with golden chains, a conquered captive, and the banner over her shall be love. I would have her go obedient, not to the requirements of a false and fatal materialism, naming itself with the names of morality and womanhood, but to the unerring instincts of her own nature. She shall not fly to the only refuge from the vacuum and despair of her life; but her great heart and her strong hands shall be wrenched from their bent by the mysterious force of an irresistible magnetism. When you have a character that can so command, a love that can so control, you have set up on earth the pillars of Heaven, and redemption draweth nigh.

V.

UT if the pursuit of a separate and independent career should not disincline girls to marriage, you think it would unfit them for its duties; that an education, an occupation, and an interest in any other than a domestic direction would produce an indifferent housewife. Is this necessary? Is it even probable? Is there any sufficient reason why a woman who has trained her judgment in a medical school, shall not go into life, not only with no disadvantage, but with positive advantage from such training? If her mind have acquired power of observation, and her fingers skill in execution, will she not be so much the better prepared for the duties of her situation, whatever they may be? The ordering of a family is not like a trade,—a thing to be learned. It is multifarious and distracting. The mistress of a household is like the sovereign of a free empire. She does not need, and cannot serve, an apprenticeship. The only way to prepare her for its duties is to enlarge her capacity to discharge them. She needs a thorough education. Everything that helps to build up mind and body,— everything that makes her healthful, hopeful, cheerful, spirited, self-reliant, energetic, strong, helps her to administer her affairs successfully. A woman who can do one thing can do another thing, and she can do it all the better for having done the other one first; so that the pursuit of a profession, instead of incapacitating her for a domestic life, makes her better fitted for it. If for a year, or two or three, she has been studying the human system, or the stars, or the flowers, or the mysteries of cloak, or bonnet, or counter, or mint, she can turn aside at the beck of the master just as well as if she had been all the while frittering herself away, and she will also be a great deal better worth beckoning to. The entrance upon a "career" does not, as many seem to think and fear, prescribe perpetual adherence to it.

A girl may have a certain end in view, and design most clearly to follow it, and she does follow it—God bless her! But Nature also has her ends, and when her unerring finger points in another quarter, "This is the way, walk ye in it," be sure the girl will go. Activity will never keep her from happiness, but it will keep her from byways and stumbling-blocks, from the traps which Nature never set, but which a sentimentalism, born of selfishness, has put in her path. And be doubly sure of this: if one or two or a dozen years of industry and resolution unfit a girl to be a wife, she would never have been a prize. Any intelligent girl can learn household science in six months, and every girl ought to have, and generally does have, at least six months' warning. Experience will do the rest for her, and do it well, if she is a girl of sense; and if not, nothing would have helped the matter. One of the best cooks I know started in life with only a cabbage for capital; and with sense and spirit, out of that solitary cabbage, with whose proper management she chanced to be acquainted, sprang pies, puddings, preserves, such as it is not well even to think of in war-times.

So much for that portion of the objection which is put forward and has a just foundation. But the main part of it is under ground. In my opinion, the real danger lies in quite the opposite quarter from the one that is sought to be defended. The trouble is not that women do not think enough about household affairs. It is that they think too much. But if one might judge from the tenor of public and private talk, one would suppose that cooking was the chief end of woman and the chief solace of man. I distinguish cooking above all the other items of the domestic establishment, because I find it so distinguished before me. Four hundred volumes of papyrus, recovered from Herculaneum, related chiefly to music, rhetoric, and cookery. The god of whom Paul told the Philippians, even weeping, is worshipped to-day. Isaac acted after his kind when he loved Esau because he did eat of his venison! To know how to cook, to keep the husband in good humor with tempting viands, to prevent his being annoyed with burnt meat, soured with heavy bread, or vexed by late dinners, is the burden of a thousand ditties besides that of our sarcastic sonneteer. Printed "Advice to Marriageable Young Ladies" informs them that "a man is better pleased when he has a good dinner upon his table, than when his wife talks good French." I should like to be absolute monarch of America long enough to enact a decree that every man who opens his mouth to tell girls to learn to make bread, shall live a week on putty and water. What! are girls then to neglect to learn to make bread? By no means. Nor to roast beef, nor to boil potatoes. But suppose General Hooker should lead out his whole army against a detachment of the Rebels, and, neglecting Lee and Jackson with their myrmidons, should expend all his ammunition and skill on a handful of the foe, would you not adjudge him worthy of court-martial? But the detachment ought to be captured. Perhaps it ought. Send out a detachment and capture it. But do not waste your whole strength on an awkward squad, and leave the main body of the enemy to ravage at will. Defeat the latter, and the former will disappear of themselves.

Now when you bring out your drums and beat your dismal tattoo about learning to cook, you are doing just this; you are devoting all your strength to the destruction of an outwork whose fall will but very remotely affect the citadel. The remedy for an ignorance of cookery is not necessarily a knowledge of cookery. What is the reason that a man has cause to complain that his wife does not know how to cook? Is it that she devoted too much of her maiden time to teaching, preaching, doctoring, and dressmaking? Ten thousand to one, no. It is because she is ignorant or because she is silly. Treat girls sensibly. Educate their observation, their perception, their judgment. Give them a knowledge of human nature: and then be yourself so noble as to command their respect, and so amiable as to secure their affection, and you will have no trouble with heavy bread. If you insist on making women ignorant and silly, be sure their ignorance and silliness will crop out. Thrust them down in one place, and they will immediately rise in another. Sooner or later, you will prove the truth of Lord Burleigh's assurance to his son, and "find to your regret that there is nothing more fulsome than a she-fool."

But the general direction of your counsel is wrong, even supposing the immediate object at which it is aimed to be right. Its tendency is to induce women to give more attention to cookery than they now do; and they already devote to it a great deal more than they ought. They do not cook too well, but too much. A few mixtures should be better arranged than now, but a great many should be left alone. Cooking is the chief concern of a very large number of New

England wives and mothers. They spend the larger part of their ingenuity in devising, and the larger part of their strength and skill and time in preparing, food which is unnecessary and often hurtful. It never occurs to them to alter their course. They do not think of it as an unjust conjugal exaction, but as a Divine allotment. It is not always the one, and seldom if ever the other; but it is a custom. We are pre-eminently an eating people. Our women are cooking themselves to death, and cooking the nation into a materialism worse than death. Suppose you have been boarding or visiting for a month or two in a stranger family, and some one asks you if they live well, what do you understand him to mean? Is he inquiring if they are honorable, if they conduct their lives on Christian principles, if they are courteous, and self-respectful and self-controlled? Are they just in their dealings, disinterested in their motives, pure in word and work? Nothing is further from his thoughts. He means—and you at once understand him—Do they have highly-spiced and numerous meats, much cake and pie, many sauces and preserves? To what degradation have we descended! To live well is to eat rich food! Honor, integrity, refinement, culture, are all chopped up into mince-pie. Heart and soul are left to shift for themselves, and the guaranty of right and righteous living is

"A fair round belly with good capon lined."

In the olden times there lived, we are told, a race of men called Bisclaverets, who were half man and half wolf; or, to speak more accurately, were half the time man and half the time wolf. Some indications in our own day lead us to believe that the race of the Bisclaverets is not wholly extinct. Some stragglers must have found their way from the shores of

Bretagne to our Western wilds, and left a posterity whose name is Legion. I copy from one of the most prominent and liberal of our religious newspapers the following "elegant extract," not original in its columns, but adopted from some other paper, with such undoubted indorsement and commendation as an insertion without comment implies:—

"The business man who has been at work hard all day, will enter his house for dinner as crabbed as a hungry bear,—crabbed because he is as hungry as a hungry bear. The wife understands the mood, and, while she says little to him, is careful not to have the dinner delayed. In the mean time, the children watch him cautiously, and do not tease him with questions. When the soup is gulped, and he leans back and wipes his mouth, there is an evident relaxation, and his wife ventures to ask for the news. When the roast beef is disposed of, she presumes upon gossip, and possibly upon a jest; and when, at last, the dessert is spread upon the table, all hands are merry, and the face of the husband and father, which entered the house so pinched, and savage, and sharp, becomes soft, and full, and beaming as the face of the round summer moon."

Are we talking about a man or a wild beast? Is it wife or female? Are they children or cubs? Does he wipe his mouth or lick his chops? "*Ventures* to ask the news"! "*Presumes* upon a jest"! The whole picture is disgusting from beginning to end. It is the portraiture of sensuality and despotism. Hunger is not a sublime sensation, nor is eating a graceful act; but both are ordained of God, and are given us with that broad blank margin which almost invariably accompanies His gifts. Religion and culture can take up the necessity, and work so deftly that it shall become an adornment; and the ordinance of eating stand for the sunniest part of life. The grossness of the act, the mere animal and mechanical function of furnishing supplies, can be so larded with wit and wisdom, with love and good-will, with pleasant talk, interchange of civilities and courtesies, and all the light, sweet, gentle amenities of life, that a bare act becomes almost a rite. The rough structure is veiled into beauty with roses and lilies and the soft play of lights and shadows. But this paragraph portrays gobbling. A woman, instead of pandering to it by service and silence, ought to lift up her voice and repress it in its earliest stages. Make a man understand that he shall eat his dinner like a gentleman or he shall have no dinner to eat. If he will be crabbed and gulp, let him go down into the coal-bin and have it out alone; but do not let him bring his Feejeeism into the dining-room to defile the presence of his wife and corrupt the manners of his children.

If you think the picture is overdrawn, I pray you to remember that I did not draw it. It is a published, and, I think, a man's sketch of manhood. I only take it as I find it. I do not myself think that materialism has attained quite that degree of repulsiveness, but it is too near it. Eating is not perpetrated, but the appetite is pampered. If a man is able to hire a cook, very well. Cooking is the cook's profession; she ought to attain skill, and her employer has a right to require it, and as great a variety and profusion of dishes as he can furnish material for. But if he is not able to hire a cook, and must depend entirely upon his wife, the case is different. Cooking is not her profession. It is only one of the duties incident to her station. It is incumbent upon her to spread a plentiful and wholesome table. It is culpable inefficiency to do less than this. It is palpable immorality to do more. No matter how fond of cooking, or how skilful or alert a woman may be, she has only twenty-four hours in her day, and two hands for her work; and one woman who has the sole care of a family cannot, if she has any rational and Christian idea of life, of personal, household, and social duties, have any more time and strength than is sufficient for their simple discharge. Overdoing in one direction must be compensated by underdoing in another. She cannot pamper Peter without pinching Paul. Much that you laud as a virtue I lament as a vice. You revel in the cakes and the pastries and the dainties, and boast the skill of the housewife; and indeed her marvels are featly wrought, sweet to the taste, and to be desired if honestly come by; but if there has been plunder and extortion, if it is a soul that flakes in the pastry, if it is a heart that is embrowned in the gravies; if leisure and freshness and breadth of sympathy and keen enjoyment have been frittered away on the fritters, and simmered away in the sweetmeats, and battered away in the puddings, give me, I pray you, a dinner of herbs. Johnny-cake was royal fare in Walden woods when a king prepared the banquet and presided at the board. Peacocks' tongues are but common meat to peacocks.

The *pâté de foie gras* is a monstrous dish. A goose is kept in some warm, confined place that precludes any extended motion, and fed with fattening food, so that his liver enlarges through disease till it is considered fit to be made into a pie,—a luxury to epicures, but a horror to any healthful person. Just such a goose is many a woman, confined by custom and her consenting will in a warm, narrow kitchen, only instead of her liver it is her life which she herself makes up into pies; but the pastry which you find so delicious seems to me disease.

The ancients buried in urns the ashes of their bodies: we deposit in urns the ashes of our souls, and pass them around at the tea-table.

Women not only injure themselves by what they neglect, but injure others by what they perform. Such stress is laid upon the commissary department, that they lose discrimination, and come to think that dainty morsels are a panacea for all the ills of the flesh, instead of being the chief cause of most of them. I knew a young wife whose husband used to come down from his study worn and weary with much brain-work, his muscles flaccid, his eyes heavy, his circulation sluggish, and she would come up from the kitchen her face all aglow with eagerness and love and cooking-stove heat, her hands full of abominable little messes which she had been plotting against him, reeking with butter and sugar, and all manner of glorified greasiness,—I am happy to say I do not know by what name she called her machinations, but I call them broiled dyspepsia, toasted indigestions, fricasseed nightmare,—and the poor husband would nibble here and nibble there, sure of grim consequences, but loath to seem a churl by indifference, and neither give nor take satisfaction. I could bear his suffering with great equanimity, for there was a poetic justice in it, though he himself was not a sinner above others, nor yet so much as many. If only those men who are continually preaching the larder could be forced, sick or well, to swallow every combination which the fertile feminine brain can devise, and the nimble feminine fingers accomplish, I should listen to their exhortations with the most lively satisfaction. But even that would not atone for the female suffering. With what disconsolate countenance would my tender, anxious young wife ring the bell and send away the scarcely-diminished dish-lings, and wonder in her fond tortured heart what next she could do to smooth the wrinkled brow and light up the dull eyes, and so revolve perpetually in her troubled mind the mysterious question that loomed up mystically before us all in our Mother Goose days, "Why didn't Jack eat his supper?"

Why? O sweet and silly little wife? Because he wanted a thorough shaking-up. Because mind and body were flabby from too long poring over his books. If you could but have performed the impossible; if you could but have parted with the feeble cant which you had learned from infancy; if you would but have driven him out alike from his study and your sitting-room, going with him, if such inducement became necessary, into the fresh air; if you would but have walked him, or worked him, or in some way kneaded him into firm, hard thew and sinew, and kept him out and active till he should have got such an appetite that cold brown bread and molasses would have seemed to him a dish fit to set before a king, you would have done him true wifely service. Then you might have come home and fed him with butter and sugar to your heart's content,— and not to the perpetual discontent and rebellion of his body.

But among all the lectures to young wives or old wives or no wives at all, I never heard or read one that counselled a woman to take her husband out walking, or rowing, or riding, or driving, or bowling, or do any other sensible thing. I have dived into oceans of nonsense, but never found the pearl.

Our New England people considers itself to have advanced much further in civilization than the aborigines, whose chief occupation, according to the histories, is hunting and fishing. But why is it

57

barbarous to devote your life to procuring food, and civilized to devote your life to cooking it? Of the two, I think I should prefer the former. The Savage may not present an inviting bill of fare; but the excitement of the chase, the close contact with nature, the wide freedom of sea and sky, the grand play of all the powers, the mighty strengthening of all the organs, the fine culture of the senses, the health and vigor of every nerve and tissue, the leap and sparkle of all the springs of life, this, surely, would be no insignificant compensation: but a continual pottering over gridirons and frying-pans is good for neither brain nor brawn. Civilization may quick upfly and kick the beam: I would much rather be a good Sioux Indian than most New England housewives.

VI.

HE much talk of fitness for marriage leads one to reflect on the advantages of living in the nineteenth century. With all the sewing-machines, washing-machines, wringing-machines, carpet-sweepers, cooking-ranges, and the innumerable devices by which labor is sought and is supposed to be saved, I do not see that there is any great gain. The requirements of civilized society rather more than keep abreast with the inventions of civilized ingenuity. Fifty years ago a bonnet cost twenty dollars. Now a comely bonnet can be bought for one dollar. But the twenty-dollar bonnet lasted ten years, and the one-dollar bonnet three months, so that, notwithstanding the superior cheapness of the material, the item bonnet costs more money than it used, and vastly more time and thought. A calico dress was not deemed unreasonable at seventy cents a yard. Lately it could be had for twelve and a half: but at seventy-five cents it was an heirloom, while at twelve and a half it stands over the wash-tub by the second year, and by the third goes into the rag-bag. The lively sewing-machine runs up a seam twenty times as swiftly as the most lively fingers: but there are twenty times as many seams to run up. Just as fast as skill "turns off" work, just so fast fashion turns it on. Nay, fashion in heaping up entirely outstrips ingenuity in lowering the pile of work; so that we do not get the benefit of our skill. The day now is no longer than the day of fifty years ago. The mother of five children seems to have no more time for educating her five children, for enjoying and training their opening lives, for studying their characters, for associating with them and acquiring their confidence, for planting unexpected roses in the little flower-plats of their years, for sitting a whole summer day with them among the beauties and wonders and delights of the woods, for spending a whole winter evening with them in games and reading, for informing her own mind and disciplining her own heart and strengthening and beautifying her own body, for cultivating the possible beneficences of society, for genial and growing acquaintance and sympathy with the poets, the philosophers, the historians, and the sages, than the mother of five children had fifty years ago. I suppose more women now-a-days know how to read and write; but do they read and write? Of the people in your village, your street, your sewing-society: how many do you find who spend as much as an hour a day in reading Milton, or Chaucer, or Spenser, or Tennyson, or Mrs. Browning? How many are there who are familiar with Hume, or Robertson, or Macaulay, or Motley, or Palfrey? How many have lingered with delight over the pages of Lord Bacon, or Jeremy Taylor, or John Stuart Mill? How many know the relation between a cat and a tiger, or what are the ingredients of buttermilk, or why yeast makes bread rise, or how the heat of the oven works, or whether a cloverhead has anything to do with a marrowfat pea? How many are interested to peer into the mysteries of the heavens above or the earth beneath or the waters under the earth? How many ever heard of the Areopigitica or the Witena-gemot, or discern any connection between Runnymede and Fort Sumter, or have the faintest opinion as to whether Runnymede is a man or a mouse? How many can tell you whether the Reformation was a revelation confronting a superstition or a fruitful branch grafted upon a barren olive-tree, or an old religion throwing off the layers of acquired corruption? How many understand the origin and bearings of Calvinism or the Nicene Creed or the Pauline Epistles? I speak, you see, not of things which have passed away leaving only a slender and hidden thread of connection, but of those which still touch life at many points. The great boast of the present day is the dissemination of knowledge: but knowledge is trash if it is not assimilated into wisdom. Knowledge which is simply plastered on to the outside of the soul and does not chemically combine to become part and parcel of the soul's substance, produces an effect little better than grotesque. Names and dates may store the memory; but why have the memory stored if you do not use its treasures? What better off am I for having a heap of isolated facts in my lumber-room if I have nothing for those facts to do? I may know in what year the battle of Hastings was fought, but unless I can locate that battle otherwhere than in geography and chronology, I might as well have committed to the charge of my memory the youthful facts of

"Onery Twoery ickery see,

Halibut crackibut pendalee.

Pin pon musket John,

Triddle traddlecome Twenty-one."

Bricks and boards are neither shelter from wind nor shade from sun. It is only when all are fitly framed together into the strength and sweetness of spirit that they become the temple of the living God, whereinto Shekinah shall come. We talk about the universal circulation of newspapers, but sometimes it seems to me that newspapers are only an enormous expansion of village gossip. Now if a murder is committed in New York we hear of it, whereas formerly we did not know it unless it were committed in the next town. But such knowledge we could very readily dispense with. Is anything added to the worth of life by learning that Bridget McArthy has been fined five dollars and costs for breaking Ellen Maloney's windows. In the old wars, it was three weeks after a victory was gained before you heard of it; now you hear of it six months before the battle is fought, and after all it turns out to be no victory, but a masterpiece of strategy.[2] What I wish to know is this: does the constant interflow of currents really deepen and broaden the channel of life? Are women any stronger of will, firmer of purpose, broader of view, sounder of judgment, than they used to be? Can they front fortune with serener brow, unawed by her malice, unflattered by her promise, unmoved by her caprice? Are they any more independent of the circumstances of life, any more concentrated in its essence? Do they think more deeply, love more nobly, live more spiritually? Are they any more divorced from the lust of the flesh, the lust of the eyes, and the pride of life; any more wedded to whatsoever things are true, whatsoever things are honest, whatsoever things are just, whatsoever things are pure, whatsoever things are lovely, whatsoever things are of good report?

I think we are in a transition-state. The increased facilities of labor are improvements, and we shall by and by reap the fruits of them; but we have hardly yet done so. We have lassoed our wild horse, but we have not harnessed him. He shows us wonderful freaks of strength, but he drags us quite as often as we drive him. "Sweet Puck" has been caught, and made to put his girdle round about the earth in forty minutes; in

> "one night, ere glimpse of morn,
>
> His shadowy flail hath threshed the corn,
>
> That ten day-laborers could not end."

But he is not yet tamed down into a trustworthy domestic drudge. If he does not actually transmute himself into a Robin Goodfellow, that bootless makes the breathless housewife churn, and the drink to bear no barm, and mislead night-wanderers, he yet annuls his work, shutting the eyes of the ten day-laborers so that they do not gain rest for his interference; his earth-girdle binds no bundle of myrrh for the well-beloved. Our great diffusion of knowledge has not given us corresponding mastery. Our knives are sharper, but we only whittle. Knowledge is poured abroad, but it is not absorbed. Yet the hour approaches. By and by, out of this wishy-washy chaos, slowly shall arise the coast-line of a new continent whereon the redeemed shall walk: meanwhile, do not let us deceive ourselves. The millennium is not yet come. We are scarcely beyond the multiplication-table of our mathematics. We are blind and blundering, and for all our skill and science, we stumble through life but little wiser than our fathers. We have the swift, clean stove-oven for the cumbrous old bake-kettle, but meanwhile we have lost the fireside, and have found no substitute; and a man's life lies not in ovens or bake-kettles, but in firesides.

This truth needs to be engraven on our brains and hearts with a pen of iron and the point of a diamond. The soul is the king and not the servant of the body. Every device, every invention, every measure, that does not subserve the interests of the soul, is worthless. Every invention that may subserve those interests, but stops short of such subserviency, stops so far short of its goal. If the cooking-range only makes that mince-pie be eaten once a day instead of once a year; if steam-power only causes that fine wheat-bread shall take the place of coarse corn-bread; if sewing-machines are going to give women more tucks to their skirts, more flounces to their gowns, more dresses to their wardrobes, and not more hours to their day, we might just as well be without the sewing-machines and the cooking-ranges and the steam-power. Is a woman any better, or any better off, for having six gowns where her mother had three? Is she not worse off? She can wear but one at a time, and she is expending brain-power and heart-power, and lifting the incidents of life into the sphere of its essentials. There are women who buy dresses, and make them, and hang them up in their closets, there to remain till the fashion changes, and the dress has to be re-made without having been once worn. O terrible emptiness of life which this signalizes! O wanton and wicked waste of priceless treasures! What shall be said in the day when God maketh inquisition? I wage no war against the æsthetics of life; but I do protest that they shall be means and not ends. Let richness drape the form, and variety crown the board, and luxury fill the house, if so be you do not wrong the king, the Master. There need be no other limitation. Wrong to one's self involves and implies all other wrong. Nothing human is foreign to any man. Nothing personal is foreign to humanity. You cannot defraud yourself of your birthright without defrauding all those to whom your birthright might bring blessings. The keenest barb of your injustice to another pierces your own breast.

But the larger number of New England families earn their bread by the sweat of their brow, and must sacrifice the one or the other,—the soul or the body. They cannot command both luxury and life; and they choose—which? Look around and answer. How many houses do you know that have no carpets on the floors, no cushions in the chairs, no paper on the walls, no silks in the wardrobes, no china in the closets, but plenty of books in the library; a harp, a piano, a violin, in one corner, an easel, a box of crayons in another; an aquarium by the window, a camp-stool in the cupboard, a fishing-rod on the shelf, a portfolio on the table; where pies and fries and cakes and preserves and pickles and puddings seldom come; where flounces and velvets and feathers and embroideries are unseen, but where the walls are adorned with drawings from the mother's own hands, with bouquets, finely selected, pressed and arranged by the daughters; with cabinets of minerals gathered, classified, and labelled by the sons; and fresh flowers from the garden, cultivated and culled by the father; where the homely fare is seasoned with Attic salt; where wit and wisdom and sprightliness and fun and heart's-ease make the simple, wholesome, and plentiful meal a fit banquet for gods; where work is work, and not simply labor; where rest is change, and not simply torpidity; where the heart is rich in love, and the head rich in lore, and intellect and affection go hand in hand; where the inmates are not the creatures of the house, but the house is the dear handiwork of the inmates; where they derive no lustre from their dwelling, but shine all through it with such sweet, soft lights, that elegance waits upon their footsteps, beauty lingers upon their brows, every spot which they tread is enchanted ground, every room which they enter is the audience-chamber of a king. On the other hand, how many houses do you know where everything is in abundance except that which alone gives abundance its value? Where moss-soft carpets and heavy curtains and gilded cornices and silver and china and sumptuous fare make a glittering pageant, but work and worry and weariness, or frivolous pleasures and frivolous interests, empty life of all its priceless possessions. How many do you know where neither wealth nor worth reigns? Where hard, grinding, pinching toil is all that the evening and the morning have to give, and everything lovely to the eye and pleasant to the soul is crushed between the upper and the nether millstones? How many young couples think they could begin housekeeping without a carpet for the parlor floor? How many think of providing that parlor with a score of the rich, ripe, mellow English classics? But to the end of the days, the authors will be a joy and strength and consolation, and the carpet will be only a dusty woollen rag. No, no; we cannot give up our trappings. Such is the poverty of our life, and we may not uncover its nakedness. We must have jewels and gold to hide our squalor and our leanness. It is tinsel or nothing. Take away our fine clothes, our fine furniture, our much eating and drinking, and what is left? True,—what is left? Vacancy and desolation. Suppose the work and worry to be suddenly abrogated to the degree that the thousands of harassed women who toil with broom or needle or dish-cloth or kneading-trough from morning till night should suddenly find on their hands four hours every day of leisure,—leisure that absolutely need be filled up by no family knitting, mending, or oversight,—would it be a boon? In many cases I greatly fear not. After the first luxury of utter rest from strenuous work, I greatly fear that that four hours would be the dullest and dreariest part of the day, and its close more gladly welcomed than its commencement. But this only shows the need, not the impossibility, of reformation. If it has come to this, that we know not what to do with ourselves, shall we go on providing toys, or shall we turn about and straightway learn self-direction? Is it so that we must fill our lives with husks, because we have fed on them so long that we have no relish for nourishing food? Have we so held in abeyance our spiritual forces that they have lost their life? Have we so given ourselves to our grosser uses, that they have usurped the throne, and shall we now make no effort to depose them and restore the rightful lord? Shall we go on forming and frocking our wax dolls, and give no heed to the marble which it is our life-work to fashion into the image and likeness of God? Better Romulus and Remus, suckled by a wolf, than our puny nurslings of conventionality! O for men and women with blood in their veins, and muscles in their bodies, and brains in their skulls,—men and women who believe in their manhood and their womanhood! who will be as valiant, as aggressive, as enduring in peace as they are showing themselves in war, who dare stand erect, who will walk their own paths, who brave solitudes, who see things and not the traditions of things, who will blow away, with one honest breath, our shabby gew-gaw finery! America was founded on the rights of man: why do we set our affections on silks and satins? Why entangle our young limbs with the fetters of an old civilization, golden though they be? Never had any nation such opportunity as ours. Here is the race-course ready, the battle-ground prepared. It needs only that we be swift and strong. There are no morasses of old prejudice to beguile our feet, no tangle of old growths to retard our progress. We have no institutions to fight against: all our institutions fight with us. No garter, no ribbon, no courtly presentation, is demanded as our stamp of rank; the badge of each man's order is set on his brow and breast. Worth needs not to have flowed down through musty ages if it would receive its meed; every man bears his seal direct from God. Humanity is more accounted of than a coat of arms. We have only to be noble, and we belong at once to the nobility. It is ourselves alone that will fail if there be failure; not opportunity. It is for us to rise to the height of the great argument. It is only that we reverence ourselves, that we esteem man as of greater mark than his meat or his raiment. Give us full and free development. Tear away these gilded fetters, and let the children of God have free course to run and be glorified. Throw off allegiance to trifles, and with the heart believe, and with the mouth make confession, and with the upright life attest: There is no God but God.

This can be done only when women and men will work together to the same end. It is not to be done by stripping away the restraints of fashion and society and leaving life bare of its proprieties. Deformity is not lovely by being exposed. What we are to do is to supplant those restraints by the gentle growths of a larger and finer culture; to replace meagreness with rounded beauty; to make the life so rich and full that all else shall seem poor in comparison; to show it so fair and fertile that every luxury shall seem but its natural outgrowth, its proper adornment; to make the soul so simply dominant as to give their laws to fashion and society instead of receiving laws from them, and so have fashion and society for its nimble servitors instead of being itself their creature and slave. Is it not so now? Who dares bend social life to his uses? Who dares run counter to its caprices? Who dares stand on his own dignity and defy its frown or sneer? But, you say, this adaptation of one's self to others is what Christianity requires. This self-seeking, this self-elevation, is directly opposed to the spirit of the Gospel, which demands that every one seek not his own, but the things which are another's. Not at all. You can in no other way benefit your generation than through your own heart and life. Can a stream rise higher than its fountain? Can a corrupt tree bring forth good fruits? The Apostle says: Let no man seek his own, but every man another's wealth. Does that mean that a farmer must not plough his own field, or plant his own corn, or hoe his own potatoes, but go over to till his neighbor's farm and leave his own fallow? But it is written, "He that provideth not for his own house hath denied the faith, and is worse than an infidel," and common sense need not be propped up by revelation, for it stands firmly on the same ground. You say a woman must not be thinking of herself, her own growth, and good all the time. So do I. But is she to obtain and exhibit self-forgetfulness by self-culture, or self-neglect? Will you be most likely to forget your head by thoroughly combing and brushing your hair every morning, or by brushing it not at all? Does not health consist in having your organs in such a condition that you do not know you have organs? A dyspeptic man is the most subjective person in the world. He thinks more about himself in a week than a well person does in a year. The true way for women and men to be thoroughly self-forgetful, is to be so thoroughly self-cultured, so healthy, so normal, so perfect, that all they have to do is their work. Themselves are perfectly transparent. No headaches and heartaches interpose between themselves and their duties. They are not forced back to concentrate their interest on a torpid liver, or tubercled lungs. They are not wasting their power by working in constant jar and clash. They are at full liberty to bring means to bear on ends. And just in proportion as sound minds have sound bodies, will people be able to forget themselves and do good to others.

Now—the connection between some of my paragraphs may be a little underground, but it is always there. If you don't quite see it, you must jump. If I should stop to say everything, I should never get through. I am not sure I shall, as it is— now, such has been the amount of gluttony, and all manner of frivolity and materialism, indirectly but strenuously inculcated by literature, that we are arrived at a point where they are almost the strongest grappling-hooks between the sexes. Understand: I am not saying that dress is frivolity. Dress is development. A woman's dress is not her first duty, but it follows closely on first duty's heels. She should dress so as to be grateful to her husband's eye, I grant, nay, I enjoin: and he is under equally strong obligations to dress so as to be grateful to her eye. But this is scarcely a matter of expense. It need not cost, appreciably, more to be neat and tasteful than it does to be dowdy and slouching. But, I have heard women say, variety in dress is necessary in order that a husband may not be wearied. But does a man ever think of having several winter coats or summer waistcoats, so that his wife may not weary of him? Does she ever think of being tired of seeing one hat till it begins to look shabby? And if a man buys his clothes and wears them according to his needs,—which is quite right,—why shall not a woman do the same? Is there any law or gospel for forcing a woman to be pleasing to her husband, while the husband is left to do that which is right in his own eyes? Or are the visual organs of a man so much more exquisitely arranged than those of a woman, that special adaptations must be made to them, while a woman may see whatever happens to be *à la mode*? Or has a man's dress intrinsically so much more beauty and character than a woman's, that less pains need be taken to make it charming?

But granting to variety all the importance that is claimed for it, are we using the lever to advantage? Suppose the gown is changed every day, while the face above it never varies, or varies only from one vapidity to another, and what is gained? If variety is the desideratum, why not attempt it in the direction in which variety is spontaneous, resultant, and always delightful? You may flit from brown merino to blue poplin, and from blue poplin to black alpaca, and be queen of all that is tiresome still. But enlarge every day the horizon of your heart: be tuneful on Monday with the birds; be fragrant on Tuesday among your roses; be thoughtful on Wednesday with the sages; be chemical on Thursday over your bread-trough; be prophetic on Friday with history; be aspiring on Saturday in spite of broom and duster; be liberal and catholic on Sunday: be fresh and genial and natural and blooming with the dews that are ready to gather on every smallest grass-blade of life, and a pink-sprigged muslin will be new for a whole season, yes, and half a dozen of them. Take example from the toad: swallow your dress; not precisely in the same sense, but as effectually. Overpower, subordinate your dress, till it shall be only a second cuticle, not to be distinguished from yourself, but a natural element of your universal harmony.

What are you going to wear to church this summer? I say church, because I am speaking now to people whose best dress is their Sunday dress. I am not writing for the Newport and Niagara frequenters, who know no currency smaller than gold eagles. You will not have many new clothes because it is "war-times," but you must have a silk mantle; that will cost fifteen dollars. You could have bought one last summer for ten dollars, but silk is now higher. You will have a barege dress, which, with the increased price of linings and trimmings and making, will cost before it is ready to be worn fifteen more. Your gloves will be a dollar and a half, and your bonnet, whitened and newly trimmed with last summer's ribbon, will be three dollars or so. The whole cost will be about thirty-five dollars. But suppose, instead of a barege gown and silk shawl, you had bought a pretty gingham and had it made in the same way, dress and mantle alike, and had taken that for your summer outfit; and had substituted for your kid gloves a pair of Lisle-thread at sixty-two cents. The gingham will last longer than the barege, and will be good for more uses after it is outworn as a dress. It will last as long in the mantle as the shape of the mantle will be fashionable, and then it will make over as economically, and into a larger number of articles. The Lisle-thread gloves will last as long as the kid, and will be much better on the whole, because they will wash. "But I should make a figure, walking up the broad aisle in a gingham mantilla!" Be sure you would, and a very pretty figure too. For you look, in it, perfectly fresh and tidy; and because you have not been fagged and fretted with its great cost you will be quite happy and pleased, and that pleasure will beam out in your face and figure, and your young, elastic tread; and there is not a man in church who will suspect that everything is not precisely as it should be. Men judge in generals, not in particulars; and the few who are conversant with minutiæ, and look beyond the facts of becomingness or unbecomingness into the question of texture and fabric, are such microscopic sort of men that you do not value their opinion one way or the other. You are triumphant so far as the men are concerned.

The women will not let you off so easily. Mrs. Judkins will think you are "very odd"; but how much better to be oddly right than evenly wrong! Mrs. Jenkins will call it *real mean*, when you are as well able to dress decently as she is! But you are the very plant and flower of decency. Mrs. Perkins will hate to see people try to be different from other folks. Ah! Mrs. Perkins, when the vapor from your heated face goes down to-morrow meeting the vapor that comes steaming up from your foaming tub, will you find it any consolation for your heat and fatigue that you went to church yesterday and are broiling over your wash-tub to-day "like other folks." Meanwhile you, by your gingham, have saved ten dollars. Ten dollars! I am lost in amazement when I think of the good that may be accomplished with ten dollars! For ten dollars you can hire a washerwoman all summer and save—absolutely add to your life six hours every Monday for three months; look at the reading, the writing, the conversation, the enjoyment that can be crowded into an hour, and then multiply it by seventy-five, and say whether your gingham dress be not a very robe of royalty. And besides the good you do yourself, and the good that will shine from you upon all around you, you will be helping to solve the great problem of the age: you will be helping to give employment to the thousands of women who are perishing for lack of something to do, and dragging society down with them. You will be setting supply and demand face to face. If you could but induce a few of your neighbors to join you,—which they will be glad to do when they see how happy and fresh it makes you,—the employment you would furnish would comfortably support some destitute unmarried woman, or some childless widow, and go far towards providing bread and butter, perhaps shoes and stockings, possibly spelling-books, to a family of children. There are, possibly, as many women who need to do more than they are doing as there are who need to do less, and you will be helping to restore or create the desired equilibrium. Or, if you choose instead, ten dollars will take your rustic little ones into the city to stock and startle their minds with ideas from the navy-yard, the museum, the aquarial gardens, the picture-galleries; or it will take your civic little ones into the country and set them down in the midst of orchards and blooms and birds, and all the pure sweet influences of long summer days. It will give you four or five drives with your husband and children,—drives that involve fascinating white baskets; napkins spread out on the grass, hungry mouths, chattering tongues, and oh! such happy hearts. Or you can go to the beach and hear the little monkeys scream for joy and terror in the rushing, lapping, embracing waves, and see them roll over and over in the soft sand, and gather untold wealth of worthless shells and heaps of shining sand for back-yard gardens. For ten dollars you can buy picture-books, long-desired toys, flowers and flower-stands for winter, roots for bedding in summer, and still have enough left to give an extra lemon to a score of wounded soldiers in a hospital ward. You can buy yourself leisure to become acquainted with your children and to make them acquainted with the brightest phases of yourself. You can put into their lives such sunny memories as no after bitterness can efface; such sunny memories as shall wreathe you with a glory in the coming years when your head is laid low in the grave. O my friend, I can almost see the light of the celestial city shining through that ten dollars,—and you talk about a silk cape!

Mind, I counsel no penuriousness, no mean retrenchment for accumulation, no domestic pillage, no mere selfish gratification. I suggest intelligent and high-minded economy for the purpose of liberal expenditure. I would take in sail where only sensualism and ostentation blow; but I would spread every rag of canvas to catch the smallest breath of an enlarged and Christian happiness. I would cease to pinch the angel, that the beast may wax fat. I would keep the beast under, that the angel may have room.

Do you say that the picture is fanciful? Everything is fanciful till it is put in practice. Fancy is often but the foreshadow of a coming fact.

If some such course as this is not possible, if we must inevitably and perpetually move on in the same rut in which we move now, then, in a thousand and a thousand cases, life seems to me not worth the living.

VII.

T is not simply that women are chained to a body of
death. Men are equally victims. The world is kept
back from its goal. One member cannot suffer
without involving all the members in its suffering.

Marriage, in its truest type, is love spiritualizing
life; the union of the mightiest and subtlest forces
working the noblest results. Marriage in its
commonest manifestations is a clumsy mechanical
contrivance. Marriage is too often mirage,—far off,
in books, in dreams, lovely and divine; approached,
it resolves itself into washing and ironing and
cooking and nursing and house-cleaning and making
and mending and long-suffering from New Year to
Christmas and from Christmas on to New Year, to
the great majority of all the women I know anything
about. I do not mean simply the dull, uninteresting
women, of whom there are really not many, but the
bright and intellectual, capable of adorning any
station, of whom there are more than you think,
because, buried under household ruins, you scarcely
catch a glimpse of what they long to be and what
they might be. And they do not like it. Volumes may
be written and spoken, extolling the tidy kitchens,
the trim wives, the snowy table-cloths, and telling us
how beautiful a woman is when doing her house-
work; and a few foolish women will be found to
accept it all and work the harder. Hundreds of years

ago, when a person I know was inconceivably young, and found great delight in hanging about the kitchen during the seed-time and harvest of pies and preserves, to glean up the remnants of mince-meat and various mixtures left in the pans, a tiny relative much more acute than he used to practise upon his approbativeness by soliloquizing to himself while both their spoons were clattering around the sides of the tin pan with frantic rapidity, "Now Peggoty isn't going away, and let me have the rest. Peggoty is going to stay and eat it all up." The result was that Peggoty used immediately to walk off and leave his cormorant kinsman to the undivided booty. Just about as astute as the kinsman, and just about as silly as Peggoty, are the men who prepare and the women who suck the thin pap of our milk-and-water novels and newspapers. But the latter are growing fewer and fewer every day. Some women have a natural taste for cooking. Some women are specially skilled in sewing. Some women are born with a broom in their hands, and some find the sick-room their peculiar paradise: but I never saw or heard of any woman who had a natural fondness for being worked and worried from morning till night, hurrying from pillar to post, and conscious all the time that things were left in an unfinished state, from sheer want of time to complete them properly. Within a week, a woman, a model housekeeper, devoted to her family,—a woman who never wrote a word for print, nor ever addressed so much as a female meeting of any kind, a woman whose husband looks upon strong-mindedness as a species of leprosy, to be lamented rather than denounced, but at any cost kept from spreading,—has told me that, if it were not for the talk it would make, she would shut up her house, take her whole family, and go to a hotel to board from June to October, so worn and wearied is she with her household duties. Yet her family consists of only three members, and her husband is full of loving-kindness and consideration. Another woman, equally accomplished in all domestic arts and graces, and equally happy in her conjugal relations, once told me that she has seen from her window a carriage of friends coming up the road to her house, and has been forced to wipe away the tears before she could go to the door to greet them; so utterly disheartened was she at the prospect of still further weight upon her already overburdened shoulders. Yet she was no misanthrope, no nun. She loved society, and was fitted to shine in it; but the inexorable, unremitting labor of her household was such, that it was impossible for her to receive from society the solace which it ought to give and which it has to give. So heavily pressed the yoke, that a party of friends was no pleasure to look forward to, but only more cake to be made, more meat to be roasted, more sheets to be washed.

Women are accounted the weaker sex; but there is no comparison to be made between the labor of the weaker and the stronger. Of fathers of families and mothers of families, the real wear and tear of life comes on the latter. If there is anxiety as to a sufficiency of support, the mother shares it equally with the father, and feels it none the less for not being able to contribute directly to the supply of the deficiency; forced, passive endurance of an evil is quite as difficult a virtue as unsuccessful struggle against it. If there is no anxiety in that direction, the occupations of men can scarcely give them any hint of the peculiar perplexing, depressing, irritating nature of a woman's ordinary household duties. Pamphleteers exhort women to hush up the discords, drive away the clouds, and have only smiles and sunshine for the husband coming home wearied with his day's labor. They would be employing themselves to much better advantage, if they would enjoin him to bring home smiles and sunshine for his wife. She is the one that pre-eminently needs strength and soothing and consolation. She needs a warm heart to lean on, a strong arm, and a steady hand to lift her out of the sloughs in which she is ready to sink, and set her on the high places where birds sing and flowers bloom and breezes blow. The husband's work may be absorbing and exhaustive, but a fundamental difference lies in the simple fact, that a man has constant and certain change of scene, and a woman has not. A man goes out to his work and comes in to his meals. Two or three times a day, sometimes all the evening, always at night and on Sunday, he is away from his business and his place of business. The day may be long or short, but there is an end to it. A woman is on the spot all the time, and her cares never cease. She eats and drinks, she goes out and comes in, she lies down and rises up, tethered to one stone. It does not seem to amount to much, that a man closes his shop and goes home; that he unyokes his oxen, ties up his cows, and sits down on the door-step: but let the merchant, year after year, eat and sleep in his counting-room, the schoolmaster in his school-room, the shoemaker over his lapstone, the blacksmith by his anvil, the minister in his study, the lawyer in his chambers, with only as frequent variations as a housekeeper's visiting and tea-drinkings give her, and I think he would presently learn that he needs not to possess powers acute enough to divide a hair 'twixt north and northwest side, in order to distinguish the difference. A distance of half a mile, or even a quarter of a mile, breaks off all the little cords that have been compressing a man's veins, and lets the blood rush through them with force and freedom. It is change of scene, change of persons, change of atmosphere, and a consequent change of a man's own self. He is made over new.

But his wife moils on in the same place. Dark care sits behind her at breakfast and dinner and supper. The walls are festooned with her cares. The floors are covered with them as thick as the dust in the Interpreter's house. *He* shakes off the dust from his feet and goes home: *her* home is in the dust. What wonder that it strangles and suffocates her?

Moreover, a man's occupation has uniformity, or rather unity. His path lies in one line; sometimes he has only to walk mechanically along it. Rather stupid, but not wearing work; for generally if he had been a man upon whom it would have worn he would have done something else: always he has power to bring everything to bear on his business. If it is mental labor, he has the opportunity of solitude, or only such association as assists. His helpers, and all with whom he is concerned, are mature, intelligent, trained, and often ambitious and self-respectful and courteous. He can set his fulcrum close to the weight, and all he has to do is to bear down on the lever.

The wife's assistants, if she has any, are unspeakably in the rough, and little children make all her schemes "gang a-gley." The incautious slam of a door will shatter the best-laid plans, and the stubbing of a chubby toe sinks her morning deep into the midday. Children are to a man amusement, delight, juvenescence, a truthful rendering of the old myth, that wicked kings were wont to derive a ghoul-like strength by transfusion of the blood of infants. The father has them for a little while. He frolics with them. He rejoices over them. They are beautiful and charming. He is new to them, and they are new to him, and by the time the novelty is over it is the hour for them to go to bed. He feels rested and refreshed for his contact with them. They present strong contrasts to the world he deals with all day. Their transparency shines sweetly against its opacity. Even their little wants and vanities and bickerings are to him only interesting developments of human nature. His power is pleased with their dependence; his pride flatters itself with their future; his tenderness softens to their clinging; his earthliness cleaves away before their innocence, and he thinks his quiver can never be too full of them.

This is the poetry, and he reads it with great delight; but there is a prose department, and that comes to the mother. She has had the cherubs all day, and she knows that the trail of the serpent is over them all. She sees the angel, in their souls as well as he, often better; but she sees too the mark of the beast on their forehead,—which he seldom discovers. His playthings are her stumbling-blocks. The constancy of her presence forbids novelty, and throws her upon her inventive powers for resources. All their weariness and fretfulness and tumbles and aches are poured into her lap. She has no division of labor, no concentration of forces; no five or ten hours devoted to housework, and two or three to her children, taking them into her heart to do good like a medicine. They patter through every hour to stay her from doing with her might any of the many things which her hands find to do. Nothing keeps limits; everything laps over. God has given her a love so inexhaustible, that, notwithstanding the washings and watchings, the sewing and dressing which children necessitate, notwithstanding the care, the check, the pull-back, the weariness, the heartsickness, which they occasion, the "little hindering things" are—my pen is not wont to be timid, but it shrinks from attempting to say what little ones are to a mother. But divine arrangement does not prevent human drawback; and looking not at inward solace, but outward business, it remains true that the business of providing for the wants of a family is not of that smooth, uncreaking nature to the mother that it is to the father. Let a man take two or three little children—two or three? Let him take one! —of one, two, three, or four years of age, to his shop, or stall, or office, and take care of him all the time for a week, and he will see what I mean.

I do not say that a man's work may not be harder for an hour, or five or ten hours, more exhaustive of mental and vital power, more exclusive of all diversions than his wife's for the same time. It may or may not be; quite as often the latter as the former: but I do say that severe prearranged, intermittent labor wears less upon the temper, the nerves, and the spirits, that is, upon body and soul, than lighter, confused, unintermitting labor. Work that enlists the energies and the enthusiasm will weary, but the weariness itself is welcome, and brings with it a satisfaction,—the pleasant sense of something accomplished. The multiplicity of a woman's labors distracts as well as wearies, and each one is so petty that she has scarcely anything to look back on. Not one of them is great enough to brace and stimulate, and all together they form a multitudinous heap, and not a mountain. It is a round of endless detail; little, insignificant, provoking items that she gets no credit for doing, but fatal discredit for leaving undone. Nobody notices that things are as they should be; but if things are not as they should be, it were better for her that a millstone were hanged about her neck,

&c.!

In a community, you find the husbands devoted to different pursuits. Baker, miller, farmer, advocate, clerk,—each one has a peculiar calling for which he is supposed to have a special taste, fitness, or motive, perhaps all; but their wives have no room for choice. Whether they have a gift of it or not, they have the same routine of baking and brewing and house-cleaning. Suppose the woman does not like it? The supposition is not an impossible, not even an unnatural one. Woman's-sphere writers confound distinctions; they seem to think that woman was not created in the garden in native honor clad like man, but rather, like the turtle, with her house on her back, and that a modern American house and its belongings; so that if she dislikes any of the conclusions which such a house premises, it is as unnatural and unwomanly as if she should be coarse or cruel. Womanliness, in their vocabulary, implies fondness of and pleasure in domestic drudgery. Their ideal woman is enamored of wash-tubs and broom-handles and frying-pans. But modern housekeeping is no more woman's sphere than farming is man's sphere, nor so much. If you go back far enough, you will find that man was directly and divinely ordained to that very pursuit. The Lord God took the man, and put him into the garden of Eden, *to dress it and to keep it*. His sphere was expressly marked out. He was to be a gardener, a farmer, a tiller of the soil. What of the woman? "The Lord God said, It is not good *that the man should be alone*: I will make him an help meet for him." What kind of help was meant is here implied, but is more clearly discovered further on by Adam's own interpretation: "The woman whom thou gavest *to be with me*." She was made for society, to be company for him; to talk and laugh and cheer and keep him from being lonesome. Not a word about housekeeping. Adam is concerned to put the very best face on the matter, and he does not say, "the woman whom thou gavest to train up the vines, to pare the apples, to stone the raisins, to gather the currants, to press the grapes, to preserve the peaches," or for any other purposes of an Eden household. It is simply "thou gavest *to be with me.*" Whatever may have come in afterwards to modify the original arrangement, came for "the hardness of your hearts." But here, before the fall, is seen, in all its beauty and simplicity, the original plan. You have the whole "woman question" in a nutshell. Yet people who are fond of quoting the Bible manage to skip this. They go back to the curse, "thy desire shall be to thy husband, and he shall rule over thee," and there they stop. Their nature is nature accursed, and even that is silent on the point of menial service: they do not go back to nature innocent, where it is excluded by implication. But if the Bible is proof on one side, it is proof on the other. If the husband is made to be the head of the woman, he is also made to be her serving-man. Nay, even the silence of the curse is more golden than the speech of man, for the same allotment of penalty which lays upon her the sorrow of conception lays upon him the sorrow of toil: so that every man whose wife is obliged to eat bread in the sweat of her brow is out of his sphere, and has failed of his "mission." He lays upon the shoulders of a weak woman his own burden as well as hers. And every man who is not a farmer is out of his sphere, and should put himself into it before he casts a single stone at any woman; and he is as much more guilty as his sphere is more accurately defined.

So much for the revelation of the word; now for the revelation of nature.

Naturally, I suppose women's tastes are not any more likely to be uniform than men's tastes. The narrow range of their lives has undoubtedly tended to keep them down towards one standard, but every new-born child is a new protest of nature,—a new outburst of individuality against monotony, so that the work is really never done, and never comes anywhere near being so far done as that all women, or the majority of women, should choose the life of a housekeeper. As far as my observation goes, the best women, the brightest women, the noblest women, are the very ones to whom it is most irksome. I do not mean housekeeping with well-trained servants, for that is general enough to admit a "brother near the throne"; but that, alas! is almost unknown in the world wherein *I* have lived; and a woman who is satisfied with the small cares, the small economies, the small interests, the constant contemplation of small things which many a household demands, is a very small sort of woman. I make the assertion both as an inference and an observation. A noble discontent—not a peevish complaining, but an inward and spiritual protest—is a woman's safeguard against the deterioration which such a life threatens, and her proof of capacity and her note of preparation for a higher. Such a woman does not do her work less well, but she rises ever superior to her work. I know such women.

You talk about the mother-instinct. The mother-instinct makes a mother love her children, but it does not make her love to destroy herself with unremitting toil for them. It makes her do it, but it does not make her love to do it. And because, in her great love, she will do it when the necessity is laid upon her,—a wicked perversion of God's good gift often lays the necessity upon her when God does not. The mother-instinct in woman corresponds to the father-instinct in man; and the wifely love to the husbandly love. Each is strong enough to bear joyfully all that God lays upon it, and patiently much that he does not lay and never intended to be laid. But he who counts upon that strength, for the purpose of abusing it, is guilty of a high crime against humanity. Each sex has the same uniformity in its loves, and would undoubtedly have the same variety in its tastes if it were not hindered. Men do not themselves believe so much as they profess in this menial gravitation. If they did, they would never lecture women so much about it. The very frenzy and frequency of their exhortations are suspicious. They join together what God has not joined. They claim identity where he has established diversity. Women are continually and publicly admonished of their household obligations, but who ever heard an assembly of men admonished of theirs? Yet men are as often derelict in furnishing provision for their families as women are lax in its administration. And while the husband may do his part in the way which seems good in his own eyes, the wife must do hers in only one way, whether it seem good or bad. The wise woman must tread "the old dull round of things" as well as the foolish woman, and then she is so footsore that she cannot enter upon that higher path which is open only to her, and shut to the foolish woman. The low necessities usurp the throne of the lofty possibilities. Oh! for this what tender consideration should she not receive! Confined to the uninteresting routine of domestic drudgery, while her tastes incline and her powers fit her for other things, no admiration is too deep, no sympathy too warm. The gentlest and most thoughtful attention is her smallest due. Let men fancy for a moment that at marriage they must give up the law, the pulpit, the machine-shop, the farm, in which they excel, and which is adequate to purse and pleasure, and turn hod-carrier or road-mender, and they may have a glimpse of the sacrifice which many a gifted woman has made. If she made it unwittingly, marrying before she knew her powers, or the life which marriage involves, a generous pity and love will smooth her path as much as may be, and press back the unexpected thorns. If she made it wittingly, choosing, in her strong love, to lay upon the altar her pleasant things, so much the more will a generous man constrain her to forget, in the fervor and efficacy of his love, the fruit which once her soul longed for. If he cannot prevent the sacrifice, he can cause that it shall not have been made in vain.

Again, a man receives immediate and definite results from his work. He has salary or wages,—so much a day, a year, a job. He is Lord High Chancellor of the Exchequer and irresponsible. His wife gets no money for her work. She has no funds under her own control, no resources of which she is mistress. She must draw supplies from her husband, and often with much outlay of ingenuity. Some men dole out money to their wives as if it were a gift, a charity, something to which the latter have no right, but which they must receive as a favor, and for which they must be thankful. They act as if their wives were trying to plunder them. Now a man has no more right to his earnings than his wife has. They belong to her just as much as to him. There is a mischievous popular opinion that the husband is the producer and the wife the consumer. In point of fact, the wife is just as much a producer as the husband. Her part in the concern is just as important as his. She earns it as truly, and has just as strong a claim and just as much a right to it as he; if possible she has more, for she ought to receive some compensation for the gap that yawns between work and wages. It is much more satisfactory to receive the latter as a direct result of the former, than as a kind of alms. Many a woman does as much to build up her husband's prosperity as he does himself. Many a woman saves him from failure and disgrace. And, as a general rule, the fate and fortunes of the family lie in her hands as much as in his. What absurdity to *pay* him his *wages* and to *give* her money to go shopping with!

A woman who went around to make a collection for a small local charity, told me that she could not help noticing the difference between the married and the unmarried women. The latter took out their purses on the spot and gave their mite or mint without hesitation. The former parleyed and would see about it, gave rather uncertainly, and must speak to Edward before they could decide. Now it may well be that a woman who has only her own self to provide for can give more liberally than one upon whose purse come the innumerable requisitions of a family. The mother may be forced to make many sacrifices, and yet be so blessed in the making that there shall be no sacrifice. The pleasure shall overbalance the pain. But there is no reason why a married woman should hesitate, or be embarrassed, or consult Edward as to the expenditure of a dime or a dollar, any more than an unmarried one. There may be more calls on the purse, but she ought to be mistress of it. She ought to know her husband's circumstances well enough to know what she can afford to give away, and she ought to be as free to use her judgment as he is to use his. In any unusual emergency, each will wish to consult the other; but he does not think of asking her as to the disposal of every chance quarter of a dollar, neither should she think of asking him. If circumstances make it necessary to sail close to the wind, sail close to the wind; but let both be in the same boat.

All this miserable and humiliating halting arises from the miserable and humiliating notion that the husband is the power and the wife the weight. It comes out, more convenient in substance, but just as objectionable in shape, in the wife's "allowance." The husband *allows* her so much a year for her expenses. If it means simply that so much is set aside for that purpose, very well; only it would sound rather strange to say that she allows him so much to carry on his business. A woman does not wish to be conversant with the details of her husband's shop any more than he wishes to understand the details of her kitchen: but he desires to know enough of that to be sure of prompt, sufficient, and agreeable meals, and a tidy house, at a cost within his means. So she should know with sufficient accuracy the extent and sources of their income to be able to arrange her ordinary disbursements without constant recurrence to him. He does not take his dinner as a boon from her. He feels under no obligations for it. He does not consider himself on his good behavior out of gratitude. It is a regular institution, a blessing entirely common to both, and excites no emotion. So should her money be,—as regularly and mechanically supplied as the dinner, exciting no more comment and needing no more argument. Whether it is kept in her pocket or his may be of small moment; but as she does not lock up the dinner in the cupboard, and then stand at the door and dole it out to him by the plateful, but sets it on the table for him to help himself: so it is better, more pacific, that he should deposit the money in an equally neutral and accessible locality.

I portray to myself the flutter which such a proposition would raise in many marital bosoms; would that they might be soothed. It is well known among farmers that hens will not eat so much if you set a measure of corn where they can pick whenever they choose, as they will if you only fling down a handful now and then, and keep them continually half starved. At the same time they will be in better condition. So, looking at the matter from the very lowest stand-point, a woman who has free access to the money will not be half so likely to lavish it as the woman who is put off with scanty and infrequent sums. She who knows how much there is to spend will almost invariably keep within the limits. If she does not know, her imagination will be very likely to magnify the fountain, and if but meagre supplies are forthcoming, she will attribute it to niggardliness, and will consider everything that can be got from her husband as legal plunder; and with under-ground pipes and above-ground trenches it shall go hard but she will drain him tolerably dry. Then he will inveigh against her extravagance, and so not only lose his money, but his temper, his calmness, and his complacency, all the while blaming her when the fault is chiefly his own. If he had but frankly acquainted her with the main facts; if he had but permitted her to look in and see what was the capacity of the reservoir, instead of leaving her to sit under the walls, knowing nothing of its resources but what she could learn from the occasional spouting of a single small pipe, he would have avoided all the trouble. It is so rarely that a wife will recklessly transcend her reasonable income, that I do not think it worth while to suggest any provision against the evil. It is an abnormal and sporadic case, to be treated physiologically rather than philosophically. The man has unfortunately allied himself to a mad woman, or he has found to his regret that there is nothing more fulsome than a she-fool.

It irks me to say these things. It is almost a profanation to connect such cold-blooded business matters with a relation which is supposed to involve, and which should involve, the highest, the purest, the fairest traits of human life. In true marriage there is indeed no need of these considerations. A complete and perfect marriage breaks down all barriers, and fuses each separate interest into one. In such there is no mine and thine, but unity and identity. For perfect marriages I do not write; but for the imperfect, and the marriages not yet contracted. Let us have another standard set up, another starting-point established, another goal fixed, that we may run without weariness, and walk without faintness, and be crowned at last with a laurel worth the wearing. A ten years' wife once said to a young lady who was spending money rather freely,—money which was, however, her own, for which she had to depend upon no one,—"You ought to lay up something for yourself. You should have a little money—if only five hundred dollars, it will be better than nothing— in the bank, so that when you are married you will have something of your own to go to, and not have to depend entirely upon your husband. You will be a great deal happier to have something that you can do what you choose with, and not feel that you must account for every cent, and make it go as far as possible." But it seems to me that this is *felo de se.* Doubtless, people often find that they have married the wrong person; but it is supposed to be a mistake, and not a walking into the ditch with eyes open. If a girl knows, or even suspects, or entertains the possibility beforehand, that she is going to marry a man from whom it is necessary to provide for herself a pecuniary refuge, why does she marry him at all? If she deliberately unites herself to one who she believes, or even fears, will not receive her as a trust from God, bone of his bone and flesh of his flesh, she forfeits all sympathy and pity, whatever may befall her. If the husband whom she is to take threatens to be greedy, or unsympathizing, or selfish, or stolid, her best defence against him is, not to put money in a bank, but to keep herself out of his reach. It is impossible to conceive of happiness in marriage, where the financial wheels do not run—I will not say smoothly, but evenly. The road may be rough, roundabout, and steep, without precluding wholesome and hearty happiness; but if one wheel drags while the other turns, if one goes back while the other goes forward, if for any reason the two do not move by parallel lines in the same direction, the whole carriage is bewitched, the whole journey is embittered, the whole object is baffled.

It is marvellous to see the insensibility with which men manage these delicate matters. It is impossible for a man to be too scrupulous, too chivalrous, too refined, in his bearing towards his wife. Her dependence should be the strongest appeal to his manhood. The very act of receiving money from him puts her in a position so equivocal, that the utmost affection and attention should be brought into play to reassure her. The velvet touch of love should disguise the iron hand of business. A sensitive woman is fully enough alive to her relations. There is need that every gentle and tender courtesy should assure and convince her that the money which she costs is a pleasure and a privilege. Her delicacy, her self-respect, her confidence in his appreciation, are the strongest ties that can bind her to himself. Let them but be sundered, and he has no longer any hold on happiness, any safeguard against discord. Let chivalry be forgotten, let sensitiveness be violated, let money intrude into the domain of love, and the spell is broken. Your stately silver urn is become an iron kettle.

Yet men will deliberately, in the presence of their wives, *to* their wives, groan over the cost of living. They do not mean extravagant purchases of silk and lace and velvet, which might be a wife's fault or thoughtlessness, and furnish an excuse for rebuke; but the butcher's bill, and the grocer's bill, and the joiner's bill. Man, when a woman is married, do you think she loses all personal feeling? Do you think your glum look over the expenses of housekeeping is a fulfilment of your promise to love and cherish? Is it calculated to retain and increase her tenderness for you? Does it bring sunshine and lighten toil, and bless her with knightly grace? Do you not know that it is only a way of regretting that you married her? It is a way of saying that you did not count the cost. You may not present it to yourself in that light, but in that light you present it to her. And do you think it is a pleasant thing to her? You go out to your shop, or sit down to your newspaper, and forget all about it. She sits down to her sewing, or stands over her cooking-stove, and meditates upon it with an indescribable pain. I do not say that every kind of uneasiness regarding expense is or ought to be thus construed. There may be an uneasiness springing directly from love. A strong and great-hearted affection frets that it cannot minister the beauty and the comfort which it longs to do, or defend against the emergencies which a future may bring. But this uneasiness is rarely if ever mistaken. Love can usually find a way to soothe the sorrows of love, and a wife's hand can almost always smooth out the wrinkles from the brow which is corrugated only for her. The complaint which I mean is of quite another character. Women know it, if men do not;—the women who have suffered from it, for it is pleasant to think that there are women to whose experience every such sensation is entirely foreign. These very men who complain because it costs so much to live will lose by bad debts more than their wives spend. They will, by sheer negligence, by a selfish reluctance to present a bill to a disagreeable person, by a cowardly fear lest insisting on what is due should alienate a customer, by culpable mismanagement of business, by indorsing a note, or lending money, through mere want of courage to say "No," or of shrewdness to detect dishonesty or incapacity, lose money enough to foot up half a dozen bills. They will waste money in cigars, in oyster-suppers, in riding when walking would be better for them, in keeping a horse which "eats his head off," in buying luxuries which they would be better off without, in sending packages and luggage by express, rather than have the trouble of taking them themselves, in numberless small items of which they make no account, but of which the bills make great account. If one might judge from the newspapers, extravagance is a peculiarity of women. So far as my observation goes, the extravagance of women is not for a moment to be compared with the extravagance of men.[3] A man is perversely, persistently, and with malice aforethought, extravagant. He is extravagant in spite of admonition and remonstrance. Where his personal comfort or interest is concerned, he scorns a sacrifice. He laughs at the suggestion that such a little thing makes any difference one way or another. He has not even the idea of economy. He does not know what the word means. He does not know the thing when he sees it.

Women take to it naturally. A certain innate sense of harmony keeps them from being wasteful. Their extravagance is the exception, not the rule. They are willing to incur self-denial. They do not scorn to take thought and trouble, and be put to inconvenience, for the sake of saving money. The greater animalism of man also comes out here in full force. If sacrifice must be, a woman will sacrifice her comforts before her taste. The man will let his tastes go, and keep his comforts, and call it good sense. A woman's extravagance is to some purpose. A man's to none. She buys many dresses, but she gives her old ones away, or cuts them over for the children, and works dextrously. A man buys and destroys. Look at the manner in which men manage the national housekeeping, and see whether it is men or women who are extravagant. Look at the clerkships in the departments, look at members of Congress browsing among government supplies, look at army and navy; walk through a camp: see the barrels of good food thrown away, see the wood wasted, see the tools wantonly destroyed. I think the wives of the soldiers could support themselves comfortably on the fragments of the soldiers' feasts. Nobody complains. A great nation must not look too closely after the pennies. A great army always makes great waste, say the newspapers that exhort women against extravagance, as if it were as much a law of nature as gravitation. Why not say housekeeping is always wasteful, and fall back on that as a primal law of nature also? Because housekeeping is not always wasteful, you say. Precisely. Housekeeping is nearly always economically conducted, and your animadversions amount just to this: because women are generally prudent, they are to be chided for all shortcomings. But men are always wasteful, therefore they must be let alone. Only be universally bad, and you shall be as unmolested as if you were good. You say that it is easier to be economical in a family than in an army. Perhaps so; but if the soldiers, instead of being men, were women, do you for a moment imagine that there would be any such waste? Let all other circumstances be unchanged. Let all the cost come upon the government just as it does. Let all provisions be furnished in the same abundance as now, and I do not believe there would be much more waste than there is in average families. I do not believe you could force women at the point of the bayonet to such reckless prodigality as men indulge in. It is against their nature. It hurts them. It violates God's law, written in their hearts. They would also be too conscientious to do it. They would not consider the fact that "Uncle Sam foots the bills" a reason why a saw should be tossed aside on the first symptom of dulness, and a new one bought. They would not throw away a half loaf because there were plenty of whole ones, but keep it and steam it. And not only would there be a great deal less waste, but there would be a great deal better supply. If women had charge of the commissariat, I do not believe there would have been one half so much friction as there has been. Hungry regiments would not get to the end of a long march and find nothing to eat. Sick soldiers would not be expected to recover health from salt pork and muddy coffee. Experience or no experience, red tape or no tape, women would have managed to bring hungry mouths and hot soups together, and to furnish delicate food for delicate health. They would not only have supplied the soldiers at less cost to government, but the less cost would have produced a larger bill of fare. How did the English army fare till Florence Nightingale came by and knocked their granary doors open? That my remarks are not mere theory, or rather that my theory is founded on truth, is abundantly proved by a statement printed in the North American Review for January, 1864, long after my words were written. It is from an article on the Sanitary Commission.

"At this moment, the only region in the loyal States that is definitely out of the circle is Missouri. The rest of our loyal territory is all embraced within one ring of method and federality. This is chiefly due to the wonderful spirit of nationality that beats in the breasts of American women. They, even more than the men of the country, from their utter withdrawal from partisan strifes and local politics, have felt the assault upon the life of the nation in its true national import. They are infinitely less *State-ish*, and more national in their pride and in their sympathies. They see the war in its broad, impersonal outlines; and while their particular and special affections are keener than men's, their general humanity and tender sensibility for unseen and distant sufferings is stronger and more constant.

"The women of the country, who are the actual creators, by the labor of their fingers, of the chief supplies and comforts needed by the soldiers, have been the first to understand, appreciate, and co-operate with the Sanitary Commission. It is due to the sagacity and zeal with which they have entered into the work, that the system of supplies, organized by the extraordinary genius of Mr. Olmstead, has become so broadly and nationally extended, and that, with Milwaukee, Chicago, Cleveland, Cincinnati, Louisville, Pittsburg, Philadelphia, New York, Brooklyn, New Haven, Hartford, Providence, Boston, Portland, and Concord for centres, there should be at least fifteen thousand Soldiers' Aid Societies, all under the control of women, combined and united in a common work,—of supplying, through the United States Sanitary Commission, the wants of the sick and wounded in the great Federal army.

"The skill, zeal, business qualities, and patient and persistent devotion exhibited by those women who manage the truly vast operations of the several chief centres of supply, at Chicago, Boston, Cleveland, Philadelphia, Pittsburg, and New York, have unfolded a new page in the history of the aptitudes and capacities of women. To receive, acknowledge, sort, arrange, mark, repack, store, hold ready for shipment, procure transportation for, and send forward at sudden call, the many thousand boxes of hospital stores which, at the order of the General Secretary at Washington, have been for the past two years and a half forwarded at various times by the 'Women's Central' at New York, the Soldiers' Aid Society of Northern Ohio, at Cleveland, the Branches at Cincinnati and at Philadelphia, or the Northwestern Branch at Chicago, has required business talents of the highest order. A correspondence demanding infinite tact, promptness, and method has been carried on with their local tributaries, by the women from these centres, with a ceaseless ardor, to which the Commission owes a very large share of its success, and the nation no small part of the sustained usefulness and generous alacrity of its own patriotic impulses.

"To collect funds (for the supply branches have usually raised their own funds from the immediate communities in which they have been situated) has often tasked their ingenuity to the utmost. In Chicago, for instance, the Branch has lately held a fair of colossal proportions, to which the whole Northwest was invited to send supplies, and to come

98

in mass! On the 26th of October last, when it opened, a procession of three miles in length, composed of wagon-loads of supplies, and of people in various ways interested, paraded through the streets of Chicago; the stores being closed, and the day given up to patriotic sympathies. For fourteen days the fair lasted, and every day brought reinforcements of supplies, and of people and purchasers. The country people, from hundreds of miles about, sent in upon the railroads all the various products of their farms, mills, and hands. Those who had nothing else sent the poultry from their barnyards; the ox, or bull, or calf, from the stall; the title-deed of a few acres of land; so many bushels of grain, or potatoes, or onions. Loads of hay, even, were sent in from ten or a dozen miles out, and sold at once in the hay-market. On the roads entering the city were seen rickety and lumbering wagons, made of poles, loaded with mixed freight,—a few cabbages, a bundle of socks, a coop of tame ducks, a few barrels of turnips, a pot of butter, and a bag of beans,—with the proud and humane farmer driving the team, his wife behind in charge of the baby, while two or three little children contended with the boxes and barrels and bundles for room to sit or lie. Such were the evidences of devotion and self-sacrificing zeal the Northwestern farmers gave, as in their long trains of wagons they trundled into Chicago, from twenty and thirty miles' distance, and unloaded their contents at the doors of the Northwestern Fairs, for the benefit of the United States Sanitary Commission. The mechanics and artisans of the towns and cities were not behind the farmers. Each manufacturer sent his best piano, plough, threshing-machine, or sewing-machine. Every form of agricultural implement, and every product of mechanical skill, was represented. From the watchmaker's jewelry to horseshoes and harness; from lace, cloth, cotton and linen, to iron and steel; from wooden and waxen and earthen ware, to butter and cheese, bacon and beef;—nothing came amiss, and nothing failed to come, and the ordering of all this was in the hands of women. They fed in the restaurant, under 'the Fair,' at fifty cents a meal— fifteen hundred mouths a day, for a fortnight—from food furnished, cooked, and served by the women of Chicago; and so orderly and convenient, so practical and wise were the arrangements, that, day by day, they had just what they had ordered and what they counted on,—always enough, and never too much. They divided the houses of the town, and levied on No. 16 A Street, for five turkeys, on Monday; No. 37 B Street, for twelve apple-pies, on Tuesday; No. 49 C Street, for forty pounds of roast beef, on Wednesday; No. 23 D Street was to furnish so much pepper on Thursday; No. 33 E Street, so much salt on Friday. In short, every preparation was made in advance, at the least inconvenience possible to the people, to distribute in the most equal manner the welcome burden of feeding the visitors, at the fair, at the expense of the good people of Chicago, but for the pecuniary benefit of the Sanitary Commission. Hundreds of lovely young girls, in simple uniforms, took their places as waiters behind the vast array of tables, and everybody was as well served as at a first-class hotel, at a less expense to himself, and with a great profit to the fair. Fifty thousand dollars, it is said, will be the least net return of this gigantic fair to the treasury of the Branch at Chicago. It is universally conceded that to Mrs. Livermore and Mrs. Hoge, old and tried friends of the soldier and of the Sanitary Commission, and its ever active agents, are due the planning, management, and success of this truly American exploit. What is the value of the money thus raised, important as it is, when compared with the worth of the spirit manifested, the loyalty exhibited, the patriotism stimulated, the example set, the prodigious tide of national devotion put in motion! How can rebellion hope to succeed in the face of such demonstrations as the Northwestern Fair? They are bloodless battles, equal in significance and results to Vicksburg and Gettysburg, to New Orleans and Newbern."

Men, have you read this paragraph? Please to read it again! Think of all your inveighing against female extravagance and incapacity, and read it yet again. Put on sackcloth and ashes, and read it aloud to your wife, to your mother, to your daughter, to your sister, to your grandmother, to your aunt, to your niece, to your mother-in-law, and all your relatives-in-law, and to every woman who suffers your presence, and then lay your hand on your mouth, and your mouth in the dust, and cry, "Woe is me! for I am undone." Inexperience? Had Mrs. Hoge and Mrs. Livermore any more experience in feeding fifteen hundred mouths a day than the quartermaster of a regiment? Have the women of Chicago generally devoted their lives to trafficking in tame ducks, loads of hay, threshing-machines, and beef and bacon? Yet you have the very essence of business tact in "nothing came amiss, and nothing failed to come"; and the very essence of economy in "always enough, and never too much"; and the crowning glory—write it on the posts of thy house, and on thy gates; teach it diligently unto thy children, and talk of it when thou sittest in thine house, and when thou walkest by the way, and when thou liest down, and when thou risest up; bind it for a sign upon thine hand, and let it be as a frontlet between thine eyes—"the ordering of all this was in the hands of women."

This ascription of female extravagance, whether made publicly in newspapers or privately in family conclave, is not only false and fatal, but it is fatal in the very innermost and vital points of life. What is destroyed is not an adventitious thing, but the spring of all satisfaction. The relations between a man and his wife decide the weal of his life. The whole chain of his circumstances can be no stronger than the link between him and her. He may be ever so rich or renowned, but he can bear no heavier weight of happiness than that link can sustain. The newspaper paragraphs do the harm of confirming individual men in their notions that it is the wife who incurs the unnecessary expense, and so divert their attention from their own duties, and urge them on in their evil courses to their own undoing. But a man is just as powerful for good as he is for evil. By as much as he can alienate his wife from himself by his petty financiering, by so much can he draw her to his heart by a gentle chivalry. Invested by the law with power, he has only to transmute it into love to secure a loyalty capable of any sacrifice. Let a wife read in her husband's face and bearing how grateful is her society, how precious her life, how sweetest of all pleasures to him is the knowledge of her pleasure; let her feel that she is to him something different from all earthly interests,—something above and beyond all other joys; let her see that, with her coming, money ceased to be mere current coin, that labor acquired a new dignity, and prudence a new charm, because they all might minister to her convenience or delight; let her see that she adjusts, harmonizes, and completes his life; that she is the central sun, about which all minor interests and plans revolve; and—what have you gained? A good housekeeper? A well-ordered household? More than this. An empire. Supreme dominion. You have only to be tender and true, and nothing can sweep away the golden mist through which, whatever you may be to others, you shall appear to her eyes a knight without fear and without reproach.

Wrong opinions concerning the relations between husband and wife are also occasionally expressed in another and opposite manner. A wife comes into the possession of property. The husband, determined not to encroach upon her rights, leaves the disposal of the property to her. He insists that it shall be invested in her name. He will take no responsibility as to the mode of investment. This may be done from honorable motives. The man means to be just and blameless; and if he is conscious of innate weakness or wickedness, or if the marriage be an ill-assorted one, he may be pursuing the best course. There may also be outside, merely business reasons which make it the best course. But to do it simply from a notion of justice, is as far as possible from what ought to be. The man shows himself entirely at fault regarding the range of justice. If life were what it should be, the law would be right in recognizing for the woman no existence separate from her husband. Love is but the fulfilling of that law. The reason why such a law is unjust is, that life is so constant a violation of the higher spiritual law, that this lower one which embodies it works mischief. It fits the righteous theory only, not the wicked facts. But law is for the evil, not for the good. There is no enactment that a man shall possess his own property. The enactments are to punish those who attempt to wrest his property from him. There need be no enactment that a man shall be master of his wife's possessions; he has but to be to her a true husband, and all that she has is his. The law should punish him for neglect of duty and disregard of claims, by a forfeiture of property. If the law this day completely reversed the position of husband and wife, it would make no jot or tittle of change in their actual position, where they love each other as they ought. Women naturally have a distaste to business, and an indifference to money. Of their own motion, they would leave such things in the hands of men, if the instinct of self-preservation did not force them to interference. In addition to this generic negative willingness, the happy wife has a positive delight in enriching with every blessing the man she loves. When Aurora gave her love with all lavishment, and prayed Romney,

"If now you'd stoop so low to take my love,

And use it roughly, without stint or spare,

As men use common things with more behind,

To any mean and ordinary end,—

The joy would set me like a star, in heaven,

So high up, I should shine because of height

And not of virtue,"—

did she make a mental reservation to herself of the money which her books had brought her?

What the law should do, is to step in and guard woman against the possible disastrous consequences which may spring from the spontaneous self-abnegation of love. What it should not do, is to guarantee to the miser, the spendthrift, the tyrant, debauchee, or vampire, the things which *a man* would possess of his own inalienable right. What a husband should do, is to show himself great enough

104

and good enough to know and feel that, in love, giving and receiving wear the selfsame grace. What he should not do, is to talk of justice when they twain should be one flesh.

VIII.

OMAN'S rank in life depends entirely on what life
is. Her importance is decided when it is decided
what service is important. If money is the one thing
needful, and its acquisition the chief end of man, the
wife's position is very inferior to her husband's. The
greater part of the money is earned in his, and often
spent in her department. He does the work that is
paid for, and he belongs to the sex that is paid. She
does the work that is not paid for, and she belongs to
the sex that is pillaged. Men go out and gain money:
wives stay at home and spend it. The case is against
them—if that is the whole case. But if money is only
means to an end; if happiness, intelligence, integrity,
are more worth than gold; if a life ruled by the law of
God, if the development of the divine in the human,
if the education of every faculty, and the enjoyment
of every power, be more lovely and more desirable
than bank stock, then the woman walks not one whit
behind the man, but side by side, with no unequal
steps. He furnishes and she fashions the material
from which grace and strength are wrought. Her
work is in point of fact incomparably fairer, finer,
more difficult, more important than his. It is not
money-getting alone, or chiefly, but money-
spending, that influences and indicates character. A
man may work up to his knees in swamp-meadows,
or breathe all day the foul air of a court-room; but if,
when released, he turns naturally to sunshine and

apple-orchards and womanly grace, swamp-mud and vile air have not polluted him. He is a clean-souled man through it all. But if a man find rest from his work in mere eating and drinking, if the money which he has earned goes to gross amusements and coarse companions, he shows at once the lowness of his character, however high may be his occupation.

Those hands which have the ordering of house and home, have a large share in the ordering of character. The man who provides the house does an important part, but she who refines it into a home is the true artist. To whom is the palm awarded, to the painter who, from ochre and lead, lays on the rough canvas the lovely landscape, touched with a beauty borrowed from his own soul, or the huckster who sells him ochre, lead, and canvas, or even the successful shoddy-contractor who pays five thousand of his Judas Iscariot dollars, that he may hang it in a bad light in his dining-room till such day as he shall have the grace to go and hang himself? It has been said that in the highest departments women have never produced a masterpiece. Painting has its old masters, but no old mistresses. Jenny Lind may entrance the world from her "heaven-kissing hill," but on the mountain-tops Mendelssohn and Beethoven stand uncompanioned. Sappho plumed her wings, but plunged quickly from the Leucadian cliff, and Milton soars steadfastly to the sun alone. We shall see about this one day, but meanwhile life itself is higher than any of the arts of life, and in living no man has risen to loftier heights than a woman, and the mass of men are infinitely lower than the mass of women, and would be lower still if it were not for female assistance. With all the help which they receive from women, they are perpetually lapsing into brutality, and whenever they go off into a community by themselves, they go headlong downwards, following their natural gravitation.

It is women that make men fit to live. They often confess it themselves without meaning anything by it. I take advantage of the confession; as the malignant Minister in Titan "retained the habit, when an open-hearted soul showed him its breaches, of marching in upon it through those breaches, as if he himself had made them." In toasts and festive speeches none can be more bland than they. With sweet and smiling, arch and gracious humility, they dwell upon the refining and elevating influence of "lovely woman," as if it were a pretty thing to be growling and snappish and stroked into quiescence and acquiescence by a soft hand,—as if a midsummer-night's dream were a midwinter-day's truth, and man were content to be Bottom the weaver, with his ass's head stuck full with musk-roses by fairy Titanias. But I say it not as a man gallantly towards women, nor as a woman angrily towards men, but as a simple statement of fact by an unconcerned spectator, and far more in sorrow than in anger. What is proffered as compliment I accept and reproduce as truth, and if men will not stand convicted of false dealing, let them show their faith by their works, and yield themselves, plastic and unresisting, to the hands that will mould them to fairest shapes.

Over against this mistaken notion stands its opponent notion, equally mistaken, more extensive, circulated by men, adopted by women, and doing its mischievous work silently and surely. Public opinion, floating about in novels and periodicals, lays upon the shoulders of women burdens which they are not able to bear, which they were never intended to bear, and which ought never to be laid upon them. Before marriage, society agrees to make men grasp the laboring oar. They must choose and woo and win; while the woman's strength is to sit still. But after marriage the scene suddenly shifts. The wife must take the wooing and winning into her hands. She must make home pleasant. She must rear the children. She must manage society. She must incur the responsibility of the welfare and happiness of the family. The husband is on the one side a wild animal who must be managed but not controlled; on the other, a piece of rare china, which must be carefully handled and kept from all rough contact.

"It is the wife who makes the home, and the home makes the man," says the country newspaper, in its domestic column.

"If a wife would make the husband delighted with home, she must first make home delightful. She must first woo him there by all the arts of affection,—by cheerfulness, tidiness, orderliness without excess: by a clean-swept hearth, a bright fire, flowers upon the mantel, a well-set table and well-cooked food. She must be careful of imposing restraints upon his tastes, inclinations, movements, and render him free of every suspicion of domestic imprisonment. If his masculine tastes, as they will, draw him from home at times, to the club, to the lodge, or the political meeting, or elsewhere, let her second them with that ready cheerfulness which will prove one of the strong cords to draw him back to home as the centre of his earthly joys," says its virtuous neighbor.

"I have heard women speak of their rights. If they had made the men of the world what God intended they should make of them, there would have been no need of this complaining," says the orthodox heroine in the orthodox novel.

"What makes a man feel at home in the house?... Is it to leave him absolute master of his rightful position, the large liberty to go and come, trusting for her part religiously in the virtue and the sovereign power of her love,—knowing, as if she had read it out of Holy Writ, for her own heart has told her" (*her* being the heroine aforementioned, now become the hero's wife) "that, if she shall ever cease to hold the love and trust which she has won, the fault, as the loss, is hers?"

"She" (*she* being the aforesaid orthodox heroine and orthodox submissive wife, now become the orthodox devoted mother),—"She had the consciousness that it was hers to make of this child what she would!"

I have spoken before of the comparative work of the husband and wife, considered merely as labor. I refer now to the comparative moral weight belonging to their respective positions.

All masculine and all orthodox feminine tractates on female education, all male lectures on female duties, all anniversary orators to female schools, ring the changes on the importance of educating girls to be good wives and mothers, with the persistency of the old song which shuttled back and forth some twenty times or more to tell us that "John Brown had a little Indian." But were the graduating class of a college ever exhorted to be good husbands and fathers? Are fathers ever admonished to teach their sons domestic virtues, to make them fond and faithful and good providers for the wives they may one day possess? But I should like to know if girls have any stronger tendency to become wives and mothers, than the boys have to become husbands and fathers? Are they any more likely to be bad wives and mothers, than boys are to be bad husbands and fathers? Is the number of incompetent wives obviously greater than the number of incompetent husbands? Is the number of injudicious mothers obviously greater than the number of injudicious fathers? And where the wife and mother is incompetent and injudicious, does it generally seem to be owing to too great strength of mind and culture of intellect, and too little domestic education, or is it owing to weakness of character? It is not a remote, but it seems to be an entirely unobserved truth, that for every wife there is a husband, and for every mother there is a father; and so far as my observation extends, domestic mismanagement and unhappiness, in an overwhelming majority of cases, are owing to the shortcomings of the husband, and not of the wife, or to the wife in an inferior and resultant measure. "There is blame on both sides," say the observers, oracularly, and this most superficial of all superficial generalizations is supposed to be an impartial and exhaustive summary. It is just as much a summary as the statement that two and two make four. Two and two do make four, but it is nothing to the purpose here. To say that there is blame on both sides, is simply saying that neither a man nor a woman is perfect, which nobody ever maintained. So long as humanity is humanity, it is not probable that one person will be entirely sinless and another entirely sinful; but there are, and will continue to be, many cases in which the blame on one side is much more heavy and condemning than the blame on the other. The man's blame is most often one of aggression, of the first provocation, of unprincipled and heartless behavior, of cruel disappointing and thwarting, of a giant's strength used giantly. The woman's is a blame of imprudence, of weakness, of disappointment, unwisely met and impatiently or otherwise ill-borne; of an inability to manage with sagacity, and so to master by superior moral power the wild beast that has clutched her,—a blame that is negative rather than positive, passive rather than active, and not to be compared with the other in point of heinousness. Why, then, do you bear down so hard on the woman's duty and leave the man to go his way unadmonished? If you do not enforce on college-boys the duty of providing for their future families, why do you enforce on seminary-girls the duty of directing their future families? If you do not educate young men to make good husbands, why should you educate young women to make good wives? If you do not exhort young men so to live and learn as to make their wives happy and train their children aright, why should you exhort young women to study to make their husbands happy and train their children aright? Because, you say, in the words already quoted, "It is the wife that makes the home, and the home makes the man." It is nothing of the sort. It is the wife and the husband together that make the home, and the man was already made. The most that wife and home in conjunction can do is to modify the man. If a husband be intemperate, or given over to money-getting, or money-saving, or money-spending,—if he be ill-tempered, indelicate, ignorant, obstinate, arrogant,—no wife, be she ever so prudent, wise, affectionate, can make the home what it ought to be. At best she can only mend it. Her energies are wasted. The ingenuity, the love, the care, that should be expended in making it happy are sacrificed in the attempt to make it as little unhappy as possible. With the best of husbands and the best of wives there are always evils enough lying in wait. Danger, disease, sin, are ever ready to spring upon the happy home, even when both the keepers stand guard at the portals; how, then, can you expect the wife to ward off even her own part of these, when you lay upon her the husband's part, and he himself is the greatest evil of all?

And what right have men to depend upon home and wife to "make" them? What is a man doing all the twenty or thirty years before he is married, that he has not made himself? And on what grounds does he come to her for completion? How came she to be any more finished than he? or any more capable of putting the finishing touches to another? Are wives generally mature and experienced, while husbands are young and inexperienced? Have wives generally more knowledge of the world, and more opportunities to become self-possessed and firmly and evenly balanced than husbands? Or is the masculine material naturally and permanently more plastic than the feminine? Let us know the pretext upon which a full-grown man charges a delicate woman, who has had little if anything to do with him until he became a full-grown man, with the cure of his soul? If there is anything to be done in the way of education and reformation, one would naturally suppose that it is the stronger sex which should educate and reform the weaker. It would seem as if the sex that is looked up to and sets itself up as sovereign should mould the sex which looks up and recognizes it as sovereign. Where, in the Bible, does a man find any warrant for laying himself to the account of his wife? When God calls every man to judgment, will he be able to pass over his shortcomings to his wife? The first man tried it, but with very small success. "The woman whom thou gavest to be with me," whimpered Adam; but it was a sorry refuge of lies, and did not avail to stay the curse from descending heavily upon his head. The plea that did not avail the first man is not likely to avail the last, nor any man between. "If thou art wise, thou art wise for thyself, but if thou scornest, thou alone shalt bear it." As a matter of fact, neither the wife makes the husband nor the husband the wife, but they both influence each other. She softens him and he strengthens her; or if, as not unfrequently happens, her nature is the stronger, she communicates to him of its strength. In a true marriage, delicacy is imparted on the one side and vigor on the other, to whichever side they originally belonged. Where the union is founded upon truth, there is always a tendency to equilibrium, woman supplying the spiritual, man the material element. She raises a mortal to the skies; he draws an angel down.

And no more than it belongs to the wife to make the home and the husband, does it belong to the mother to train up the children in the way they should go. The family is a joint-stock concern, so established both by nature and revelation. Where, in the Bible, do we find that the mother can make of her child what she will, or that God gave the making of the men of the world into her hand? In Holy Writ, the father's duties loom up as largely as the mother's, and if there is any difference it is not one that discriminates in his favor or in favor of his release from duty. Fathers and mothers in the Bible receive equal honor and equal deference, but the instruction and guidance of the children are much more definitely and repeatedly attributed to and inculcated upon and implied as belonging to the father than the mother. He is recognized as the head. At his door lies the responsibility. Ahaziah walked in the ways of his mother, but of his father also when he did evil in the sight of the Lord. It is the sins of the fathers, not of the mothers, that are visited upon the children. It was the fathers, not the mothers, who were to make known to the children the truth of Jehovah. It was the instruction of his father that Solomon commanded his son to hear, and the law of his mother which he commanded him not to forsake, —an arrangement which modern opinions seem inclined to reverse. It is the fathers who are pronounced to be the glory of children, not the mothers; and glory implies action. A father may die, and his dying prayer and his conscientious life, both commending his family to God, may descend upon them in ever-renewing blessing. Such is the promise of the Lord. A father may neglect his children, and the mother's care and love be so blessed of Heaven that they shall be burning and shining lights in the temple of the Most High. But this is God's uncovenanted mercy, and the father has no right to expect it. Yet one not seldom hears or sees anecdotes which imply that such neglect of children is not a crime,—a crime against children, against mothers, against society, against God. In times of financial disaster I have more than once heard of men's consoling themselves for the ruin of their business by playfully declaring that they should now go home and get acquainted with their children. But the non-acquaintance with children, of which many fathers are guilty, is not a theme to be lightly spoken of. Is it a small thing to give life to a soul that can never die; that, through unending ages, in happiness or in misery, clothed with glory or with shame, beautiful, strong, upright, or disfigured and deformed, must live on and on and on, forever and forever? Is it a small thing to give life to a sentient being, that must know even the experience of this world? That may be bowed down with guilt, remorse, wretchedness, bringing other souls with it to the dust, or may be upborne through a pure, happy, and beneficent career, bearing other souls with it to the skies? How dare a man look upon these helpless, hapless souls, and know that to him they owe their being, with all its dread possibilities; that upon him may fall the curse of their ruined lives, and—neglect them? How dare he leave them to another? To no other do they belong. His duty he cannot delegate. After country, which includes all things, his first duty is to his family. He is a father, and at no price can he sell his fatherhood.

I see notices of Female Prayer-Meetings. The mothers of a regiment assemble to pray for their sons who have gone to the war. There are Mothers' Guides and Mothers' Assistants and Mothers' Hymn-Books. But where are the Fathers' Hymn-Books? Where are the Paternal Prayer-Meetings? When do the Fathers of Regiments assemble to pray for their soldier-sons? If boys need their mothers' prayers, they need also their fathers' prayers. Does the fervent, effectual prayer of righteous women avail so much that righteous men can feel they have nothing to do but give themselves up to their farms and their merchandise, to buy and to sell and to get gain? Can men wait upon the Lord by proxy? Shall we bring political economy into religion, and arrange a wise division of labor by which the wife shall serve God, and the husband shall serve Mammon,—the wife do the praying and the husband see to the marketing,— he make sure of this world and she look out for the next? It is a nice little arrangement, but—He that sitteth in the heavens shall laugh; the Lord shall have it in derision.

But fathers must attend to their business. They must earn money to support the family. They must provide wherewith to keep the pot boiling. Certainly they must; but it requires no more time, or attention, or ingenuity, or vitality, or strength, or spirits, or endurance, no more expenditure of any of the forces of life, to go out and earn something to put into the pot, than it does to stay at home and boil it. If the mother, with her harassing cares, the never-ending details of her never-ending work, can find time for studying her maternal relations and responsibilities, and comparing her experience with that of others for purposes of improvement and the highest efficiency, and for joining in social prayer for the blessing of God on her efforts, the father can find time for similar study, effort, and prayer. If she can leave her baby, he can leave his books. If she can leave her kitchen, he can leave his counting-room. His bench, his desk, his fields, his office, are no more exacting than her nursery, her laundry, her work-basket. Women will go to the mothers' meeting who have to sit up till one o'clock in the morning to darn the little frock, and patch the old coat that must be worn that day; and sometimes they do it from stern necessity, without having the consolation of any mothers' meeting to go to. Let men but be as earnest in their purpose, as sincere in their belief, let them feel that the souls of their children are in their hands as keenly as mothers feel their responsibility, and business would straightway relax its claims and withdraw into the background, where it belongs. If a great general is come to town, if a famous regiment is to have a reception, if a long-looked-for statue has safely crossed the sea and is to be set up, if a foreign fleet lies in the harbor and is to send its officers on shore, if a young Prince is to pass through the city on his way home, men rush together in masses so dense as to endanger limb and life. Business is the last thing that interposes any obstacle to seeing and hearing that which a man determines to see and hear.

Business? What is man's business? Is it to take

care of that which is temporary or that which is permanent; that which belongs to matter, or that which belongs to mind; that which he shares in common with the beasts, or that which allies him to the angels,—nay, more, which constitutes in him the image and likeness of God? A man's business is to support his family. Certainly. He that provideth not for his own household hath denied the faith, and is worse than an infidel. I agree to that with all my heart. But what is he to provide? Food, raiment, shelter? These first, for without these is nothing; but these not last, for he who stops here and turns his powers into another channel is guilty of high crime. If his children were calves, lambs, chickens, he would do so much for them; because they are human beings, he must do somewhat more. But how many of the fathers who make business their plea for not watching over their children, who are away from home from seven in the morning till seven at night, who from year's end to year's end, except on Sunday and perhaps two or three festive days, see their children only at hurried meals, and snatch a kiss, perhaps, after they are in bed and asleep, who know no more about the inward and hourly life of their own than of their neighbor's children,—how many of these fathers are spending their time and talents in the sole business of getting food, clothes, and shelter, or even books and educational opportunities for their families? How many of these men earn just that and no more? It is not the support of families, it is not business, it is not necessity alone, on which they lavish themselves. It is their own pride or luxury or inclination. They wish to extend their business, to acquire wealth, or a competence, to be known as enterprising, public-spirited men, to be chosen on committees and sent to the legislature, all right, if rightly come by, but terribly wrong, worthless, perishable with the using, and of no important use, if children are to be given in barter for them.

"This is all very well to talk about," you say; "but a man cannot do anything in this world without money, and he cannot make money unless he sticks to his business." Ah, my friend! so far as the best things of this world are concerned, you cannot do anything with money, and you cannot make good men and women unless you stick to your children. Will money give you back the little baby-soul whose tender unfolding had such sweetness and healing for you, but which you lost because you would not stop long enough to look at it in your mad world-ways? Will money give you the saving influence over your boy which might have kept him from vicious companions and vicious habits,—an influence which your constant interest, intercourse, and example in his boyish days might have established, but which seemed to you too trivial a thing to win you from your darling pursuit of gains? Will money make you the friend and confidant of your daughter, the joy of her heart, and the standard of her judgment, so that her ripening youth shall give you intimacy, interchange of thought and sentiment, and you shall give to her a measure to estimate the men around her, and a steady light that shall keep her from being beguiled by the lights that only lead astray? Will it give you back the children who have rushed out wildly or strayed indifferently from the house which you have never taken pains to make a home, but have been content to turn into a hotel, with only less of liberty? Will money make you the heart as well as the head of your family,—honored, revered, beloved?

If your firm transacts business on a capital of a hundred thousand instead of half a million dollars, what is it but a little less paper, fewer clerks, and narrower rooms? Though your farm have but fifty instead of two hundred acres, there is just as much land on the earth. Suppose you argue before a jury only two cases to-day instead of three, there are a dozen young advocates who will be glad of the crumbs that fall from your table, and Fate will mete out her sure, rough-handed justice. With half the business you are doing now, could not you and your family be comfortably and decently fed, clothed, and sheltered? House, dress, and furniture might not be so fine, but something of more worth than they would be finer. A family's support does not necessarily involve sumptuous fare, purple and fine linen, damask and rosewood. If the choice lies between Turkey carpets, or even three-ply, under a child's feet, and a father's hand clasping his to guide his steps, what man who believes—I will not say in immortality, but in virtue,—what father who is not utterly unworthy to bear the sacred name, can for one moment waver?

Every man, and especially every father, should aim to have a character that shall alone have weight both with his fellow-citizens and his children. His integrity should be so unimpeachable that his motives shall be unquestioned. So far as his reputation is truthful, it should be firmly grounded on moral virtues and moral graces, so that his word shall have a force quite independent of his surroundings. He should be strong enough to be able to live in a plain house, and wear plain clothes, and deny himself, not only luxuries, but comforts and beauties, for the sake of his children's society and improvement, without forfeiting the respect and esteem of his neighbors or inflicting any pain of mortification upon his children. You cannot do anything in this world without money, if money is your sole or your chief claim to consideration; but, in the face of ten thousand denials, I would still maintain that it is possible to attain a character and a standing that shall set money at defiance. He who refuses to believe this, and acts upon a contrary belief, shows not only a want of real inward dignity, but of a knowledge of history and of life. A picture of Raphael, fitly framed and hung, is a treasure to be prized beyond words; but with no frame at all, and hung in the dreary parlor of a village inn, it is worth more, and would be more widely sought and more highly prized than a palaceful of commonplace paintings. Let all the accessories be as beautiful as you can command; but at all events make sure of the picture. He is not a wise man who expends all his energies on the frame, and trusts to luck for the painting.

Nor is it any excuse to say that you must lay up provision against the future. No one has any right to sacrifice the present to the future. You do not know that you will have any future. "The present, the present, is all thou hast for thy sure possessing." You may forego present luxuries for future needs or for future luxuries, but you may not forego present needs for future possibilities. If besides performing the duty of today you can also lay up money for to-morrow, it is well; but to slight a certain to-day for an uncertain to-morrow, is all ill. Provide, if you can, means to send your boy to college, to educate your daughter, to shelter your old age; yet, remember, before those means can be used, the boy, the girl, the man, may lie each in his silent grave; but though there may never be a college student, a ripening maiden, a gray-haired man, there is now a little boy, a little girl, who stand in need of their father; and a father is of more worth to his son than a college, of more worth to his daughter than many tutors. Train them in the way they should go, going yourself before them with a steady step, and trust God for that future against which you are unable to provide.

And this remember: the very best provision against the future is investments in heart and muscle and brain. Money without them is worthless. They without money are still inestimable riches. If your son at twenty-one is alienated from his father, dissipated, headstrong, weak, a source of anxiety and trouble to his family, he will pierce your heart through with many sorrows, though you have hundreds of thousands of dollars laid up for him in the bank. If your daughter is a frivolous, woman, the silks with which your wealth enables you to adorn her, the society with which it may perhaps enable you to surround her, will only set her folly in a stronger light. But if your children stand on the threshold of their manhood and their womanhood, strong, self-poised, mailed for defence and armed for warfare, glad and grateful for the love that has forged each weapon and taught its skilful handling, no king on his throne is so blessed as you. They have all that they need to conquer the world. Your money may be a snare to your child, your wisdom never. If you lose your money, it is gone forever. The child whom your love is enriching with youthful health and promise may go before you suddenly out of the world, but your labor and your love are not lost. Somewhere, under a warmer sun than this, his earthly promise bursts into the full blossom and the mellow fruit of performance more beautiful than eye can see or heart conceive.

The adequate care and guidance of the family which he has founded is a man's business in life.

Farming, preaching, and shopkeeping are secondary matters, to be regulated according to the needs of the family. The family is not to be regulated by their requirements. And a family's needs are not gay clothing and rich food, but a husband and father. It is the great duty of his life to be acquainted with his children, to know their character, their tastes, their tendencies, to know who are their associates, and what are their associations, what books they read, and what books they like to read, to gratify their innocent desires, to lop off their excrescences and bring out their excellences, to know them as a good farmer knows his soil, draining the bogs into fertile meadows and turning the watercourses into channels of beauty and life. He may furnish his children opportunities without number, but the one thing beyond all others which he owes them is himself. He may provide tutors and schools; but to no tutor and no school can he pass over his relationship and its responsibilities. If he is a stranger to his children, if they are strangers to him, he shall be found wanting when he is weighed in the balance.

Niebuhr, we are told by his biographer, "considered the training of his children, especially of his son, as the most imperative duty of his life, to which all other considerations, except that of very evident and important service to his country, ought to be subordinated. In ordinary times he placed private duties above public ones." Before the child was born his fatherly fondness was planning schemes for the future. "In case it should be a boy, I am already preparing myself to educate him. I should try to familiarize him very early with the ancient languages, by making him repeat sentences after me, and relating stories to him in them, in order that he might not have too much to learn afterwards, nor yet

123

read too much at too early an age; but receive his education after the fashion of the ancients. I think I should know how to educate a boy, but not a girl; I should be in danger of making her too learned.... I would relate innumerable stories to the boy, as my father did to me; but by degrees mix up more and more of Greek and Latin in them, so that he would be forced to learn those languages in order to understand the stories." By and by, when the child is eight months old, we find him curtailing his literary investigations because he is "moreover, just now, too much occupied with Marcuccio." When "Marcuccio" is five years old his father writes: "We have daily proofs of Marcus's noble nature; still I am well aware that this affords us no guaranty, unless it be guided with the most watchful care.... I succeed with teaching as well as I could have ventured to hope.... I am reading with him Hygin's Mythologicum,—a book which, perhaps, it is not easy to use for this purpose, and which, yet, is more suited to it than any other, from the absence of formal periods, and the interest of the narrative. For German, I write fragments of the Greek mythology for him.... I give everything in a very free and picturesque style, so that it is as exciting as poetry to him; and, in fact, he reads it with such delight that we are often interrupted by his cries of joy. The child is quite devoted to me; but this educating costs me a great deal of time. However, I have had my share of life, and I shall consider it as a reward for my labors if this young life be as fully and richly developed as lies within my power."

If Niebuhr, one of the most learned men of his time, ambassador of Prussia to Rome, with all the business to transact, not only of Prussia, but of all the petty German powers that had no minister of their own, engaged in minute and abstruse historical investigation bearing upon a work with which he was occupied and which may be said to have revolutionized Roman history,—if his time was not too valuable to bestow upon the amusement, the affection, and the education of a baby, where shall we find, in America, a man whose valuable time shall be a sufficient reason for the neglect of his children? It may not be necessary or desirable to copy Niebuhr's course with exactness. His residence in Rome devolved upon him a larger part of the mental education of the boy than would have been necessary at home. I am also inclined to think that he was too careful and troubled, and did not have faith enough in Nature and God. But the point which I wish to show is, that, in the midst of his numerous and important duties, he found time for his child; and if he could do so much, surely those who have not one tenth part of his duties and responsibilities, either in number or weight, can find time to do the far less service which devolves upon them. If they cannot, there is but one resource. If a man is not able to be both statesman and father, both merchant and father, or lawyer and father, or farmer and father, he ought to elect which he will be, and confine himself to his choice. If he is too much absorbed in scientific pursuits, or if he is not a sufficiently dextrous workman to be able to secure from his bench time enough to attend to other interests, he ought not to create other interests. No man has any right to assume the charge of two positions when he has the ability to perform the duties of but one. If he alone bore the evil consequences of his shortcomings, he would be less blameworthy, but the chief burden falls upon his children and upon the state. Reckless of moral obligation, mindful only of his own selfish impulses, the fruits of his recklessness and selfishness are,—not houses that tumble down upon their builders, machinery that cannot bear its own strain, garments that perish with the first using,— these are bad enough, but these are harmlessness itself compared with the evils which he causes. The harvest of his headlong wickedness is living beings who must bear their life forever. He bids into the world, tender little innocent souls, knowing that he cannot or will not stand guard over them to ward off the fierce, wild devils that lie in wait to rend them. Plastic to his touch, they may be moulded to vessels of honor or vessels of dishonor, for the promise of God is absolute, yea, and amen. Yet he turns aside to fritter away his time over newspapers, to talk politics, to buy and sell and get unnecessary gain, and leaves them to other hands, to chance comers, to all manner of warping and hardening influences, so that their after-lives must be one long and bitter struggle against early acquired deformity, or a fatal yielding and a fatal torpor whose end is deadly dismay.

But in popular opinion and by common usage all is thrown upon the mother. By all tradition she is the centre, the heart, the mainspring, of the household. From what newspaper, what book, what lecture, would you learn that fathers have anything to do at home but to go into their slippers and dressing-gowns, and be luxuriously fed and softly soothed into repose? The care and management of the children fall upon the mother. Who does all the fine things in the pretty nursery rhymes? "My mother." It is her sphere, divinely circled. All the fitnesses of her life point in that one direction. All men's hands are so many finger-posts saying, "This is the way, walk ye in it."

It is the mother's sphere to take motherly care of

her children. It is the father's sphere to take fatherly care. Neither can leave his duties to the other without danger. The family system is a combination of the solar and the binary systems. All the little bodies whirl around a common centre, but that centre is no solitary orb. It is two suns, self-luminous, revolving around each other, and neither able to throw upon its mate the burden of its shining.

Many fathers seem to think that they have nothing to do with their children except to caress them and frolic with them an hour or two in the evening, until they are old enough to be assistants in work. But just as soon as there is the fatherly relation, there is the fatherly duty. A baby in a house is a well-spring of pleasure; but it is also a well-spring of care and anxiety immeasurable, of whose waters there is no reason why the father should not drink as deeply as the mother. The glory, the honor, the immortality, will shed a full light upon him, and he also

"With heart of thankfulness should bear

Of the great common burden his full share."

I have seen a great deal of pleasantry played off against the doctrines of woman's rights in newspapers, pictorial and otherwise; the wife is represented as being immersed in public employments, while the meek, sad husband stays at home and minds the baby. I do not know that any important ends would be answered by an indiscriminate female-haranguing in the market-place; but I do know that it would be a great deal better for all concerned if fathers would pay more attention to the little ones. Womanly gentleness and tenderness, and long-suffering to-baby-ward reads sweetly in books, rounds graceful periods from melodious lips, and is the loveliest of all modes of levying black mail. But when you come down to matters of fact, a fractious child is just as likely to be quieted by its father's lullaby as by its mother's, if you pin the father down to lullabies. Men who are inclined to take care of their children never find any hinderance in their manhood. Male nurses for children are no less efficient than female nurses. It is not his sex, but his selfishness, that makes man's unfitness. He will not endure the tedium of soothing and tending his child. He knows the mother will, and he lets her do it. Her fitness is a good excuse for his self-indulgence. But if he is disposed to take the trouble, he can do it often as well as she; often better, for the mother's weaker and wearier nerves and greater sensitiveness act on the little one and increase its irritability, while the father's strength and calmness are a sort of soporific. Somebody says that a mother's arm is the strongest thing in the world. It upbears the child as she walks back and forth through the long night-hours soothing its restlessness and pain, and never tires. Vastly well spoken. Suppose, O smooth-tongued Seignior, you take a turn with the baby yourself, and see whether your arm tires. If it does, do not for one moment indulge in the pleasing illusion that hers does not. It is made of flesh and blood and bones just like yours, and like causes produce like effects. But what *is* true is, that her unselfish mother-love is so strong that she keeps on, notwithstanding the ache. Go and do thou likewise. I do not say that fathers will not. Many do, and what man has done man may do. Leave female endurance to poetry, and remember that in actual life the laws of bone and muscle are as fixed as any other laws of natural philosophy, and that action is surely followed by fatigue. Walk you the floor with the baby in your arms, if he must be carried, at least two hours to her one, because your arms were stronger to begin with, and because hers have an added weakness from the advent of this little round-limbed Prince. Do not, above all things, betake yourself to a remote and silent part of the house and dream your pleasant dreams, while the mother loses her sleep and her rest by the ailing and fretful baby. But a man's rest must not be broken. Why not as well as a woman's? He must have a clear head and a firm hand to transact the next day's business. But what is she going to do? The cases are so innumerable as to form a very insignificant proportion wherein the American mother is not also cook, laundress, seamstress, housekeeper, and chambermaid, with sometimes one awkward, ignorant, inefficient Irish servant, rarely two, and not rarely none at all. As a matter of moral economy the care of a baby is enough to occupy any woman's time, and is all the care she ought to have. As I have before said, even under the curse, this is the arrangement that was made for her. Her motherhood frees her from toil; but man's care is heavier than God's curse, and she too often bears on her own head both her punishment and his. If he makes such provision for her that she has absolutely no other than her maternal duties, she can afford, perhaps, to lose her rest at night, since she can make it up in the daytime; and unquestionably nature has fitted babies to mothers more closely than to fathers; but to lay upon her, besides the care of her children, all manner of other cares, and then leave her with aching nerves and weakened frame and failing heart to worry it out as she may, is a culpable cruelty for which no amount of pretty sentiment is the smallest atonement.[4]

There are so many ways where there is a will! There are so many opportunities for usefulness, if a man would only improve them. How many times does the merchant, the lawyer, the busy business man, stop at the street-corners, or in his own haunts, to chat with friends? How many hours there are in the twenty-four when a man might run down from his study, come in earlier from his shop, take a recess from his fields, and rest himself and his wife by giving the little one a ride in the basket-wagon, or the elegant carriage, or amusing it on the carpet, while tired mamma lies down for a much-needed nap, or turns off a greater amount of belated mending or cooking than she could do in four hours with baby. And what benefit would not the man himself receive, what gradual diminution of his selfishness in thus waiting upon the helplessness of this little creature. Under what bonds for the future and for virtue does it not lay him? Let him look down upon his baby with earnest eyes, and inwardly resolve to be himself a man pure and honorable as he wishes this boy to be; let him remember to bear himself toward all women as he would have all men bear themselves to the tiny woman in his arms.

There are men who assume and act on the assumption that their days must be kept free from childish interlopers. They are aggrieved, their personal rights are infringed upon, they have a most heavy and undeserved yoke to bear if the children are not hustled out of their way,—as if children were a kind of luxury and plaything of women in which they may be indulged, if they will be careful to confine them to their own department, nor ever let them encroach on the peculiar domains of the lord of the manor. There are women weak enough to give in to this assumption, and make it a rule that the children are not to disturb their father. Before he comes into the house the crying baby must be hushed at any cost, or removed beyond his hearing. The little ones are not allowed to enter his study, they must not play in the hall near it, nor in the garden under his window, because the noise disturbs him. When the mood takes him, he takes them. He goes into the nursery and has a merry romp with them, and when he is tired of it or they begin to take too many liberties, he goes out again and thinks his children are very charming. Or possibly he never goes into the nursery at all,—a lack of interest which would be very unwomanly in a woman, but is not the the least unmanly nor absolutely unknown in a man. It is a great affliction to the mother, if, in consequence of a temporary neglect of picket-duty, he puts his head into the kitchen or sewing-room, to say with heroic self-control, "Carrie, the children are so in and out that it is impossible for me to do anything." An impatient upward look from his newspaper causes her a shiver of dread. Small table-skirmishes are put to an untimely end by mamma's hurrying the unlucky belligerents out of sight and sound of their outraged sire, and the one Medo-Persic law of the family is at all risks to rescue the father from every inconvenience and annoyance from the children. The kind, devoted woman shuts them carefully up within her own precincts. They may overrun her without stint. They may climb her chair, pull her work about, upset her basket, scratch the bureau, cut the sofa, run to her for healing in every little heart-ache; but no matter. They are kept from disturbing papa. I am amazed at the folly of women! Kept from disturbing papa? Rather hound them on, if there must be any intervention! Put the crying baby in his arms the moment he enters the house, and be sure to run away at once beyond his reach, or with true masculine ingenuity he will be sure at the end of five minutes to find some pretext for delivering the young orator back into your care. So far from carefully withholding the children from the paternal vicinage, at the first symptoms of exclusiveness, put a paper of candy and a set of drums at his door to toll the children thither. But this only in extreme cases. If he is ordinarily reasonable, the right course is to do neither, but let things take their own way. Except in case of illness or some unusual and pressing emergency, the little ones ought not to be kept from either of their lawful owners. The serenity of one is no more sacred than the serenity of the other. The father must simply take the natural consequences of his children. If they drift into his current, he must bear them on. He ought to experience their obviousness, their inconvenience, their distraction. It is no worse for a chubby hand to upset the inkstand on his papers, than for it to upset the molasses-pitcher upon the table-cloth. It is no worse for his experiments, his study, his reading, to be interrupted, than it is for his wife's sewing. He can write his letters, or stand behind the counter, or make shoes, with a baby in his arms, just as well as she can make bread and set the table with a baby in her arms. Let him come into actual close contact with his children and see what they are and what they do, and he will have far more just ideas of the whole subject than if he stands far off and, from old theories on the one side and ten minutes of clean apron and bright faces on the other, pronounces his euphonious generalizations. His children will elicit as much love and admiration and interest as now, together with a great deal more knowledge and a great deal less silly, mannish sentimentalism.

IX.

UT whatever may be the opportunities and capabilities of infantine gymnastics, there is always one way in which fathers may indirectly, but very powerfully, influence their children, and that is through the mother. When her little children are around her, she needs above all earthly things the strength, support, society, and sympathy of her husband. It is wellnigh impossible to conceive the demand which a little child makes upon its mother's vitality. In Nature's plan, I believe, the supply is always equal to the demand. The new, fresh life gives back through a thousand channels all the life it draws. But if the mother is left alone, in such a solitude as is never found outside of marriage, but often and often within it; if she is left to seek in her baby her chief solace, unhappy is her fate. The little one exhausts her physical strength, and the inattentive and abstracted—alas! that one may not seldom say, the unkind and overbearing husband fails to supply her with moral strength, and her weary feet go on with ever-diminishing joy. All this is unnecessary. All this is contrary to the Divine economy. Every child ought to be a new spring of life, an El Dorado, fountain of immortal youth. Whether it shall be or not lies, if you look at it from one point, wholly with the husband, or if you look at it from another, wholly with the wife. On the one hand, each is all-powerful. On the other, each is powerless. But the husband has always the advantage of strength, out-door activities, and continual commerce with the world, and consequent variety. The wife, surrounded by her children, is in danger of giving herself up to them entirely. She will incessantly dispense her life without being careful to furnish herself for such demands by opening her soul to new accessions. Here is where her husband should stand by her continually to encourage and stimulate. If she is not strong enough to go out into the world, let him bring the world home to her. He should by all means see to it that her heart and soul do not contract. Every child, every added experience, should have the effect of expanding her horizon, deepening and enlarging her sympathies, and enabling her to gather the whole earth into her motherly love. Her little world ought to be a type of the great world. The wisdom which she gathers in the one, she ought to turn to the good of the other,— a good that will surely come back again in other shapes to her family world. So, every family should be both a missionary centre and the medium through which, in never-ending flow, all good and gracious influences shall pour. Every family should rise and fall with the pulse of humanity, and not be a mere knob of organic matter, without dependencies or connections. But the father should see to this. He should gently lure the mother out of her nursery into such broad fresh air as she needs for healthy growth. What that shall be is a question of character and culture. A lyceum lecture, a sewing-society, an evening party, a concert, a county fair, may be elevation, amusement, improvement to her. Or he may do her most good by helping her to be interested in reading, either in the current or in classic literature. Or, best of all, he may charm her with his own companionship, beguile her with pleasant drives, or walks and talks, keeping her heart open on the husband side, and so continually alive, while maintaining also the oneness which marriage in theory creates. It is this respect in which husbands are perhaps most generally deficient. They do not talk with their wives. If a neighbor is married, they tell of it. If a battle is fought, or a village burnt down, they communicate the fact; but for any interchange of thought or sentiment or emotion, for any conversation that is invigorating, inspiring, that causes a thrill or leaves a glow, how often does such a thing occur between husband and wife? What intellectual meeting is there,—what shock of electricities? When a definite domestic question is to be decided, the wife's judgment may be sought, and that is better than a solitary stumbling on, regardless of her views or feelings; but this sort of bread-and-butter discussion of ways and means is not the gentle, animated play of conversation, not that pleasant sparkle which enlivens the hours, that trustful confidence which lightens the heart, that wielding of weapons which strengthens the arm, that sweet, instinctive half unveiling which increases respect and deepens love and fills the heart with inexpressible tenderness. Yet there is nobody in the world with whom it is so important for a man to be intimately acquainted as his own wife, while such intimate acquaintance is the exception rather than the rule. Ever one sees them going on each in his own path, each with his own inner world of opinions and hopes and memories, one in name, miserably two in all else.

Men often have too much confidence in their measuring-lines. They fancy they have fathomed a soul's depths when they have but sounded its shallows. They think they have circumnavigated the globe when they have only paddled in a cove. They trim their sails for other seas, leaving the priceless gems of their own undiscovered. To many a man no voyage of exploration would bring such rich returns as a persevering and affectionate search into the resources of the heart which he calls his own. Many and many a man would be amazed at learning that in the tame household drudge, in the meek, timid, apologetic recipient of his caprices, in the worn and fretful invalid, in the commonplace, insipid domestic weakling he scorns an angel unawares. Many a wife is wearied and neglected into moral shabbiness, who, rightly entreated, would have walked sister and wife of the gods. Human nature in certain directions is as infinite as the Divine nature, and when a man turns away from his wife, under the impression that he has exhausted her capabilities, and must seek elsewhere the sympathy and companionship he craves or go without it altogether, let him reflect that the chances are at least even that he has but exhausted himself, and that the soil which seems to him fallow might in other hands or with a wiser culture yield most plenteous harvests.

There is another point which should be kept in solemn consideration. The deportment of children to their parents is very largely influenced by the deportment of parents to each other. It is of small service that a child be taught to repeat the formula, "Honor thy father and thy mother," if, by his bearing, the father continually dishonors the mother. The Monday courtesy has more effect than the Sunday commandment. Every conjugal impoliteness is a lesson in filial disrespect. If a son sees that his father is regardless of his mother's taste, does not respect her opinions, or heed her sensitiveness or care for her happiness; or if, on the other hand, he sees that she is held in ever-watchful love, he will be very likely to follow in the same path. There are of course exceptions. A gross and brutal abuse may work an opposite effect by the law of contrarieties, but in ordinary cases this is the ordinary course of events. In common Christian families a boy will appraise his mother at his father's valuation. If the husband takes the liberty of speaking to her sharply, the son when irritated will not think it worth while to repress his inclination to do the same. If the husband is not careful to pay her outward respect, let it not be supposed that his son will set him the example. But if the husband cherishes her with delight, if his behavior always assumes that the best is to be reserved for her, the best will be her incense from the whole family, and no son will any more allow himself to indulge any evil propensity in her presence than he would pluck out his right eye. And in the delicacy, the refinement, the gentleness and warmth and consecration of her presence all this courtesy and consideration will come back to them a hundred-fold in constant dews of blessing.

As with habits so with principles. The mother's influence is strong, but the stories told of its strength are often hurtful in their tendency. It is not the strength of the mother's, but of the father's influence, that needs to be held up to prominence. By Divine sufferance, mothers can do much to abrogate the evil consequences of paternal misdoing,—but paternal misdoing is not for that any the less evil. If the husband laughs at his wife's temperance notions, and thinks wine-sipping to be elegant and harmless, his boy will sip wine elegantly and fancy his mother old-fashioned; and with his father's appetite, but without his father's strength, and with more than his father's temptations,—in the great city, homeless, bewildered, and dazzled,—he will rush on to a bitter end. If the husband thinks religion a thing beautiful and becoming to woman, but unnecessary to manly character, his son will not long go to church and to Sunday school when he feels in his veins the thrill of approaching manhood. I know a community where not a man can be found to superintend the Sabbath school, and a woman, noble and whole-souled, takes its charge upon herself. The fathers do not disbelieve in Sunday schools, or they would not suffer their wives and children to go. They do not believe in them, or they would go themselves. They are simply indifferent,—and indifferent in a matter so important, that indifference is guilt. Will the young men of that community be likely to fear God and keep his commandments? Will they be likely to acknowledge the claims of a religion which their fathers despise? If they grow up hardened, selfish, headstrong, unfortified against assault, will it be the fault of the mothers who are struggling against wind and tide, or of the fathers who are lazily lounging at oar and rudder?

People in general are not half married. Half? If one would mathematically approximate the truth, he must multiply his denominator far beyond reach of the digits; and, what is still worse the fraction that is married is, in a vast majority of cases, not only the least, but the lowest. It is not the intellect, the spirit, the immortality, that is married, but that alone which is of the earth, earthy.

Xenophon, in his *Memorabilia Socratis*, presents to us Ischomacus, an Athenian of great riches and reputation, repairing to Socrates for help in extricating him from domestic entanglements. In laying the case before the philosopher, Ischomacus informs him that he told his wife that his main object in marrying her was to have a person in whose discretion he could confide, who would take proper care of his servants, and expend his money with economy,—which was certainly very frank.

But that was twenty-three hundred years ago, and people have grown less material and more spiritual since then. No man now would hold out to a woman such inducement to marriage. Certainly not. Men now wait till the Rubicon is passed, and then lay down their pleasant little programmes in the newspapers,—general principles for private consumption. The popular voice, speaking in your everywhere circulating newspaper, says: "A man gets a wife to look after his affairs, and to assist him in his journey through life; to educate and prepare their children for a proper station in life, and not to dissipate his property. The husband's interest should be the wife's care, and her greatest ambition to carry her no farther than his welfare or happiness, together with that of her children. This should be her sole aim, and the theatre of her exploits in the bosom of her family, where she may do as much toward making a fortune as he can in the counting-room or the workshop."

Is this very much more commanding than the attitude of Ischomacus? Does Anno Domini loom with immeasurable grandeur above Anno Mundi? Ischomacus wanted his wife to manage his fortune. Young America wants his to help make one. Is it a very great stride in advance, considering we have been twenty-three centuries about it? This extract I take from a religious newspaper, and it is pagan to the heart's core; yes, and in these matters the Church is as pagan as the World. Because a man is folded in the Church, one has no more expectation of finding in him spiritual views concerning marriage than if he belonged to the World. Unmitigated selfishness, worldliness, greed, and evil-seeking are the roots and fruits of such a "religious" paragraph. Church and World are both gone aside and altogether become filthy. The holy sacrament is profaned alike by churchman and worldling. It is tossed on the spear-point of levity, it is clutched under the muck-rake of materialism, it is degraded and defiled till its pristine purity is wellnigh lost, and only a marred and defaced image rears its foul features from the mire. That it does not always cause disgust, is because the goddess is so chiefly hidden that women do not recognize the lineaments of the demon which has usurped her place. Miasma has polluted the atmosphere so long that people do not know the feeling of untainted air. O, it is good to speak your mind, be it only once in a lifetime! Now I wish I had walked softly all my days, that, with all the force of a rare indignation, I might just this once crush down that hateful, that debasing, that vile and leprous thing which flaunts the name of marriage, but does not even put on the white garments of its sanctity to hide its own shame. Leer and laugh, coarse jest, advice, insinuation, interpretation, and conjecture beslime the surface of our social life and work abomination. Nature and unconsciousness become impossible, and one is swallowed up in stagnant depths, or borne above them only with an inward, raging tempest of irrepressible loathing. A blessing rest upon this pen-point that stamps black and heavy into receptive paper the wrath which it is not lawful otherwise to express. Sentiments the most repulsive, the most insulting to womanhood and to a woman, may be coolly, carelessly, unconsciously tossed at you by and in society, and you must smile and parry with equal nonchalance. Thank Heaven for Gutenberg and

Dr. Faustus, that whatsoever has been spoken in darkness may be heard to its shame in the light, and that which has been spoken in the ear may be proclaimed upon the house-tops with the detestation it deserves!

X.

TAY for a moment the pressure with which—though, perhaps, all unknown to themselves—you force women under the yoke of marriage, and let us look without passion at a few palpable, commonplace facts. Women must marry because they need a protector. They are weak, and cannot safely go down life's pathway without a strong arm to lean on. What kind of protection do wives actually find? I once looked into an old-fashioned house and I saw a woman, the mother of seven sons, heating her oven with the boughs of trees, which she could manage only by resting the branching ends on the backs of chairs while the trunk ends were burning in the oven, and as they broke into coals the boughs were pushed in, till the whole was consumed. When her dinner was preparing, she would also take her pails and go through the hot summer morning a quarter of a mile to the spring for water. Was this "protection, freedom, tender-liking, ease." This was not in a brutal and quarrelsome, but in a united and Christian family; father and mother members of an Orthodox church in good and regular standing, owners of broad lands and plenty of money, the sons rather famous for their filial love and duty. It was not an unnatural thing, and excited no comment. The seven sons, all their lives, held their mother in affectionate remembrance, but it never occurred to them to leave the hay-fields in order to cut wood or fetch water.

This was sixty or seventy years ago, before any of you, my young readers, were born.

Once a rich man built a barn, and of course he had "a raising." To the raising came the men and women from all the country-side, as was their wont. For the men was a supper provided with lavish abundance. Before they came in, thirty women sat down to supper. Of course, when came the men's turn to be served, these women gave assistance at the tables, but all the previous cooking and arrangement had been done by the women of the family, without outside help. Besides the hot meat supper, the men were furnished with unlimited drink; cider, rum, and brandy were carried out to them by the pailful. An experienced carpenter from an adjoining village declared that he would take the timber in the woods, hew it and frame it, and raise it for what the mere festivities of raising cost. To perform one little piece of work, the men laid upon the shoulders of women a burden ten times heavier than their own, and incurred an expense which, if put upon their large, square, bare dwelling-house, would have given it beauties and conveniences, whose absence was a continual and severe drawback to the women's comfort. They turned the woman's work into hard labor, that they might turn their own into a frolic. Were those women protected? That was only one instance, but that was the common machinery used in raising barns. That, too, was long ago.

Once there existed a village containing four schools, which were in session three months in the summer and three months in the winter. At the beginning and end of the terms, the "committee," of whom there were two in each "district," used to visit the schools attended by the greater part of the adult male population of the district. At the conclusion of this visit, one of the district committee at the beginning of the term, and one at the end, was always expected to invite the other seven committeemen and all the visiting neighbors to his house to dinner. The hard-working farmer's wife, or the butcher's, or the shoemaker's wife, with her four, five, seven, little children around her, and no servant, prepared her three roast turkeys, her three plum-puddings, and all the attendant dishes; and the ten, twenty, thirty stalwart farmers, butchers, shoemakers, booted and burly, filed into her best room, swallowed her roast turkeys and her plum-puddings, with no assistance from her except the most valued service of flitting around the table to keep their plates supplied, and then filed away to visit another school and swarm into another best room, leaving her to the bones, and the dishes, and the six little children. And this is man's protection. But this was the old times, you say. Yes, and you look back upon it with a sigh, and call it the "*good old times.*"

Well, the times have changed. They are no longer old, but new. Have we changed with them? In a town I wot of, the doctors have a periodical meeting. They assemble in the evening by themselves in a parlor, discussing no one knows what, among themselves, till ten or eleven o'clock, when they emerge into the dining-room and have a grand set-to upon lobster salads, stewed oysters, ices, and all manner of frothy fanfaronade. A minister is going to be ordained in a country village, and the village families round about heap up their tables and bid in all comers to feasts of fat things. A conference of churches is held in the meeting-house, and the same newspaper paragraph that notes the logical sermon and the gratifying reports of revivals, notes also the good things which the hospitable citizens provided, and the urgency with which strangers were pressed to partake. One would suppose that the reasoning of the fastidious old Jews was suspected to have descended to our own day and race, and that the sons of men must always come eating and drinking, or people will say they have a devil.

Every advance in science or skill seems to be attended by a corresponding advance in the claims of the cooking-range. The palate keeps pace with the brain. The one presents a claim for every victory of the other. The left hand reaches out to clutch what the right hand is stretched out to offer to humanity.

Now you all think this is very strange,—a most remarkable way of looking at things, a most inhospitable and cold-blooded view to take of society. What! begrudge a little pains to give one's friends a pleasant reception! and that only once a year, or a month! It is such a thing as was never heard of. You have always looked upon the affair as one of pleasure. The houses which, you have entered opened wide to you their doors. You met on all sides smiles, welcome, and good cheer. You never for a moment dreamed or heard of such a thing as that you were considered a trouble, a visitation. Perhaps you were not. Very likely you were held in honor; but these customs are burdensome for all that. You must remember that by far the greater part of American housewives are already overborne by their ordinary domestic cares. This makes the whole thing wear a very different aspect from what it otherwise would. If a cup is half full, you can pour in a great deal more, and only increase the cup's worth, for to such end was it created; but if it is already brimmed, you cannot add even a teaspoonful without mischief, and if you suddenly dash in another cupful, you will make a sad mess of it. Now when these various convocations occur, the note of preparation is sounded long beforehand, and the wail of weariness echoes long afterwards. This is simply a statement of fact. I am not responsible for the fact. I did not create it, and I wish it were otherwise; but so long as it is a fact, it is much better that it should be known. The woman who welcomed you so warmly, entreated you so tenderly, entertained you so agreeably, had no sooner shut the door behind you, when you had started for the church, than the sunshine which radiated from your presence went suddenly behind a cloud of odorous steam that rose up from stew-pan and gridiron. While you were listening to the eloquent address, she was flying about to have the dishes washed and the next meal ready. When, after your hour's pleasant talk in the evening over the day's doings, you were sleeping soundly in her airy chambers, she, as noiselessly as possible, till eleven and twelve o'clock at night, was sweeping her carpets and dusting her furniture in the only time which she could rescue from the duties of hospitality for that purpose. I maintain that, however agreeable are these social conventions, they are bought too dearly at such a price. A great many women who suffer from such causes never think of complaining. They are hospitable from the bottom of their hearts; but however sincere their welcome, pies do not bake themselves. Never a cow went in at one end of an oven to come out at the other a nicely-browned sirloin of beef. Never a barrel of flour and a bowl of yeast rushed spontaneously together and evoked a batch of bread, nor did the hen-fever at its hottest height ever produce bantam or Shanghai that could lay eggs which would leap lightly ceiling-ward to come down an omelet. All these things require time

146

and pains, and generally the time and pains of people who, by reason of the stern necessities of their position, have none of either to spare. It is not just to say that these emergencies come only once in a great while, and are therefore too insignificant to be reckoned. The same injudiciousness which crops out in a conference of churches this week will reappear in a town-meeting next week, and in a mass-meeting the week after, and a teachers'-meeting the week after that. The same marital ignorance and inconsiderateness that brings on one thing will bring on another thing, and, except in the few cases where money and other ample resources enable one to secure adequate service, the wrong side, the prose side, the hard side of these pleasant "occasions" comes on the wife; who, whether she meet it gladly, or only acquiescently, or reluctantly, is surely worn away by the attrition. However welcome society may be to her, she cannot encounter these odds with impunity, and in a majority of cases the odds are so heavy that she has neither time nor spirits to enjoy the society. All this wear and tear is unnecessary. The doctors would be better off to go home without their hot suppers. There is seldom, in cities, any necessity for feeding masses of people, because professional feeding-houses are always at hand, and people seldom congregate in the country except in summer, when each man might, with the smallest trouble, carry his own sandwich, and eat it on the grass, surrounded by his kinsfolk and acquaintance, with just as much hilarity as if he were sitting in a hard-cushioned high chair in a country-house parlor. Enjoyment would not be curtailed on the one side, and would be greatly promoted on the other.

The Essex Institute has its Field-meetings,—its pleasant bi-weekly summer visits into the country, and is everywhere welcome. During the morning it roams over the fields, laying its inquisitive hands on every green and blossoming and creeping thing. The insects in the air, the fishes in the brook, the spiders in their webs, the butterfly on its stalk, feel instinctively that their hour is come, and converge spontaneously into their little tin sarcophagi. At noonday hosts of heavy baskets unlade their toothsome freight, and a merry feast is seasoned with Attic salt. In the afternoon, the farm-wagons come driving up, and the farm-horses lash their contented sides under the friendly trees, while city and country join in the grave or sparkling or instructive talk which fixes the wisdom caught in the morning rambles. At night, young men and maidens, old men and children, go their several ways homeward, just as happy as if they had left behind them a dozen family-mothers wearied into fretfulness and illness by much serving. They depend upon no one for entertainment and owe no tiresome formalities. Go, all manner of convocations, and do likewise.

Note, if you please, that it is not feasting which is objectionable. Truly or falsely, eating has always been held to be the promoter and attendant of conviviality, the mouth opening the way at the same time to the palate and the brain. If men can provide feasts without laying burdens upon their wives, let them do it and welcome; but if the material part of the feast cannot be accomplished without so serious an increase of a wife's labor as to destroy or diminish her capacity for enjoying the mental part, it ought not to be attempted.

You may say that women are as much to blame in this thing as men; that the great profusion, variety, and elaborateness of their meals are as much of their own motion as of men's; that they are indeed proud of and delight in showing their culinary resources; that they gather sewing-circles of their own sex without any hint, help, or wish from the other, and make just as great table-displays on such occasions as on any others that I have mentioned,—all of which may be very true. So the Doctor Southsides for many years maintained that slavery must be a good thing, because the slaves were content in it. So the Austrian despots point to peasants dancing on the greensward as the justification of their paternal government, their absolute tyranny; as if degradation is any less disastrous when its victims are sunk so low as to be unconscious of their situation,—as if, indeed, that were not the lowest pit of all. How came women, made as truly as man in the image and likeness of God, to be reduced to the level of sacrificing time, ease, intellectual and social good, to the low pride of sensual display? Is it not the fault of those whose walk and conversation have made the care of eating and drinking the one thing needful in a woman's education, the chief end of her life; who have not hesitated to degrade the high prerogatives of an immortal soul to the gratification of their own fleshly lusts; who have manoeuvred so adroitly that the tickling of their own palates has become a more important and a more influential thing than the building up of the temple of the Holy Ghost? Profusion and variety and elaborateness are of the wife's own motion; but the more profuse, varied, and elaborate her display, the more you praise her. The more ingenuity her feast displays, the more ingeniously you combine words and exhaust your rhetoric to express approbation and delight. Your continued and conjoint praise is a far stronger incentive than the clubs and thongs with which husbands have been sometimes wont to urge their wives to action, and which you recognize as force.

You do not compel her, but, directly and indirectly, with an almost irresistible potency, for years and years you have enjoined it upon her, till your moral pressure has become as powerful as any display of physical strength could be. And having, in French fashion, set up a cook on the shrine of your worship, is it an extenuation of your offence, that women now vie with each other in striving to merit and attain such an apotheosis? Having caused your female children to pass through the kitchen-fire to the Moloch of your adoration, are you so illogical as to suppose that they will come out without any smell of fire upon their garments?

You are not to blame for the thistle-field. You did not make the thistles grow. No; but you planted the seed, you watered the soil, you supplied all the conditions of growth; and when the Lord of the vineyard cometh seeking fruit, and findeth only thistles, what shall he do but miserably destroy those wicked men and give the vineyard unto others?

These are only the difficult hills over which you urge women to climb when you urge them on to marriage. Of the levels between, of the plains over which lies the every-day path of the great majority of married women, I have spoken with sufficient distinctness in another connection. Whether they are the wives of inefficient or of enterprising men makes small difference. The overwhelming probability is, that your blooming bride will encounter a fate similar to that of the prince in the fairy-tale, who, enchanted by an ugly old witch, was compelled to spend his life sitting inside a great iron stove; only, instead of sitting comfortably inside, she will be kept in perpetual motion outside. Poverty or wealth, ignorance or education, in the husband, may affect the quality, but scarcely the quantity, of the wife's work. Hard, grinding, depressing toil is not the peculiar lot of the poor housewife. It is the "protection," the "cherishing," which men "well to do in the world" award their wives,—the thriving farmers, the butchers, the blacksmiths, who "get a good living," and perhaps have "money at interest." What advantageth it a woman to be the wife of a "rising man"? He rises by reading, by reasoning, by attention to his business, by intercourse with intelligent people, by journeys, by constant growth, and constant contact with stimulating circumstances; but she is tied down by the endless details of housekeeping and the nursery. Growth, intelligence, and rising in the world are not for her. His increasing business and fair political prospects only bring more cares to her, and bring them long before any permanent increase of income justifies, or can command, anything approximating to adequate assistance in the home department. And his increase of business, his widening circle of acquaintance, are sure to take him more away from home, to absorb more of his time and his thoughts, and so not only create heavier burdens, but call to other tasks the strength that ought to bear them. The selfsame circumstances which raise the man depress the woman. If he does not make especial effort to upbear her with himself, the result will presently be, that, while he rides on the crest of the wave, she is engulfed in the trough of the sea. There is small reason to suppose he will make the effort. It is the men in "comfortable circumstances," shrewd, with an eye to the main chance, who often sin most deeply in this respect. Their main chance does not include husbandly love, wifely repose. It is a part of their "business talent" to turn their wives to account just as they turn everything else. She is a partner in the concern. She is a part of the stock in trade. She is one of the stepping-stones to eminence or competence. All that she can earn or save, all the labor or supervision that can be wrested from her, is so, much added to the working capital; and so long as she does not lose her health, so long as she remains in good working order, they never suspect that anything is wrong. If she were not doing the house-work or taking care of the children, she would not be doing anything that would bring in money, or nearly so much money, as her economy and foresight save. Even if she does lose her health, her husband scarcely so much as thinks of laying the sin at his own door. It was not hard work or low spirits, it was rheumatism or slow fever, that brought her down. If her life lapses away, and she descends into the grave before she has lived out half her days, her sorrowing husband lays it to the account of a mysterious Providence, and—"the world is all before him where to choose."

Have I drawn a cold, harsh picture? The coldness and harshness are not alone in the drawing. It spreads before you every day and all around you: a picture whose figures throb with hidden life,—a very *tableau vivant*. What else can be expected from our social principles? What kind of husbands do you look for in men who have set their affections on fortune or fame? What kind of husbands can a society turn out that publicly and shamelessly avows the preservation and increase of property to be the object of marriage? A people's practice is sometimes, but very rarely, better than its principles. If wealth or position be the chief goal of a man's ambition, he only acts consistently in harnessing his wife along with all his other powers and possessions to his chariot. Looking at it dispassionately, freed from the glamour which popular opinion throws upon our eyes, it would seem to be better for a woman to marry the Grand Turk, since a friendly bowstring might put a period to her trouble, or she might hope to be tied up in a sack and safely and quietly deposited in the Bosphorus; while in America there is no such possibility. You must live on to the end, come it never so tardily.

And how far extends even so much protection as this,—the protection which consists in appropriating a woman's time and strength, and deteriorating both her mind and body by incessant, chiefly menial, and not unfrequently repulsive toil, and giving her in return—food, clothing, and shelter, which, if female labor were justly paid, she could earn by one fourth of the effort, and which is often bestowed with more or less reluctance and unpleasant conditioning, as a favor rather than a right? Look around upon all the people whose circumstances you know, and see if the number of families is small whose support depends partly upon the mother? Do you know any families which depend chiefly or entirely upon the mother? Do you know any, where the husbands are invalids, and have laid by nothing for a rainy day? any, where the husbands are lazy and inefficient, and perhaps intemperate, and neglect to provide for their families? any, where they have been unfortunate and lost all, and only the mother's courage and energy supply deficiency? any, where the husband has died insolvent, and the survivor struggles single-handed against the tide? any, where the husband's death was the lifting of an incubus, which removed, the family seemed at once to be prosperous and happy? Do you ever see a woman, with a family of children and a husband, taking the entire care of her household, and, besides this, earning a little money at knitting or sewing or washing? Judging from my own observation, setting aside inability from disease, where you find one woman who is a dead-weight upon her energetic husband, you will find seven men who are a dead-weight upon their energetic wives.

But all this is "protection." All this is the superior sex cherishing the inferior; the chivalrous sex defending the helpless; the strong caring for the delicate; the able providing for the dependent. To all this you urge women when you goad them on to marriage. And you do well to apply your goad. You are wise in your generation, when you create such an overwhelming outside pressure; without it, women would not go down quick into the pit. Left to their own unprejudiced reason, to their own clear eyes and rapid and just conclusions, they would not choose, the greatest of all evils,—a living death. In vain is the net spread in the sight of any bird. If you cannot help this state of things, where is your logic? If you can help it, where is your conscience?

XI.

OU will say that I have left the main element out of the calculation; that I have looked at marriage only in respect of its material combinations, in which light it appears but as a body without the soul; whereas, in its real wholeness it is penetrated by love which transforms all common scenes, persons, and duties "into something rich and strange." But will truth permit one to view it otherwise? Is marriage, as we see it practically carried out, penetrated with this vivifying and spiritualizing element? Love, indeed, calls nothing common or unclean; but, as a matter of homely fact, is there love enough in ordinary housekeeping to keep it sweet? The first year or two runs well, but how much living love survives the first olympiad? How much outlasts a decade? In marriages openly mercenary, we do not count on finding affection; where they are entered into honestly, are they followed by different results? If a woman marries for money, or station, or respectability, she may compass her ends, but if she marries for love, are not the odds against her? Motive affects her character, but scarcely her fate. Her love will be wasted on a thankless heart; she may consider herself fortunate if it be not trampled under a brutal, or perhaps only a heedless foot. Love in marriage! Marriage is the grave of love. Look at best for association, habit, support, tranquillity, freedom from outside compassion, in marriage, but do not look for love.

On such a topic as this the truth must be felt rather than proved, yet authority is not wanting. So eminent and trustworthy a man as Paley, in his Moral and Political Philosophy, having spoken of the necessity that a man and wife should make mutual concession, adds: "A man and woman in love with each other do this insensibly; but love is neither general nor durable; and where that is wanting, no lessons of duty, no delicacy of sentiment, will go half so far with the generality of mankind as this one intelligible reflection, that they must each make the best of their bargain."

This work was published in 1785. We have all studied it at school, under the guidance of men and women, married and single. Its positions have been variously, frequently, and sometimes successfully assailed. But I have never heard a whisper breathed or seen a line written impugning his statement, that love is neither general nor durable. This statement is not made under the influence of passion, or to compass any purpose, but is simply the basis of an argument,—a general truth, as if he should say that man is endowed with a conscience.

In that most fascinating of biographies, the "Memoirs of Frederic Perthes," written by his son, and published in Edinburgh, we have a very charming picture of home life. Perthes, a man known throughout Germany, the intimate friend of her most distinguished scholars and statesmen, is the husband of Caroline, a woman whose character, indirectly but minutely and impressively portrayed in her husband's memoirs, seems to be without flaw. Fresh, simple, truthful, sensible, sympathetic, affectionate, educated, and accomplished, the qualities of her head and heart alike command something deeper than respect. As daughter, wife, mother, and woman she is equally admirable. Her letters to her husband and her children are as full of wisdom as of love. Everywhere she shines white and clear and pure as the moon, yet warm, beneficent, and bountiful as the sun. It is only as the wife of Perthes that we know her; but, magnificent as Perthes unquestionably was, he pales before the most beautiful, most gracious, most womanly woman whom he won to his heart and home. No suspicion of her own exceeding excellence ever seems to have dawned upon her own mind. Her Perthes was the object of her deep respect and her lasting love. This fact of itself shows that he must have been a man of extraordinary conjugal merit. His relations to her must have been of a very rare delicacy. He must have bestowed an attention and been capable of an appreciation far beyond the ordinary measure, or such a woman as his wife could not have written after several years of marriage, "The old song is every morning new, that, if possible, I love Perthes still better than the day before." If one may not find satisfaction in the contemplation of a marriage passed under circumstances so favoring, where shall he look for satisfaction? Nevertheless, listen to a story lightly told by her son, the biographer, the learned law-professor of the world-renowned Bonn,—told as the old prophets are supposed to have frequently uttered their prophecies, with but the most vague and imperfect comprehension of what it was that they were saying.

"With her lively fancy, and a heart ever seeking sympathy, she felt it to be hard that Perthes, laden with cares, business, and interests of all kinds, could devote so little time to her and the children. 'My hope becomes every day less that Perthes will be able to make any such arrangement of his time as will leave a few quiet hours for me and the children. There is nothing that I can do but to love him, and to bear him ever in my heart, till it shall please God to bring us together to some region where we shall no longer need house or housekeeping, and where there are neither bills to be paid nor books to be kept. Perthes feels it a heavy trial, but he keeps up his spirits, and for this I thank God.' To these and kindred feelings which she had long cherished in her heart Caroline now gave expression in letters which she wrote to Perthes during his absence. After eighteen years of trial and vicissitude, her affection for her husband had retained all its youthful freshness; life and love had not become merely habitual, they remained fresh and spontaneous as in the bride. She always gave free utterance to her feelings, in a manner at once unrestrained and characteristic, and felt deeply when Perthes, as a husband, addressed her otherwise than he had done as a bridegroom. During Perthes's detention for some weeks in Leipsic, this state of feeling found expression on both sides, half in jest and half in earnest. 'You indeed renounced all sensibility for this year, because of your many occupations,' wrote Caroline a few days after her husband's departure; 'but I, for my part, when I write to you, cannot do so without deep feeling; for the thought of you excites all the sensibility of which my heart is capable. Not a line have I yet received. Tell me, is it not rather hard that you did not write me from Brunswick? At least I thought so, and felt very much that your companion G. should have written to his newly-married wife, and you not to me. It is the first time you have ever gone on a journey without writing to me from your first resting-place. I have been reading over your earlier letter to find satisfaction to myself, in some measure at least, but it has been a mixed pleasure. Last year, at Blankenese, you promised me many happy hours of mutual companionship. I have not yet had them; and yet you owe many such to me,— yes, you do indeed.' Perthes answered: 'You write, telling me that I have renounced all sensibility for this year. This is not true, my dearest heart; it is quite otherwise. I think that, after so many years of mutual interchange of feeling and of thought, and when people understand each other thoroughly, there is an end of all those little tendernesses of expression, which represent a relationship that is still piquant because new. Be content with me, dear child, we understand each other. I did not write to you from Brunswick, because we passed through quickly. Moreover, it is not fair to compare me with my companion, the bridegroom; youth has its features, and so also has middle age. It would be absurd, indeed, were I now to be looking by moonlight under the trees and among the clouds for young maidens, as I did twenty years ago, or were to imagine young ladies to be angels. Nor would it become *you* any better if you were to be dancing a gallopade, or clambering up trees in fits of love enthusiasm. We should not find fault with our having grown older; only be satisfied, give God the praise, and exercise patience and forbearance with me.'"

Can anything be more natural than Caroline's gentle remonstrance? Can anything be more hopeless than Perthes's shuffling reply? Lonely wife, languishing for a draught of the olden tenderness, and with nothing to medicine her weariness but the information that it had all come to an end; reaching out for a little of the love that was her life, and met by the assertion that climbing trees was not becoming to a woman of her age! It is good to know that she replied with spirit, though still with no diminution of her immeasurable love. "Your last letter is indeed a strange one. I must again say, that my affection knows neither youth nor age, and is eternal. I can detect no change, except that I now *know* what formerly I only hoped and believed. I never took you for an angel, nor do I now take you for the reverse; neither did I ever beguile you by assuming an angel's form or angelic manners. I never danced the gallopade, or climbed trees, and am now exactly what I was then, only rather older; and you must take me as I am, my Perthes;—in one word, love me, and tell me so sometimes, and that is all I want."

Men, you to whose keeping a woman's heart is intrusted, can you hear that simple prayer,—"Love me, and tell me so sometimes, and that is all I want"?

Perthes, shamed out of his worldliness into at least an attempt at sympathy, replies: "Your answer was just what it ought to have been; only don't forget that my inward love for you is as eternal as yours is for me; but I have so many things to think of."

Undoubtedly, after all his evasion, the truth came out at last,—"I have so many things to think of." It was the best excuse he could offer, and it is a great pity he had not brought it forward in the beginning. He had suffered the cares of this world and the deceitfulness of business to choke his love; but it would have been far more honorable to himself and far more comfortable to his wife to confess it frankly, than to affirm his indifference and neglect to be the natural course of events. A love overgrown with weeds may be revived, but for a love lost by natural decay there is no resurrection. "I did not write to you from Brunswick, because we passed through quickly." Did he pass through any more quickly than his companion G., who found time to write to his newly-married wife? "We understand each other thoroughly, and therefore there is an end of all those little tendernesses of expression"; but there was no end of them on Caroline's part. Her understanding was not less thorough than his, yet her love craved expression. "My inward love for you is as eternal as yours for me"; yet just before he had been pleading his increasing years as an excuse for his diminishing tenderness, while Caroline's stanch heart declared, "My affection knows neither youth nor age, and is eternal. I can detect no change, except that I now *know* what formerly I only hoped and believed." Shortly afterwards, while spending a summer at Wandsbeck for her health, almost daily letters were exchanged between herself and her husband. "While those of Perthes were devoted to warnings and entreaties to take care of her health, (a cheap substitute for affection which Perthes was not alone in employing,) the few lines in which Caroline was wont to reply were full of expressions of love, and of sorrow on account of their necessary separation. 'I am seated in the garden,' she writes, 'and all my merry little birds are around me. I let the sun shine upon me, to make me well if he can. God grant it! if it only be so far as to enable me to discharge my duties to my family.'—'I hope, my dear Perthes, that you will again have pleasure in me; the waters seem really to do me good. Come to-morrow, only not too late. My very soul longs for you.'—'You shall be thanked for the delightful hours that I enjoyed with you yesterday,' she writes, after a short visit to Hamburg, 'and for the sight of your dear, kind face, as I got out of the carriage.'—'I only live where you are with me. Send Matthias to me, if it does not interfere with his lessons: if I cannot have the father, I must put up with the son.'—'The children enjoy their freedom, and are my joy and delight.... But you, dear old father! you, too, are my joy and delight. Let me have a little letter; I cannot help longing for one, and will read it, when I get it, ten times over.'—'It is eighteen years to-day since I wrote you the last letter before our marriage, and sent you my first request about the little black cross. I have asked for many things in the eighteen years that have passed since then, dear Perthes, and what shall I ask to-day? You can tell, for you know me well, and know that I have never said an untrue word to you. Only you cannot quite know my indescribable affection, for it is infinite. Perthes, my heart is full of joy and sadness,—would that you were here! This day eighteen years ago I did not long for you more fervently or more ardently than now. I thank God continually for everything. I am and remain yours in time, and, though I know not how, for eternity, too! Be in a very good humor, when you come to-morrow. Affection is certainly the greatest wonder in heaven or on earth, and the only thing that I can represent to myself as insatiable throughout eternity.'"

Do these extracts indicate that many years of mutual interchange of feeling and thought had put an end to little tendernesses of expression? Does his love seem as eternal as hers? It is true that he falls back upon "inward" love; but we only know saints in their bodies. Inward love that denies outward manifestation may satisfy men, but it will never pass current with women. Little children, who have been idle during their study-hour, will often excuse their failures by declaring that they "know, but cannot think." No teacher, however, is imposed on. A scholar that does not know his lesson well enough to recite it, does not know it at all. A love that does not, in one way or another, express itself sufficiently to satisfy the object of its love, is not love. To satisfy the *object* of its love, I say, for love can never satisfy itself. It was not love that Perthes's letter contained, but an apology for its absence.

What men love is the comforts of the married state, not the person who provides them,—wifely duties rather than the wife. A man enjoys his home. He likes the cheery fireside, the dressing-gown and slippers, the bright tea-urn and the brighter eyes behind it. He likes to see boys and girls growing up around him, bearing his name and inheriting his qualities. He likes to have his clothes laid ready to his hand, stockings in their integrity, buttons firm in their places, meals pleasant, prompt, yet frugal. He likes a servant such as money cannot hire;— attentive, affectionate, spontaneous, devoted, and trustworthy. He likes very much the greatest comfort for the smallest outlay, and certainly he likes to be loved. His love runs in the current of his likings, and is speedily indistinguishable from them; but does he love the woman who is his wife? Would he say to her, as poor Tom sadly pleaded in "A Half-Life and Half a Life,"—"But I love you true and if you can only fancy me, I'll work so hard that you'll be able to keep a hired girl and have all your time for reading and going about the woods, as you like to do"? Would he say, as Von Fink said to Lenore, —"You will have no need to make my shirts, and if you don't like account-keeping, why let it alone"? Listen, for it is good to know that a man has lived and written who did not look for his domestic happiness entirely in a bread-pan and a work-basket. "Just as you are, Lenore,—resolute, bold, a little passionate devil,—just so will I have you remain. We have been companions in arms, and so we shall continue to be.... Were you not my heart's desire, were you a man, I should like to have you for my life's companion; so, Lenore, you will be to me not only a beloved wife, but a courageous friend, the confidante of all my plans, my best and truest comrade."

Lenore shook her head; "I ought to be your housewife," sighed she (the new love not yet having quite purged out the old leaven).

Fink—(but no matter what Fink did. We are concerned now only with what he said.) "Be content, sweetheart," said he, tenderly, "and make up your mind to it. We have been together in a fire strong enough to bring love to maturity, and we know each other thoroughly. Between ourselves, we shall have many a storm in our house. I am no easy-going companion, at least for a woman, and you will very soon find that will of yours again, the loss of which you are now lamenting. Be at rest, darling, you shall be as headstrong as of yore; you need not distress yourself on that account; so you may prepare for a few storms, but for hearty love and merry life as well." Would your latter-day lover sign such articles of agreement on his marriage-day?

Of course he would not. The shirts and the account-keeping are what he marries for, and it would be a manifest absurdity to annul the conclusion of the whole matter. It is not a question what women *like* to do; they must bake and brew and make and mend, whether they like it or not. Men do not marry for the purpose of making women happy, but to make themselves happy. A girl looks forward in her marriage to what she will do for her husband's happiness. A man, to what he will enjoy through his wife's ministrations. "He needs a wife," say the good women who were born and bred in these opinions and do not suspect their grossness.

"It is a grand good match; I don't know anybody that needs a wife more than he," said one of these at a little gathering, speaking of a recent marriage.

"Why?" innocently questioned another woman, who was supposed to have somewhat peculiar views concerning these things.

"O, you never want anybody to marry!" burst out a chorus of voices,—which was surely a very broad inference from one narrow monosyllable.

"But why does he need a wife?" persisted the questioner.

"For sympathy and companionship," triumphantly replied the first woman, knowing that to such motives her interlocutor could take no exception. But a third woman, not knowing that anything lay behind these questions and answers, and feeling that the original position was but feebly maintained by such unsubstantial things as sympathy and companionship, being also a near neighbor of the person in question, and acquainted with the facts, proceeded to strengthen the case by adding, "Well, he was all alone, and he wa'n't very well, and he was taken sick one night and couldn't get anybody to take care of him."

"But why not hire a nurse?"

"Well he did, and she was very good; but she wouldn't do his washing."

Only wait long enough, and you are tolerably sure to get the truth at last. It was not sympathy and companionship, after all, that the man wanted: it was his washing!

You see a most unconscious, but irrefragable

testimony concerning the relations which are deemed proper between a man and his wife in the very common use of the phrase, "kind husband." It is often employed in praise of the living and in eulogy of the dead. Compared with a cruel husband, I suppose a kind husband is the more tolerable; but compared with a true husband, there is no such thing as a kind husband. You are kind to animals, to beggars, to the beetle that you step out of your path to avoid treading on. One may be kind to people who have no claims upon him, but he is not kind to his wife. He does not stand towards her in any relation that makes kindness possible. He can no more be kind to his wife than he can be to himself. His wife is not his inferior, to be condescended to, but his treasure to be cherished, his friend to be loved, his adviser to be deferred to. It is an insult to a woman for her husband to assume, or for his biographer to assume for him, that he *could* be kind to her. Did you ever hear a woman praised for being kind to her husband? Did you ever hear an obituary declare a woman to be a dutiful daughter, a kind wife, a faithful mother? You may be sure the phrase is never used by any one who has a just idea of what marriage ought to be.

If love cannot outlast a few years of life, it is idle to lament that it is so surely quenched by death. Absence cannot be blamed for dissipating a love that has been already conquered by presence. Nevertheless, in the alacrity with which one is off with the old love and on with the new may be read the shallowness, the flimsiness, the earthliness, of that which passes for the deepest, the most lasting, and the most divine. Weary feet, aching brow, and disappointed heart are at rest; or a vigorous young life is smitten before its heyday was clouded; or the ripened sheaf is garnered at the harvest-time; but no proprieties, no shock of premature loss, nor the "late remorse of love," avails to make the impression indelible. The dead past may bury its dead out of sight; the resurrection may adjust its own perplexities; but in this world there must be good cheer. The funeral baked meats shall coldly furnish forth the marriage-table. *La Reine est morte: Vive la Reine!* And when the loving wife is gone away from the heart that entertained its angel unawares, people will tell you with a sober face how "beautifully he bears it!" "perfectly resigned!" "Christian calmness!" "kiss the rod!" It were to be wished he did not bear it quite so beautifully. When a wife is prematurely torn from her home, the only proper attitude for her husband is to sit in sackcloth and ashes. It is fit that he should be stricken to the dust. It is not becoming for him to indulge in pious reflections. Ill-timed resignation is a breach of morals. He is not to be supposed capable of a lasting fidelity, but he may be expected to be temporarily stunned by the blow. It would be more decorous for him to follow the example of the powerful and wealthy king in the fairy-tale, who, having lost his wife, was so inconsolable that he shut himself up for eight entire days in a little room, where he spent his time chiefly in knocking his head against the wall!

It is pitiful to see a strong man tottering into a wrong path from sheer lack of strength to walk in the right one, which yet he does not lack clear vision to see. But the spectacle may be profitable for doctrine, for reproof, for correction, for instruction in righteousness. Perhaps no more faithful and graphic presentation of the diplomacy that is employed in compassing a second marriage can be given than is found in the proceedings of Perthes. When, after twenty-four years of married life, his wife, the mother of his ten children, left him, he repaired to Gotha and lived three years in the family of a married daughter. In an early stage of his bereavement he writes of his loneliness, and mentions, but almost with repugnance, certainly with no apparent intention of entering it, or any intimation of a possibility of receiving joy from it, "a new wedlock." Nevertheless, the thought is there. His daughter's sister-in-law, a widow of thirty years, and mother of four children, lives next door. Presently comes down his mother-in-law to pay a visit. "She was much concerned about Perthes's situation, and one day, while they were walking in the orangery, expressed herself openly to him. She told him that he was no more a master of his own house, that soon his younger children would be leaving him, and that his strong health gave promise of a long life yet to come; that for him solitude was not good, that he could not bear it, and consequently that he ought not to put off choosing a companion for the remainder of his life." All of which of course came to him with the freshness of entire novelty. But immediately we find that at these words "the thought of Charlotte shot like lightning through his soul." So it seems that he had already outstripped his mother-in-law. She dealt, only in generals, but he had advanced to particulars. However, "he made no reply, but he had a hard battle to fight with himself from that time forth. In September he communicated to his mother-in-law the *pros* and *cons* which agitated him so much, but without giving her to understand that it was no longer the subject of marriage in general, but of one marriage in particular, which now disquieted him. After stating the outward and inward circumstances, which made a second marriage advisable in his case, he goes on to say: 'I am quite certain that Caroline foresaw, from her knowledge of my character and temperament, a second marriage for me, and I am equally certain that no new union could ever disturb my spirit's abiding union with her. [It is to be hoped that Charlotte was duly made acquainted with this fact.] My inner life is filled with her memory, and will be so till my latest day; but I must own that this is possible only while I incorporate in thought her happy soul, and think of her as a human being, still sharing my earthly existence, still taking interest in all I do; and I cannot disguise from myself, while viewing her under this aspect, that my dear Caroline would prefer my living on alone, satisfied with her memory. Again, there can be no doubt that Holy Scripture, although permitting a second marriage, does so on account of the hardness of our hearts. The civil law contains no prohibition either, and yet there has always existed a social prejudice against such a marriage, and youth, whose ideal is always fresh and fair, and women who are always young in soul, look with secret disgust upon it. I know, too, that my remaining alone would be, not only with reference to others, but in itself, the worthier course; but, on the other hand, I know it would be so in reality only if this worthiness were not assumed for the purpose of appearing in a false light to myself, to other men, and perhaps even before God, or for the purpose of cloaking selfishness under the guise of fidelity to the departed.' It was not, however, by answering this question, nor by reflecting upon the lawfulness of second marriages in general, that Perthes's irresolution was subdued, but by an increasing attachment to the lady whose character had attracted him."

Very honorable appears Perthes here, in that he

argues the case against himself with fulness and frankness, revealing to himself without disguise the weakness under which he finally falls, and conscious all the while that it is a weakness. He does not attempt to hide the fact that Caroline would have preferred to live alone in his memory, and he falls back on his only defensible ground,—the hardness of his heart. Confession is forgiveness. Let him pass on to the new bride, and the second family of eleven children that will spring up around them.

But there are men, and women too,—there are always women enough to echo men's opinions,— who assume that the spirit of the departed will be delighted in her heavenly abode to know that the husband decides not to spend his life in solitude. Some women indeed show the last infirmity of noble minds by *recommending* their husbands to take a second wife, although it seems a pity to waste one's last breath in bestowing advice which is so entirely superfluous. If a man will marry, let him marry, but let no patient Griselda "gin the hous to dight" for the "newe lady." If a man will marry, let him marry, but let him not offer the world an apology for the act. The apology is itself an accusation; a dishonor to both wives instead of one. He knows his own motives and emotions. If they are upright and sufficient, it is no matter what people say about him; he and the other person immediately concerned should be so self-satisfied as to be indifferent to outside comment. If they are not upright and sufficient, attempting to make them appear so is an additional offence.

I have said on this subject more than I intended. I meant only to state a fact clearly enough to use it. The rest "whistled itself." Practically, I do not know that I have any quarrel with any marriage that is real, whether it come after the first or fiftieth attempt. Judging from general observation, I should suppose that most people might marry half a dozen times, and not be completely married then.

If, as Perthes seems to have thought, all this is the natural course of events, why do you make all womanly honor and happiness converge in the one focus of marriage, unless like a Mussulman you believe that on such condition alone can women aspire to immortality? But even then it would be a hard bargain. Immortality is dearly bought at the price of immorality. When all other arguments fail, and you would mount to your sublimest heights of moral elevation, you assure a woman that, no matter how lofty her life may be, nor how deep her satisfaction may seem, if she fails of marriage she fails of the highest development, the deepest experience, the greatest benefit. You tell her that she misses somewhat which Heaven itself cannot supply. But, on the other hand, you have previously shown that marriage is but a temporary arrangement, an entirely mundane affair. Love belongs as completely to this world as houses and barns,—is in fact rather supplementary to them,—especially to the house. It is of the body, and not of the spirit; for the spirit lives forever, but when the body dies, love dies also. There are no claims beyond the grave. Nay, it does not reach to the grave. The delight, the spontaneity, the satisfaction, the keenness, all die out before the person dies. The pulp shrivels, and only a wrinkled skin of habit remains. But a woman is immortal. Can a mortal love satisfy an immortal heart? Is it possible that an undying soul must find its strongest development in a dying love? Does a creature of the skies incur an irreparable loss, miss an irreclaimable jewel, suffer an incurable wound, when it loses, or misses, or suffers *anything* which is but of the earth earthy? Can anything finite be indispensable to an infinite life?

Again, if this accession of toil, and this diminution and decay of perceptible love, and this falling back on inward love, is the natural course of events, why not say so in the beginning? If inward love be satisfactory at one time, why not at another, as well before marriage as after? Why, when a man has once made and received affidavit of love, should he not be content, and neither proffer nor demand manifestations? Let men be satisfied with inward love during courtship, and the honeymoon, if inward love is so all-sufficient. Not in the least. Men are not one tenth part so capable of inward love as women, —I mean of an inward love without outward expression. Their inward love becomes outward love almost as soon as it becomes love at all. They are ten times more tumultuous, more demonstrative, more *phenomenal*, than women. They are as impatient as children, and more unreasonable. They cannot, or they will not, brook delay, suspense, refusal. Women accept all these drawbacks as a part of the programme, and with "the endurance that outwearies wrong," while men fiercely, if vainly, kick against the pricks and talk about *inward love*!

And if the true object of marriage be to help accumulate or frugally to manage a fortune, to cook dinners, and act as a sewing-machine, "warranted not to ravel," say that frankly also in the beginning. Tell women plainly what you want of them. Do not lure them into your service under false pretences. Do not wait till they are irrevocably fastened to you, and then lay on them the burdens of labor and take away the supports of love, and lecture them into acquiescence through the newspapers. While there is yet left to them a freedom of choice, make them fully acquainted with the circumstances of the case, that they may be able to choose intelligently. When one does not expect much, one is not disappointed at receiving little. One is not chilled at heart by snow in winter. It is walking over sunny Southern lands, and finding frosts when you looked for flowers, that freezes the fountains of life. If you do not overwhelm a woman with your protestations, if you do not lure her to your heart by presenting yourself to her and praying her to be to you friend, comrade, and lover, when what you really want is cook, laundress, and housekeeper, she will at least know what is before her. But do not swear to her eternal fidelity, knowing that, as soon as you thoroughly understand each other, there will be an end of all little tendernesses of expression. Do not span her with a rainbow, and spread diamond-dust beneath her feet, knowing all the while that a very little time will bring for the one but a cold, penetrating rain, and will change the other into coarse, sharp pebbles that shall bruise her tender feet. Change the formula of your marriage vows, and instead of promising to love, honor, and cherish till death you do part, promise to do it only till you understand her thoroughly, and then to make the best of the bargain!

If we were forced to believe that these right-hand fallings-off and left-hand defections were indeed the legitimate workings of the human heart, the natural history of mankind, then should we be forced to believe that this world is a stupendous failure, and the sooner it is burned up the better. We should be forced to believe in the thorough degradation and destructibility of both mind and matter. For the essence of value is durability. A soap-bubble is as beautiful as a pearl and as brilliant as a diamond; for what is called practical service, for warmth, or shelter, or sustenance, one is quite as good as another. What makes their different worth is, that the soap-bubble yields up its lovely life to the first molecule that sails through the air to solicit it, while the gems outlast a thousand years. But if life is a soap-bubble, and not a pearl, shall a woman sell all that she has and buy it? What advantageth the possession of a happiness which melts in the grasp, —which is satisfactory only for the short time that it is novel? Who would care to enter a path of roses, knowing that a few steps will take him into a vast and barren desert, whence escape is impossible? If this is real life, let us rather pitch our tents in fairy-land; for then, when the Prince is at last restored to his true manly form and his rightful throne, and united to the beautiful, constant Princess, we invariably find, not only that their happiness was quite inexpressible, but it lasted to the end of their lives.

If we are to believe such propositions, we might as well call ourselves infidels, and have done with it. To deny the existence of love takes away no more hope from humanity than to deny the immortality of love. It is no worse to take away life from the soul than to give it a life which is but a protracted death. To make a distinction between earthly and heavenly love hardly affects the case. The direction of love is not love. All love is heavenly,—"bright effluence of bright essence increate." If a man gives himself to the pursuit of unworthy objects, or to the indulgence of unhallowed pleasures, a pure name need not be dragged down into the mire that his error may have a seemly christening. If that is love which fades out long before its object; if, when its object disappears behind the veil love rightly returns to earth, then are we of all creatures most miserable; for we abnegate a future. We thought it had been he which should have redeemed Israel; but thou shalt return unto the ground, for out of it wast thou taken. Dust art thou, O love, and unto dust shalt thou return.

Nay, let us have falsehood rather than truth, if this be truth. But this cannot be truth. Love sets up his ladder on the earth, but the top of it reaches unto heaven, and if the eye be clear and the heart pure, the angels of God shall be seen ascending and descending on it. The fashion of this world passeth away,

"But love strikes one hour,—LOVE."

Hear a woman's voice mingling now with angels' voices,—the voice of a woman whose pathway to the skies was a line of light shining still more and more unto the perfect day.

"I classed, appraising once,

Earth's lamentable sounds: the welladay,

The jarring yea and nay,

The fall of kisses on unanswering clay,

The sobbed farewell, the welcome mournfuller

But all did leaven the air

With a less bitter leaven of sure despair

Than these words,—'I loved ONCE.'

"And who saith, 'I loved ONCE'?

Not angels, whose clear eyes love, love foresee,

Love through eternity,

Who by To Love do apprehend To Be.

Not God, called LOVE, his noble crown-name, casting

    A light too broad for blasting!

The great God, changing not from everlasting,

    Saith never, 'I loved ONCE.'

    "Nor ever the 'Loved ONCE'

Dost THOU say, Victim-Christ, misprisèd friend!

    The cross and curse may rend;

But, having loved, Thou lovest to the end!

It is man's saying,—man's. Too weak to move

    One spherèd star above,

Man desecrates the eternal God-word Love

    With his No More and Once.

    .   .   .   .   .

    "Say never, ye loved ONCE!

God is too near above, the grave below,

    And all our moments go

Too quickly past our souls, for saying so.

The mysteries of life and death avenge

    Affections light of range:

There comes no change to justify that change,

    Whatever comes,—loved ONCE!"

XII.

EN, by reason of their hardness of heart, gravitate towards the material theory, and women, by reason of their softness of heart, lower to the same level. Men defy heaven and earth to compass self-indulgence, and women defy the divine law written in their hearts rather than thwart men. Instead of setting their faces like a flint against this tendency, they accept it, excuse it, try to think it inevitable, a matter of organization, and make the best of it. They will counsel young girls not to reckon upon receiving as much love as they give! Fatal advice! Disastrous generalization! Yet neither unnatural nor unkind, for it is the fruit of a sad and wide experience. They would gladly spare fresh souls the apples of Sodom, whose fair seeming bewrayed themselves; but they should teach them to avoid disappointment, not by counting upon bitterness, but by rejecting apples of Sodom altogether, and receiving only such fruit as cheers the heart of God as well as man. Why shall not women receive as much love as they give? Is man less capable of loving than woman? Where in nature or in revelation is the warrant for such an hypothesis? When He commands, "Thou shalt love the Lord thy God with all thy heart, and with all thy soul, and with all thy mind, and with all thy strength," is he not speaking to men as well as women? and are a man's heart, soul, mind, and strength less than a woman's? Are not husbands commanded to love their wives even as Christ loved the Church? and did he love the Church less than the Church loved him? Is not every man commanded in particular to love his wife even as himself,—to love his wife as his own body? and is a man's love to himself, his love to his own body, a feeble and untrustworthy sentiment? You find in the Bible no letting a man off from his duties of love; no letting him down. Old-fashioned as it is, written for a state of society far different from ours, often brought forward to prop up old wrongs and bluff off newly-found rights, the Bible is still the very storehouse of reforms. It contains the germs not only of spiritual life, but of spiritual living. Glows on its pages the morning-red which has scarcely yet gilded the world.

Women must not expect to receive as much love as they give! It is inviting men to esteem lightly what should be a priceless possession. It is not waiting for them to drag down the banner to the dust; it is making haste to trail it for them with malice aforethought. Men now are not too constant, too devoted to the higher aims of life; but let constancy and devotion not be expected of them, and in what seven-league boots will they stride down the broad road! It is doing them but left-handed service thus to throw the door open to weakness and wavering concerning higher interests, and a blind devotion to the god of this world. To assume that their tone may be low, is to lower their tone. Men are less good than they would be if goodness were demanded of them. The current is turbid and unwholesome, because it is not strictly required to be pure and clear. The way for women to be truly serviceable to men, is to be themselves exacting.

"Exacting"? What word is that? An exacting woman? An exacting wife? "Hail! Horrors, hail!"

The unlovely being has existed, and within the memory of men still living, but it has always been looked upon as a monster,

"Whom none could love, whom none
could thank,

Creation's blot, creation's blank!"

We have fallen on evil times indeed if such a being is to be held up for approval and imitation.

But the character of exaction depends somewhat on the nature of the thing exacted. To exact from a man that to which you have a right, and which it is his own truest interest to bestow, is neither unchristian nor unamiable. One may and should grant large room for the play of tastes; for differences of organization, opinion, habit, education; but a catholicity which admits to its presence anything that defileth is no fruit of that tree whose leaves are for the healing of the nations. The gardener who is tolerant of weeds and not untender towards misshapen, or dwarfed, or otherwise imperfect flowers will have but a sorry show for the eyes of the master. Such latitude is a source of deterioration. It is the kindness which kills. Each sex should be to the other an incitement to lofty aims. Each should stand on its own mountain-height and call to the other through clear, bright air; but such sufferance only draws both down into the damp, unwholesome valley-lands where lurk fever and pestilence. A woman cannot with impunity open her doors to unworthy guests. There may be bowing and smiling, and never-ending smooth speech, but in the end, and long before the end, they shall draw their swords against the beauty of her wisdom and shall defile her brightness. A man may go all lengths in pursuit of his own selfish comfort, but he does not the less respect those who hold themselves above it, and if women, who should be pure and purifying, mar the spotlessness of a divine sanctity and lessen the claims of an imperial dignity, thinking thereby to be meeter for profane approach, they work a work whose evil strikes its roots into the inmost life of society. From mistaken kindness woman may weave a narrow garland, but there is lost a glory from the hand that bears and the brow that wears it. If the queen is content to spend her life in the kitchen over bread and honey, and if she is satisfied that the king spend his in the parlor counting out his money, neither king nor queen will receive that homage or command that allegiance which is the rightful royal prerogative.

There is a foolish subservience, an ostentatious and superficial chivalry, an undignified and slavish deference to whims which silly women demand and sillier men grant. Yet even this is not so much the fault of the weak women as of the strong men, who surround women with the atmosphere which naturally creates such weakness. But women have a right, and it is their duty to expect, to claim, to exact if you please, a constancy, spirituality, devotion, as great as their own. Where God makes no distinction of sex in his demands upon mankind, His creatures should not make distinctions. "Men are different from women," is the conclusion of the whole matter at female debating-societies, and the all-sufficient excuse for every short-coming or over-coming; but the Apostles and Prophets find therein no warrant for a violation of moral law, no guaranty for immunity from punishment, no escape from the obligations to unselfish and righteous living. Nowhere does the Saviour of the world proclaim to men a liberty in selfishness or sin. His kingdom will never come, nor his will be done on earth as it is done in heaven, so long as men are permitted to take out indulgences. If they do it ignorantly, not knowing the true character and claims of womanhood, nor consequently of manhood, they should be taught. If they think a wife's chief duty is to economize her husband's fortunes, or to minister to his physical comforts, they should be speedily freed from the illusion. If they suppose knowledge to be ill-adapted to the female constitution, and harmless only when administered homoeopathically, they should be quietly undeceived. If they have been so trained that marriage is to them but unholy ground whereon is found no place for modesty, chastity, delicacy, reverence, how shall they ever unlearn the bad lesson but through pure womanly teaching?

But women fear to take this attitude. There are many indeed who have become so demoralized that they do not know there is any such attitude to take; but there are others who do see it, and shrink from assuming it. Women whose courage and fortitude are indescribable, who will brave pain and fatigue and all definite physical obstacles in their path, will bow down their heads like a bulrush with fear of that indefinable thing which may be called social disapprobation. Through cowardice, they are traitors to their own sex, and impediments to the other. One cannot find it in his heart to blame them harshly. The weakness has so many palliations, it is so natural a growth of their wickedly arranged circumstances, as to disarm rebuke and move scarcely more than pity; but it is none the less a fact, lamentable and disastrous. Women who know and lament the erroneous notions and the guilty actions of men concerning woman, and the culpable relations of men to women, will endeavor to hold back the opinions of a woman when they go against the current. They will admit the force of all her objections, the justice of every remonstrance, but will assure her that opposition will be of no avail. She will accomplish nothing, but—and here lies the real bugbear—but she will make men almost afraid of her!

I would that men were not only almost, but altogether afraid of every woman! I would that men should hold woman in such knightly fear that they should never dare to approach her, matron or maid, save with clean hands and a pure heart; never dare to lift up their souls to vanity nor swear deceitfully; never dare to insult her presence with words of flattery, insincerity, coarseness, sensuality, mercenary self-seeking, or any other form of dishonor. I would that woman were herself so noble and wise, her approbation so unquestionably the reward of merit, that a man should not dare to think ignobly lest his ignoble thought flower into word or act before her eyes; should not wish to think ignobly, since it removed him to such a distance from her, and wrought in him so sad an unlikeness to her; should not be able to think ignobly, being interpenetrated with the celestial fragrance which is her native air. I would have the heathen cloud-divinity which inwraps her with a factitious light, only to hide her real features from mortal gaze, torn utterly away, that men may see in her the fullest presentation possible to earth of the god-like in humanity. So powerfully does the Most High stand ready to work in her to will and to do of his good pleasure, that she may be to man a living revelation, Emanuel, God with us.

We ought to stand in awe of one another. We do not sufficiently respect personality. Every soul comes fresh from the creative hand and bears its own divine stamp. We should not go thoughtlessly into its presence. We should not wantonly violate its holiness. Even the body is fearfully and wonderfully made, and well may be, for it is the temple of the Holy Ghost; but if the temple is sacred, how much more that holy thing which the temple enshrines,— the unseen, incomprehensible, infinite soul, the essential spirit, the holy ghost. Who that cherishes the divine visitant in his own heart but must be amazed at the reckless irreverence with which we assail each other. It is not the smile, the chance word, the pleasant or even the hostile rencounter in the outer courts; it is that we do not respect each other's silences. We do not scruple to pry into the arcana. The hermit's sanctuary may lie in the huntsman's track, but he will have his pleasure though hermit and sanctuary were in the third heaven. We do not accept what is given with gladness and singleness of heart; we stretch out wanton hands to pull aside the curtain and reveal to the garish day what should be suffered to repose in the twilight of inner chambers.

When the prudent adviser, the practical man or woman, counsels, "Do not demand so much from your friends,—they won't stand it,"—am I to infer that friendship is a mercenary matter, a thing of compromise and barter? Shall I fence in my acts, words, thoughts, that I may secure something whose sole value, whose sole existence, indeed, lies in its spontaneity? Shall I haggle for incense? Am I loved for what I do, what I say, what I think, and not for what I am? Why, this is not love. I am myself, first of all, not Launcelot nor another. He who loves me can but wish me to be this in fullest measure. I will live my life. I will go whithersoever the spirit leads. He who loves me will rejoice in this and give me all furtherance. I demand all things—in you. I demand nothing—from you. "Will not stand it"? If you can hate me, hate me. If you can refrain from loving, love not. I can dispense with your regard, but there is something indispensable. You shall love me because you cannot help it, or you shall love me not at all. If I cannot compel affection in the teeth of all conflicting opinion, I renounce it altogether. If the aroma of character is not strong enough to overpower with its sweetness all unfragrant exhalations of opinion, it is a matter of but small account.

If two people should design simply to club together, to take their meals at the same table and dwell under the same roof, it would be a thing to be carefully considered; but when the question is, not of association alone, but of absolute oneness, not of similarity of tastes or habits, but of an inmost and all-prevailing sympathy, it becomes us to be wary. Mere mechanical junction is easy of accomplishment, but a chemical combination demands fine analysis and the most careful adjustment. It needs not that a globe of fire should come raging through the skies to set our world ablaze; a very slight change in the atmosphere which embraces it, a little less of one ingredient, a little more of another, and the earth and the works that are therein shall be burned up. Yet the delicacy of matter is but a faint type of the delicacy of mind. He who would pass within the veil to commune with the soul between the cherubim must assume holy garments. If the trouble seem to him too great, let him be content to tarry without. Uzzah put forth an incautious hand and touched the ark of God unbidden, and the anger of the Lord was kindled against him, and there he died by the ark of God. Now, as then, if any man defile the temple of God, him shall God destroy; for the temple of God is holy, which temple ye are.

Yet the general opinion seems to be that human beings are made by machinery like Waltham watches, and will fit perfectly when brought together at random, as the different parts taken indiscriminately from a heap of similar parts will fit and form a watch. Juxtaposition is the only necessary preliminary to harmony. On the contrary, it is true not only of prodigies, but of every member of the race that nature made him and then broke the mould. Every person is a prodigy. So great, so radical, so out-spreading, are the differences between individuals, that the wonder is, not that they quarrel so much, but that they are ever peaceful when brought together. The wonder is that so many fierce antagonisms can be soothed even into an outward quiet. Looking at it as mechanism, seeing how diverse, aggressive, and impatient are the qualities of man, and how peculiarly are his circumstances adapted to foster his peculiarities, one would say that the only security was in solitude. Indeed, young people are very apt to think so. They combine in an ideal all the charms which attract, and exclude from it all the disagreeable traits which repel them, and see reality fall so far short of their imaginary standard that they fully believe they shall never find the true Prince. And they never would, but for an inward, inexplicable suffusion of the Divine essence, whose source and action lie beyond knowledge or control, which works without instigation, but is all-powerful to create or annihilate. This, however, which is the sole explanation of the phenomenon, which is the sole conciliator between opposing forces, is generally left out of view. People scarcely seem to be conscious that there is any phenomenon. They philosophize sagaciously upon the singular skill which swings unnumbered worlds in space, and spins them on in never-ending cycle, yet marks out their paths so wisely that world sweeps clear of world and never a collision crushes one to ruin. But full as the universe is of stars, the nearest are hundreds of thousands of miles apart; while the intellectual, nervous worlds that are set going on the surface of our earth are close together. Half a dozen of them are placed as it were shoulder to shoulder. Their zigzag orbits intersect each other a hundred times a day. Is it any wonder that there is hard abrasion, that surfaces are seamed and furrowed, and that sometimes a crash startles us? Is not the wonder rather that crashes are not the order of the day, that the seams are seams and not cracks through the whole crust, and that the largest result of abrasion is smoothness and evenness and polish?

Yet, utterly unmindful of the fitness of things, people will wonder why a man and a woman who are thrown occasionally together do not—what? Attack each other in an outburst of impatience at stupidity and cross-purposes? Not at all, but "strike up a match." That is, put themselves into relations which shall turn an association whose redeeming feature is that it is casual and under control into an association that is constant and irrevocable! Masculine backwardness is not perhaps considered remarkable, as indeed there is very little of it to be remarked, but the utmost surprise is expressed on those rare occasions in which women are supposed to have declined a "desirable offer." That a woman should not avail herself of an opportunity to become the wife of a man who is well-educated, well-mannered, "well-off," seems to be an inexplicable fact. He is her equal in fortune, position, character. Commentators "cannot see any reason why she should not marry him." But is there any reason why she should marry him? The burden of proof lies upon motion, not rest; upon him who changes, not upon him who retains a position. All these things which are called inducements are no more than so many sticks and stones; you might just as well repeat the a b c, and call that inducement. The matters which bear on such conclusions are of an entirely different nature. Your "inducements" may come in by and by, when the main point is settled, to modify outward acts, but till the Divine Spirit moves, they are without form and void.

Nor are well-wishers always so careful as to take the man himself into the account. If surroundings are favorable, if to a by-stander there seems to be a sort of house-and-barn adaptation, it is enough. House and barn should at once join roof and become one edifice. It is of no importance that this holds stalls for horned oxen, and that entertainment for angels; that the one is informed with spiritual life and the other filled with hay: hay and heaven are all one to many eyes. "Why does she not marry him?" Why? Simply because there is not enough of him, or what there is is not of the right stuff. If he were twenty instead of one, she might dare promise to honor him, might dare hope to respect him. If he had just twenty times as much of *being*, or if his amplitude could be converted into fineness, he might meet her on equal ground; but being only one and such a one, she is in an overwhelming majority, and it is not republican that majorities should yield to minorities. He may be, as you say, "just as good as she," but not good for her.

These views appear in the (perhaps apocryphal) stories occasionally told of renowned personages. A poor man or an obscure man proposes to a young woman whose father is rich, and he is refused. The poor and obscure man becomes presently a great banker, a governor, president of a college, or recovers lost counties, or dukedoms in Europe. I have even heard the story repeated of the Emperor of the French and a New York young woman. Moral: Is not the woman sorry now that she did not marry the poor man? Probably not. Certainly not if she belongs to the true type. What have all these changes to do with the matter? Is he any more comfortable to live with because he is a governor? Is he any more adapted to her because he is a duke? It is barely possible that she was mistaken; but if she were, she is probably ignorant of it herself. His present state does not indicate a mistake. Only a close companionship would be likely to discover it. The qualities which make domestic content are not usually revealed by ever so brilliant public success. If they originally existed, they are little likely to have been developed. As business affairs are usually conducted, they are more likely to drown out home happiness than to create it. But all this is irrelevant. Nothing is really meant to which this is an answer. It is only the manifestation of a blindness to what constitutes attraction. The man has discovered outside advantages, and it is assumed that that is enough. She of course refused him because she had not sagacity enough to discern the shadow of his coming greatness. It does not seem to be suspected that she could have refused him because he did not suit her! What difference does it make whether a man is a clown or a king, if you do not like him? Is a great judge necessarily an agreeable person to think of? Is a world-renowned financier necessarily the person who will have most power to draw out what is good and gracious in a woman? Girls naturally give their loyalty to men, not to crowns, or ermine.

The lovely Florina was as fond of King Charming, when he came to her in the shape of a Bluebird, as when he appeared at court in royal majesty. Wicked outside opinion, it is true, warps their judgment in a very great degree, and destroys their freedom; but of their own nature, in their inmost hearts, they are true; and when they have independence enough to manifest their truth in these palpable acts, they may be safely set down as true. They acted from sincerity and dignity, not from mercenary short-sightedness. They acted from the most simple and natural causes, and what have they to regret? It is much better to be the wife of an honest and respectable American citizen than to be Empress of the French,—even looking at it in a solely worldly point of view. When we add to this that one loves the American citizen, and does not love the French Emperor, the case may as well be ruled out of court at once. There is no ground for any further proceedings.

Men and women act upon these views too much, as well in regulating as in establishing a home. They recognize and make liberal allowance for palpable, outspoken wants, yet are unmindful or contemptuous of others equally important, but less on the surface, and less sharply defined. A man who would incur self-reproach and the contempt of his neighbors by allowing his wife to suffer from lack of bread in his house, will not suspect so much as a slight dereliction of duty in allowing her to suffer from lack of beauty there. A woman who is never weary of meeting the demands upon her husband's palate, who will have the joint cooked exactly to his liking, and the dinner prompt to his convenience, would scout the thought of leaving her morning's occupation to give him her company in a two hours' drive. People will devote their lives uncomplainingly to meeting each other's wants, but will neutralize all their efforts and sacrifice happiness hand over hand by neglecting or disregarding each other's tastes. They will spend all their money in thatching the roof, but will do just nothing at all to keep the fire alive on the hearth. There are very few indeed who are not able to do both. Of course if people lavish their whole strength on gross matters, they have none left for the finer; but it is not often that gross matters *need* the whole strength. A careful observation and just views would be able, as a general thing without detriment, to wrest many an hour from vain, vulgar, useless, or harmful pursuits, to bestow it upon adornments and amenities that do not perish with the using. And if a man or a woman is so deteriorated as to prefer the indulgence of a coarse or frivolous appetite, or the inordinate indulgence of a merely natural appetite, to the gratification and cultivation of refined and elevated tastes,—the more's the pity!

XIII.

MARVEL that men who lay so little stress on the heart, by reason of the great stress they lay upon the intellect, should use their intellects to so little purpose in matters so important, and which come so closely home to their business and bosoms as those we have been discussing. I marvel that, while they see facts so distinctly, they have so little skill to trace out causes. Many instances have been given to show how far more unreasonable, intense, malignant, vulgar, and venomous is the hatred of their country shown and felt by Southern women than that evinced by Southern men. It is very commonly said that they have done more than the men to keep alive the rebellion. The coarseness and impropriety of their behavior have been relatively far greater than that of the men. Has any one ever suggested that the narrowness, the utter insufficiency of their education, the state of almost absolute pupilage bedizened over with a gaudy tinsel of tilt and tournament chivalry in which they have been kept, absolutely incapacitating them for broad views, rational thinking, or even a refined self-possession in emergencies, had anything to do with it? In a newspaper published under the auspices of one of our Sanitary Fairs, a contributor says: "I never saw a nurse from any hospital, but I asked her the question if the ladies there worked without jealousy or unkind feeling toward each other? *and I have not found the*

first one who could answer 'yes' to that question.... I know a gentleman (a noble one, too) who urged his daughter *not* to go to the hospitals, 'because,' said he, 'you will surely get into a muss: it cannot be helped; women cannot be together without it." Is it indeed an arrangement of Divine Providence, that women cannot act together without so much bickering, jealousy, petty domineering, small envies, and venomous quarrels, as to make it undesirable that they should act together at all? Is magnanimity impossible to women? Are they incapable of exercising it towards each other? Or may it not be that their lives have generally so little breadth, they are so universally absorbed in limited interests, their "sphere" has been so rigidly circumscribed to their own families, that when they are set in wider circles, they are like spoiled children? In the troubles that arise in female conventions and combinations, I do not see any inherent deficiency of female organization, but every sign of very serious deficiencies in female education.

Men make merry over the unwillingness of women to acknowledge their increasing years; over the artifices to which they resort for the purpose of hiding the encroachments of time; but the reluctance and the deception are the direct harvest of men's own sowing. It is men, and nobody else, who are chiefly to blame for the weakness and the meanness. They have decreed what shall be coin and what counters, and women do but acknowledge their image and superscription. Exceptions are not innumerous, but I think every one will confess, upon a moment's reflection, that in the general apportionment the heroines of literature are the lovely and delightful young women, and the hatred, envy, malice, and all uncharitableness are allotted to the old. Hetty Sorrels are not very common, nor Mrs. Bennetts very uncommon. Why should not women dread to be thought old, when age is tainted and taunted? Why should they not fight off its approaches, when it is indissolubly connected with repulsive traits? Women see themselves prized and petted, not chiefly for those qualities which age improves, but for those which it destroys or impairs. And as women are made by nature to set a high value upon the good opinions of men, and are warped by a vicious education into setting almost the sole value of life upon them, they logically cling with the utmost tenacity to that youth which is their main security for regard. "Youth and beauty" are the twin deities of song and story. "Youth and beauty" are supposed to unlock the doors of fate. It is no matter that in real life fact may not comport with the statements of fiction. No matter that in real life the strongest power carries the day, whether it be youthful or aged, fair or frightful. The events of real life have but small radii, but the ripples of romance circle out over the whole sea of civilization, and wave succeeds wave till the impression becomes wellnigh continuous.

(One can hardly suppress a smile, by the way, at the absurdity which this coupling sometimes presupposes. A man will think to swell your horror of rebel barbarities by asserting that they spared neither youth nor beauty, as if you like to be shot any better because you are old and ugly!)

So with tight-lacing and the new attachment of a *chiropodist* to fashionable families. Most men, it is true, harangue against the former; but if masculine sentiment were really set against tight-lacing and its results, do you think girls would long make their dressing-maids sit up waiting their return from balls, lest an unpractised hand should not unloose the lacings by those short and easy stages which are necessary to prevent the shock of nature's too sudden rebound? Or if you plead "not guilty" to this count, do you believe that girls who have been liberally educated, taught to turn their eyes to large prospects, large duties, and large hopes, could be induced so to put themselves to the torture? Was a right-minded and right-hearted loving and beloved wife, an intelligent and judicious Christian mother, a wise and kindly woman, ever known voluntarily to assume a strait-waistcoat? If girls were trained as every living soul should be trained, would it be necessary to have a "professor" go the rounds of fine houses in the morning to undo the injuries inflicted by tight shoes on the previous evening? If a girl were sagaciously managed, would she not have too much discrimination to suppose that, when a poet sings of

"Her feet beneath her petticoat

Like little mice,"

she is expected to reduce her feet to the dimensions of mice, or that, when he announces

"That which her slender waist confined

Shall now my joyful temples bind,"

she is thinking of a slenderness produced by lashing herself to the bedpost? Be sure a woman will never cramp her body in that way, until society has cramped her soul and mind to still more unnatural distortion. Lay the axe unto the root of the tree, if you wish to accomplish anything; do not merely stand off and throw pebbles at the fruit.

Society is unsparing in its censure of the girl who boasts of her "offers." There are few things which men will not sooner forgive than the revelation of their own rejected proposals. Bayard Taylor makes

Hannah Thurston recoil in disgust at Seth Wattles's hesitating suggestion: "You,—you won't say anything about this?" "What do you take me for?" exclaims immaculate womanhood. Why then is a girl's life made to consist in the abundance of her suitors? It is stamped a shame for a woman not to receive an offer, and then it is stamped a shame for her to take away her reproach by revealing that she has received one. Surely, she is in evil case!

I do not profess any overweening admiration for those qualities of character which induce the exultant publication of such personal items; but I do say that men have no right to complain. The natural results of their own course would not be any more than accomplished, if "offers" were published in the newspapers along with the deaths and marriages.

If you really wish women to be magnanimous, catholic, you must grant to them the conditions of becoming so. Just so long as their souls are cabined, cribbed, and confined, whether in a palace or in a hovel, with only such fresh air as a narrow crevice or casement may afford, they will have but a stunted and unsymmetrical development. You cannot systematically and deliberately dwarf or repress nine faculties, and wickedly stimulate one, and that a subordinate one, and then have as the result a perfect woman. You may force Nature, but she will have her revenges. He that offendeth in one point, is guilty of all. The blow that you aim at the head, not only makes the whole head sick, but the whole heart faint. When you have brought women to the point of writing such babble as,

"We poor women, feeble-natured,

   Large of heart, in wisdom small,

Who the world's incessant battle

Cannot understand at all," &c., &c,
&c.,

do you think you have laid the foundation for solid character? Lay aside your alternate weakness and severity, your silly coddling and your equally silly cautioning, and permit a woman to be a human being. Let the free winds have free access to her, bringing the fragrance of June and the frostiness of December. Fling wide open all the portals, that the sacred soul may go in and out as God decreed. Let every power which God has bestowed have free course to run and be glorified, and you shall truly find before long that the pleasure of the Lord shall prosper in the hands of women.

If the weakness and ignorance and frivolity of which I have spoken be natural, as it is insisted, if the heaven-born instincts of women do, as you in effect asseverate, lead women to devote themselves exclusively to all manner of materialism and pettinesses, and to be content with what sustenance they can find in the crumbs of love that fall from their husbands' tables; if it is unnatural and unwomanly, as you say it is, to have other inclinations and aspirations, and to experience any personal or social discontent,—why do you say so much to urge them to such devotion and content? People are not largely given to doing unnatural things. They do not need incentives, strenuous persuasion, labored and reiterated arguments, to induce them to do what their hearts by creation incline them to do; nor do they need to be held back by main force from that to which they have no natural leaning. Nobody builds a dam to make water run down hill. No tunnelling nor blasting of rocks is necessary to lure rivers to the ocean. No urging and coaxing must be resorted to before the parent-robins build a nest and gather food for their young. But the instincts of women are as strong, the nature of women is as marked, as those of birds, and there is no need of your counselling them to walk in the paths which God has appointed for their feet. No. You do not really believe what you are saying. You feel, if you do not know,—you have a dim, instinctive sense that the life which you appoint to women is not their natural life. It crushes and deforms their nature continually, and continually Nature bursts out in violent resistance, and continually with shriek and din and clamor you strive to frighten her back into her narrow torture-house, with a success all too great.

There seems to lurk in the masculine breast an unmanly fear lest the development of the female mind should be fatal to the superiority of the male mind. But a superiority which must prolong its existence by the enforcement of ignorance is of a very ignoble sort. If, to preserve his relative position, man must, by persuasion or by law, forbid to women opportunities for education and a field for action, together with moral support in obtaining the one and contesting in the other, he pays to the female mind a greater compliment, and heaps upon his own character a greater reproach, than the highest female attainments could do. He shows that he dares not risk a fair trial. If she cannot rival him, the sooner she makes the attempt, and incurs the failure, the sooner will she revert to her old position, and the sooner will peace be restored. The very discouragement by which man surrounds her shows that he does not believe in the original and inherent necessity of her present position. If this counsel be of women merely, it will come to naught of itself. You need not bring up so much rhetoric against it. But if it be of God, ye cannot overthrow it; lest haply ye be found even to fight against God.

There is another fear, equally honest, but more honorable, or rather less dishonorable. There is a belief, apparently, that the womanly character somehow needs the restraints of existing customs. It is feared that a sudden rush of science to the female brain would produce asphyxia in the female heart. It is feared that the study of philosophy, the higher mathematics, and the ancient languages would unsex women,—would destroy the gentleness, the tenderness, the softness, the yieldingness, the sweet and endearing qualities which traditionally belong to them. They would lose all the graces of their sex, and become, say men, as one of us.

From such a fate, good Lord! deliver us. I agree most heartily with men in the opinion, that no calamity could be more fatal to woman than a growing likeness to men; but no cloud so big as the smallest baby's smallest finger-nail portends it. Healthy development never can produce unhealthy results. Nature is never at war with herself. The good and wise and all-powerful Creator never created a faculty to be destroyed, a faculty whose utmost cultivation, if harmonious and not discordant, should be injurious. He made all things beautiful and beneficial in their proper places. It is only arbitrary contraction and expansion that produce mischief. It is the neglect of one thing and the undue prominence given to another that destroys symmetry and causes disaster.

There has been so little experiment made in female education, that we must reason somewhat abstractly; yet we are not left, even in this early stage, without witnesses.

On the 26th of May, 1863, died Mrs. O. W. Hitchcock, wife of one of the Presidents of Amherst College. A writer, who professes to have known her well, gives the following account of her:—

"Born in Amherst, March 8th, 1796, fitted for college and accomplished alike in the fine arts and the exact sciences in an age when the standard of female education was comparatively low, associated with Dr. Hitchcock, then unknown to the public, in the instruction of Deerfield Academy, and there the instrument of her future husband's conversion, *filling* to the full the office of a pastor's wife for five years, in Conway, Massachusetts, and for the rest of her long life sharing all her husband's labors, sorrows, joys, and honors, while at the same time she was the centre of every private, social, charitable, and public movement of which it was suitable for a lady to be the centre, she passed away from us by a death as serenely beautiful as the evening on which she died, May 26, 1863, at the age of sixty-seven, leaving a vacancy not only in the home and the hearts of her bereaved husband and afflicted children, but in the community and the wide circle of her acquaintance, which can be filled by none but Him who comforted the mourning family at Bethany. If strangers would form some idea of what Mrs. Hitchcock was, especially as a *help meet* for her honored husband, and if friends would refresh their memory of a truly 'virtuous woman,' let them read, as it were over her still open grave, the dedication, by Dr. Hitchcock, of his 'Religion and Geology' to his 'beloved wife.' Never did husband pay to wife a higher or *juster* tribute of respect and affection.

"The following is the dedication referred to. It was written in 1851:—

"'*To my beloved Wife.* Both gratitude and affection prompt me to dedicate these Lectures to you. To your kindness and self-denying labors I have been mainly indebted for the ability and leisure to give any successful attention to scientific pursuits. Early should I have sunk under the pressure of feeble health, nervous despondency, poverty, and blighted hopes, had not your sympathies and cheering counsels sustained me. And during the last thirty years of professional labors, how little could I have done in the cause of science, had you not, in a great measure, relieved me of the cares of a numerous family! Furthermore, while I have described scientific facts with the pen only, how much more vividly have they been portrayed by your pencil! And it is peculiarly appropriate that your name should be associated with mine in any literary effort where the theme is geology; since your artistic skill has done more than my voice to render that science attractive to the young men whom I have instructed. I love especially to connect your name with an effort to defend and illustrate that religion which I am sure is dearer to you than everything else. I know that you would forbid this public allusion to your labors and sacrifices, did I not send it forth to the world before it meets your eye. But I am unwilling to lose this opportunity of bearing a testimony which both justice and affection urge me to give. In a world where much is said of female deception and inconstancy, I desire to testify that one man at least has placed implicit confidence in woman, and has not been disappointed. Through many checkered scenes have we passed together, both on the land and the sea, at home and in foreign countries; and now the voyage of life is almost ended. The ties of earthly affection, which have so long united us in uninterrupted harmony and happiness, will soon be sundered. But there are ties which death cannot break; and we indulge the hope that by them we shall be linked together and to the throne of God through eternal ages. In life and in death I abide

"'Your affectionate husband,

"'Edward Hitchcock.'"

Note here everything, but specially two things

1. Mrs. Hitchcock was fitted for college, accomplished in the fine arts and the exact sciences, sympathized in her husband's tastes and understood his pursuits so thoroughly as to be able to render him essential assistance in his professional duties.

2. Note the use and connections of the word *kindness*. She relieved him of the cares of a numerous family, and so gave him leisure for his scientific researches. Does that invalidate what I have before said regarding paternal duties? On the contrary, it strengthens my words. Dr. Hitchcock, in the fulness of his beautiful fame, in the ripeness of his years, confirms the truth of my principles. He knew—the great-hearted gentleman, the beloved disciple—that these cares belonged to him by right, and that it was of grace and not of law that his wife assumed them. So impressed is he with her kindness, so filled with gratitude is his magnanimous heart,

that he even ventures to run the risk of wounding her delicacy by offering thanks in this public manner; shielding her, however, from every breath of offence by skilfully declaring her freedom from all participation in the publicity. *He* uses the word kindness properly. It was a kindness, indeed, for her to step out of her own sphere and assume the burdens of his; but her husband's love was her impelling motive, and his gratitude her exceeding great reward. Not strictly her duty, it became undoubtedly her delight. For love is lavish. Love counts no sacrifice, knows of none. For a husband who loved and recognized her, a wife would bear Atlas on her shoulders. Only when it is coldly reckoned upon as a right, coldly received as a due, does service become servitude.

Read now the dedication of that royal book "On Liberty," by John Stuart Mill, "one of the most powerful and original thinkers of the nineteenth century," a man of culture so thorough that his has been said to be the most cultivated mind of the age:

—

"To the beloved and deplored memory of her who was the inspirer, and in part the author, of all that is best in my writings,—the friend and wife whose exalted sense of truth and right was my strongest incitement, and whose approbation was my chief reward,—I dedicate this volume. Like all that I have written for many years, it belongs as much to her as to me; but the work as it stands has had, in a very insufficient degree, the inestimable advantage of her revision; some of the most important portions having been reserved for a more careful re-examination, which they are now never destined to receive. Were I but capable of interpreting to the world one half the great thoughts and noble feelings which are buried in her grave, I should be the medium of a greater benefit to it than is ever likely to arise from anything that I can write, unprompted and unassisted by her all but unrivalled wisdom."

Elizabeth Barrett Browning, we are told by encyclopedists, was educated in a masculine range of studies, and with a masculine strictness of intellectual discipline. The poets and philosophers of Greece were the companions of her mind. In imaginative power and originality of intellectual construction she is said to be entitled to the very first place among the later English poets. She had considered carefully, and was capable of treating wisely, the deepest social problems which have engaged the attention of the most sagacious and practical minds. Society in the aggregate, and the self-consciousness of the solitary individual, were held in her grasp with equal ease, and observed with equal accuracy. She had a statesman's comprehension of the social and political problems which perplex the well-wishers of Italy, and discussed them with the spirit of a statesman. This is not my pronunciamento nor my language, but those of Hon. George S. Hillard.

With a word fitly spoken this eminently strong-minded woman drew to her side a poet of poets, and he in turn drew her to his heart.

When ten years of marriage had made him so well acquainted with his wife as to give weight to his testimony, he wrote, at the close of a volume of poems called "Men and Women," "One word more,"—surely the seemliest word that ever poet uttered. He sang of the one sonnet that Rafael wrote, of the one picture that Dante painted,—

"Once, and only once, and for one only,

(Ah, the prize!) to find his love a language

Fit and fair and simple and sufficient,"—

and somewhat sadly adds:—

"I shall never, in the years remaining,

Paint you pictures, no, nor carve you statues,

Make you music that should all-express me;

So it seems: I stand on my attainment.

This of verse alone, one life allows me;

Other heights in other lives, God willing

—

All the gifts from all the heights, your own, Love.

"Yet a semblance of resource avails us—

Shade so finely touched, love's sense must seize it.

Take these lines, look lovingly and nearly,

Lines I write the first time and the last time.

.   .   .   .   .

He who writes may write for once, as I do.

"Love, you saw me gather men and women,

Live or dead or fashioned by my fancy.

.   .   .   .   .

I am mine and yours,—the rest be all men's.

.   .   .   .   .

Let me speak this once in my true person,

. . . . .

Though the fruit of speech be just this
sentence,—

Pray you, look on these my men and
women,

Take and keep my fifty poems finished;

Where my heart lies, let my brain lie also!

Poor the speech; be how I speak, for all
things.

"Not but that you know me! Lo, the
moon's self!

Here in London, yonder late in Florence.

Still we find her face, the thrice-
transfigured.

. . . . .

What, there's nothing in the moon
noteworthy?

Nay—for if that moon could love a
mortal,

Use, to charm him (so to fit a fancy)

All her magic ('t is the old sweet mythos)

She would turn a new side to her mortal,

Side unseen of herdsman, huntsman,
steersman,—

Blank to Zoroaster on his terrace,

Blind to Galileo on his turret,

Dumb to Homer, dumb to Keats—him,
even!

God be thanked, the meanest of his
creatures

Boasts two soul-sides,—one to face the
world with,

One to show a woman when he loves her.

"This I say of me, but think of you, Love!

This to you,—yourself my moon of poets!

Ah, but that's the world's side,—there's
the wonder,—

Thus they see you, praise you, think they
know you.

There, in turn I stand with them and praise
you,

Out of my own self, I dare to phrase it,

But the best is when I glide from out
them,

Cross a step or two of dubious twilight,

Come out on the other side, the novel

Silent silver lights and darks undreamed
of,

When I hush and bless myself with
silence.

"O, their Rafael of the dear Madonnas,

O, their Dante of the dread Inferno,

Wrote one song—and in my brain I sing
it,

Drew one angel—borne, see, on my
bosom!"

Have you read it a hundred times before? Are you

not grateful to me for giving you an excuse to begin on the second hundred?

O women, since the heavens have been opened to reveal these points of light, and you can infer somewhat the radiance which may wrap you about with ineffable glory, will you be satisfied again with the beggarly elements of a sordid world? Seeing on what heights a woman may stand, will you lower to the level graded by generations of silly, selfish, sensual male minds? Is it really worth while? If it is not a good bargain to lose your own soul that you may gain the whole world, what must it be to lose your soul and gain only a few stereotyped phrases? If every other man that ever lived preached a crusade for "stocking-mending, love, and cookery," and only these three whom I have mentioned bore a different banner, would it not still be better to shape your course by theirs? Is it not better to be worthy of the respect and reverence of thinkers, than to receive the serenade of sounding brass? Is it not better to heed the one true voice crying in the wilderness, than to join in the uproar of the idolatrous mob that shouts, "Great is Diana of the Ephesians!" When I lose faith in human destiny, and am almost ready to say, "Who shall show us any good?" I remember these utterances,—so lofty that one may say, not as the fulsome courtiers of old time cried, but reverently and duly, "It is the voice of God, and not of men,"— I recall these utterances, the first so heartsome and overflowing that there is no thought for niceties of phrase, but only one eager desire to pay an undemanded tribute, only a warm, imperative urgency of expression; the second inexpressibly mournful, but with such calm majesty of pain as an ancient sculptor might have wrought into passionless marble, or a Roman Senator folded beneath his mantle;—in the first, a man looking from his happy earthly home, forward and upward to a happier home in heaven; in the second, one gazing hopelessly from his waste places down into darkness and the grave; —the first believing, "Because I live ye shall live also"; the second sadly querying, "Man goeth to the grave, and where is he?"—the first become as a little child through faith; the second only as a pagan sage by reason;—the third heaping up with ever unwearied and ever more delighted hand the brightest gems of learning and fancy to adorn a beloved brow;—all turning at the summit of their renown, at the point of their grandest achievement, to do honor to a woman, the first two vindicating the intellect of wifeliness, the last the wifeliness of intellect; all breathing a magnanimity in whose presence no smallness can be so much as named;— and I say there is more strength and courage to be gained, more hope for the future and more faith in humanity to be gathered, from such a glimpse than from the contemplation of five—what? hundred? thousand? millions?—of ordinary marriages.

But to return to the question at issue,—Are these exceptional cases? It is man's own work if they are. Just as the elevation of one negro from slavery to supremacy, from stupidity to intelligence, is an indisputable proof that the elevation of the whole race is possible, so the case of one such woman as those I have mentioned settles the question for the whole sex. All may not attain the same heights, but this shows that intellectuality is open to them without destroying spirituality. Education, it seems, can do just as much for woman as for men. As careful mental training makes a man large-minded, it makes a woman large-minded. If it does not make a man narrow-souled and shallow-hearted, it will not make a woman so. If it does not unfit a man for manly duties, it will not unfit a woman for womanly duties. If ignorance and petty interests and limited views make a man trivial, obstinate, prejudiced, why is it not the same things which make a woman so? It is not necessary to determine whether there is an essential difference between the masculine and feminine brain or nature. All the difference, both in quantity and quality, which any one demands, may be granted without affecting this question of mental culture. No matter whether it be strong or weak, large or small, educate what mind there is to its highest capacity. If there is no difference, it is so much gained. If there is a difference, each mind will select from the material furnished that which is suitable for its own sustenance. Violet and apple-tree grow side by side. If the soil is poor they are both meagre; if the soil is rich, they both flourish. From the same tract one gathers his golden and mellow fruit, the other her glowing purple richness. You may put a covering over the violet and stunt it into a pale, puny, sickly thing, or you may cultivate it to an imperial beauty. But it will be a violet still. The utmost cultivation will not turn it into an apple-tree. Every plant may have a different taste and a different need from every other plant, but they all want the earth. The tiny draughts of the slender anemone are not to be compared with the rivers of sap that bear to the royal oak its centuries; but oak and anemone each demands all the juice it can quaff, and earth and sea and sky are alike laid under tribute to fill the fairy drinking-cup of the one, as well as the huge wassail-bowl of the other.

So with mind. The philosopher, the poet, the theologian, the chemist, quarry in the same mine, and each brings up thence the treasure that his soul loves. The same cloud sweeps over the farmer to refresh his thirsty lands, over the philosopher to confirm his theories, over the painter to tempt his pencil. The principle of selection that obtains in the lower ranks of Nature will not fail us in her higher walks.

It is because law, logic, science, philosophy, have been so almost exclusively in the hands of men, that they have accomplished such puerile results. With all their beauty and power, they have left our common life so poor, and vapid, and vicious, because only half their lesson has been learned. But they bear a message from the Most High, and when woman shall be permitted to lend her listening ear and bring to the interpretation her finer sense, we shall have good tidings of great joy which shall be to all people.

But what is to become of masculine domination and feminine submission? O faithless and perverse generation! Do you indeed believe that it is "natural" for woman to trust and for man to be trusted,—for man to guide and woman to be guided,—for man to rule and woman to be ruled? In whose hand, then, lies the power to change Nature? Is she so weak that a little more or less of this or that, administered by one of her creatures, can alter all her arrangements? The granite of this round world lies underneath, and the alluvium settles on the surface. Do you suppose that anything and everything you can do in the way of cultivation will have power to upheave the granite from its hidden depths and send down the alluvium to discharge its underground duties? What bands hold in their place the oxygen and nitrogen? Who says to the silex and the phosphorus, "Thus far shalt thou go, and no farther"? And do you think that, if you cannot change the quantities of these simple elements, whose processes are patent to the eye, you can change the qualities of the most complex thing in the whole world, which works behind an impenetrable veil? If you cannot add one cubit to a woman's stature, nor make one hair of her head white or black, do you think you can add or subtract one feature from her mind? Cease with high-sounding praise to extol the womanly nature, while practically you deny that there is any. Bring your deeds up to your words. Believe that God did not give to bird and brake and flower a stability of character which he denied to half the human race. Believe that a woman may be a woman still, though careful culture make the wilderness blossom like the rose,—and not only a woman, but as much more and better a woman as the garden is more and better than the wilderness. The distinctions of sex are innate and eternal. They create their own barriers, which cannot be overleaped.

Do you think that, in the examples which I have given,—and perhaps in others which your own observation may have furnished you,—there was any unusual lack of harmony or adjustment? Do you judge, from the testimony of their husbands, that Mrs. Hitchcock, or Mrs. Mill, or Mrs. Browning were any more overbearing, any more greedy of authority, any more ambitious of outside power, any more unlovely and unattractive, than the silliest Mrs. Maplesap, who never knew any "sterner duty than to give caresses"? He must have used his eyes to little purpose who has failed to see that, in a symmetrical womanhood, every member keeps pace with every other. If one member suffers, all the members suffer. Power is not local, but all-embracing. Weakness does not coexist with strength. A silly, shallow woman cannot love deeply, cannot live commandingly. I believe that a woman of intellectual strength has a corresponding affectional strength. An evil education may have so warped her that she seems to be a power for evil rather than for good; but, all other things being equal, the sounder the judgment the deeper the love. The clear head and the strong heart go together. A woman who can assist her husband in geology, or revise his metaphysics, or criticise his poetry, is much more likely to hold him in wifely love and honor, is much more likely to enliven his joy and medicine his weariness, than she who can only clutch at the hem of his robe. Her love is intelligent, comprehensive, firmly founded, and not to be lightly disturbed. Weakness may possess itself of the outworks, but is easily dislodged. Strength goes within and takes possession.

All the unloveliness and unwisdom which may have characterized the "woman's movement," and of which men seem to stand in perpetual dread, are but the natural consequence of their own misdoing. It was a reaction against their wrong. Did women demand ungracefully? It was because their entreaty had been scorned and their grace slighted. Never,—I would risk my life on the assertion,—never did any number of women leave a home to clamor in public for social rights unless impelled by the sting of social wrongs, either in their own person or in the persons of those dear to them. Every unwomanliness had its rise in a previous unmanliness.

In a vile, nameless book to which I have before referred, I find quoted the story of a rajah who was in the habit of asking, "Who is she?" whenever a calamity was related to him, however severe or however trivial. His attendants reported to him one morning that a laborer had fallen from a ladder when working at his palace, and had broken his neck. "Who is she?" demanded the rajah. "A man, no woman, great prince," was the reply. "Who is she?" repeated the rajah, with increased anger. In vain did the attendants assert the manhood of the laborer. "Bring me instant intelligence what woman caused this accident, or woe upon your heads!" exclaimed the prince. In an hour the active attendants returned, and, prostrating themselves, cried out, "O wise and powerful prince, as the ill-fated laborer was working on the scaffold, he was attracted by the beauty of one of your highness's damsels, and, gazing on her, lost his balance and fell to the ground." "You hear now," said the prince, "no accident can happen without a woman being, *in some way*, an instrument."

One might, perhaps, be pardoned for asking whether entire reliance can be placed on testimony which is dictated beforehand on penalty of losing one's head; but the anecdote indicates about the usual quantity of sense and sagacity which is popularly brought to bear on the "woman question," and we will let it pass. I have quoted the story because, by changing the feminine for the masculine noun and pronoun, it so admirably expresses my own views. As I look around upon the world, and see the sin, the sorrow, the suffering, it seems to me that, so far as it can be traced to human agency, man is at the bottom of every evil under the sun. As the husband is, the wife is. The nursery rhyme gives the whole history of man and woman in a nutshell:—

"Jack and Gill

   Went up the hill

To draw a pail of water;

   Jack fell down

   And broke his crown,

And Gill came tumbling after."

Men have a way of falling back on Eve's transgression, as if that were a sufficient excuse for all short- or wrong-coming. Milton glosses over Adam's part in the transgression, and even gives his sin a rather magnanimous air,—which is very different from that which Adam's character wears in Genesis,—while all the blame is laid on "the woman whom thou gavest to be with me." But before pronouncing judgment, I should like to hear Eve's version of the story. Moses has given his, and Milton his,—the first doubtless conveying as much truth as he was able to be the medium of, the second expressing all the paganism of his sex and his generation, mingled with the gall of his own private bitterness; but we have never a word from Eve. That is, we have man's side represented. But Eve will awake one day, and then, and not till then, we shall know the whole. Meanwhile, it is well for men to go back to the beginning of creation to find woman the guilty party. If they stop anywhere short of it, they will be forced to shift the burden to their own shoulders. A woman may have been originally one step in advance of man in evil-doing, but he very soon caught up with her, and has never since suffered himself to labor under a similar disadvantage. I cannot think of a single folly, weakness, or vice in women which men have not either planted or fostered; and generally they have done both. But they do not see the link between cause and effect, and they fail to direct their denunciation to the proper quarter.

It only needs to trust nature! Learn that women crave to pay homage as strongly as men crave to receive it. The higher women rise the more eagerly will they turn to somewhat higher. It cannot be sweeter for a man to be looked up to than it is for a woman to look up to him. Never can you raise women to such an altitude that they will find their pride and pleasure in looking down. Women want men to be masters quite as much as men themselves wish it; but they want them first to be worthy of it. Women never rebel against the authority of goodness, of superiority, but against the tyranny of obstinacy, ignorance, heartlessness. The supremacy which a husband holds by virtue of his character is a wife's boon and blessing, and she suns herself in it and is filled with an unspeakable content. It is the supremacy of mere position, the supremacy of inferiority, that galls and irritates; that breaks out in conventions and resolutions and remonstrances, in suicide and insanity and crime. "The women now-a-days are playing the devil all round," I heard a man say not long ago, in speaking of a woman hitherto respectable, who had left husband and children and eloped with some unknown adventurer. And I said in my heart, "I am glad of it. Men have been playing the devil single-handed long enough, I am glad women are taking it up. *Similia similibus curantur.*" Things must, to be sure, be in a very dreadful condition to require such "heroic treatment," but things are in a very dreadful condition, and if men will not amend them out of love of justice and right and purity, I do not see any other way than that they must be forced to do it out of a selfish regard to their own household comfort. Let my people go, that they may serve me, was the word of the Lord to Pharaoh, but Pharaoh hardened his heart and would not let the people go. Not until there was no longer in Egypt a house in which there was not one dead did the required emancipation come. Then with a great cry of horror and dread were the children of Israel sent out as the Lord their God commanded. Let my people go, that they may serve me, seems the Lord to have been saying these many years to the taskmasters of America; but who is the Lord, the taskmasters have cried, that we should obey his voice to let Israel go? We know not the Lord, neither will we let Israel go. Now on summer fields red with blood, through the terrible voice of the cannonade bearing its summons of death, we are learning in anguish and tears who is the Lord; and if men choose not to do justly and love mercy and walk softly with women, it is according to analogy that women shall become to them the scourge of God. The very charities, the tendernesses, the blessing and beneficent qualities against which they have sinned shall become thongs to lash and scorpions to sting,— and all the people shall say amen!

I am so far from being surprised when women occasionally run away from their husbands, that I rather marvel that there is not a hegira of women; that our streets and lanes are not choked up with fugitives. I do not believe in women's leaving their husbands to live with other men; it is infamy and it is folly: but I do believe most profoundly in women's leaving their husbands. It may be their right and their duty. I think there is not the smallest danger in the state's putting all possible power of this nature into the hands of women; because a woman's nature is such that she will never exercise this power till she has borne to the utmost, cruelty, malignity, or indifference; and, in point of morality, indifference is just as good ground for separation as cruelty. Love is the sole morality of marriage, and a marriage to which love has never come, or from which it has departed, is immorality, and a woman cannot continue in it without continually incurring stain. I do not think she has a right to marry again; not even a legal divorce justifies a second marriage; but she has a right to withdraw from the man who imbrutes her. If the law does not justify such action, she is right in taking the matter into her own hands. There is no power on earth that can make a woman live with a man, if she chooses not to live with him, and has a will strong enough to bear out her choice; and when she finds that she ministers only to his selfishness, when she discovers that her marriage is no marriage at all, but an alliance offensive to all delicacy and opposed to all improvement, she is not only justified in discontinuing it, but she is not justified in continuing it. The position which a woman occupies in such a connection is fairer in the eyes of the law, but morally it is no less objectionable than if the marriage ceremony had never taken place. A prayer and a promise cannot turn pollution into purity.

Is this a movement towards violating the sanctity of marriage? It is rather causing that marriage shall not with its sanctity protect sin. When a slaver, freighted with wretchedness, unfurls from its masthead the Stars and Stripes, that it may avoid capture, does it thereby free itself from guilt, or does it desecrate our flag? Who honors his country, he who permits the slave-ship to go on her horrible way protected by the sacred name she has dared to invoke, or he who scorns to suffer those folds to sanction crime, tears down the flag from its disgracing eminence, unlooses the bands of the oppressor and bids the oppressed go free?

But are there not inconstant, weak women, who would take advantage of such power, and for any fancied slight or foolish whim desert a good home and a good husband? Well, what then? If a silly woman will of her own motion go away and live by herself, I think she pursues a wise course and deserves well of the Republic. I do not believe her good husband will complain. On the contrary, he would doubtless adopt a part at least of the Napoleonic principle, and build a bridge of gold for his fleeing spouse. Such power will never make silly women, though it may possibly render them more conspicuous, and that will be a benefit. The more vividly a wrong is seen and felt, the more likely is it to be removed. The remedy for the mischief which Lord Burleigh's she-fool may do is, not to bind her to your hearth, but to keep her away from it altogether; and better than a remedy, the preventive is, so to treat women that they shall not be fools. If the ways of male transgressors against women can be made so hard that they shall, in very self-defence, set to and mend them—Heaven be praised!

But what of the Bible? Is not the permanency of the marriage connection inculcated there? No more than I inculcate it. I certainly do not see it enforced in any such manner as to weaken my position. Its permanency is assumed rather than enjoined; but a basis of essential oneness is also assumed, which is the sufficient, the true, and the only true and sufficient basis. "Therefore," says Adam, "shall a man leave his father and his mother, and shall cleave unto his wife: and they shall be one flesh." But if, instead of cleaving to his wife, a man cleaves away from his wife, and instead of being one flesh, the twain become twain,—I do not see that Adam has anything to say on the subject. I suppose Eve looked so lovely to him, and he was so delighted to have her, that it never occurred to him to make any provision against the contingency of his abusing her. I have not made any especial research, but I do not remember anything in the precepts or examples of the Bible that enjoins the continuance of association

218

in spite of everything. In principle it is presumed to be perpetual, but in practice the Bible makes certain exceptions to perpetuity,—lays down rules indeed for separation. "What God hath joined together let not man put asunder," says our Saviour, which surely does not mean that what greed or lust or ambition has joined together woman may not put asunder. When a young man and a maiden, drawn towards each other by their God-given instincts, have become one by love, no mere outside incompatibility of wealth or rank, or any such thing, should forbid them to become one by marriage. For what God hath joined together let not man put asunder. But the God who would not permit an ox and an ass to be yoked together to the same plough, never, surely, joined in holy wedlock a brute and an angel; and if the angel struggles to escape from the unequal yoke-fellow to whom the powers of evil have coupled her, who dare thrust her back under the yoke with a "Thus saith the Lord"? Christ himself does not pronounce against the putting away of wife or husband, but against the putting away of one and marrying another. St. Paul's words regarding the Christian and the idolater can hardly be applied in our society, but so far as they can be applied they confirm my views. "Let not the wife depart from her husband," he says, and immediately adds, "*but and if she depart, let her remain unmarried*, or be reconciled to her husband." Precisely. For no trivial cause should the wife give her husband over to be the prey of his own wicked passions; but if he is so bad, if he so degrades her life that she must depart, let her remain unmarried.

It may be said that the interests of children would be compromised by this mode of procedure. But the interests of children are already fatally compromised. The interests of children are never at variance with those of their parents. If it is for the interest of the mother to leave her husband, it is not for the interest of her children that she should stay with him. Whatever mortification or disgrace might come to a few children would not be the greatest harm that could happen to them, and in the end all children would be the gainers.

"I hold that man the worst of public foes

Who, either for his own or children's sake,

To save his blood from scandal, lets the wife

Whom he knows false abide and rule the house."

True. For "man" put "woman," and for "wife" "husband," and it will be no less true. Of one thing be sure. The interests of children need not block the wheels of legislation. The mother will take them into as earnest consideration as any assembly of men. If they are not safe in her hands, they will not be safe in any hands.

Furthermore notice, the chief stress of Scriptural prohibition is laid on men. The rules and restraints are for men. Very little injunction is given to women. The Inspirer of the Bible knew the souls which he had made, and for the hardness of men's hearts hedged them about with restrictions, and for the softness of women's hearts left them chiefly to their own sweet will. The great Creator knew that women would never be largely addicted to leaving their husbands for trifling causes, nor indeed are serious causes often sufficient to produce such results. The rack and wheel and thumb-screw of married life are generally less powerful than the patience of the wifely heart. But his Maker knew, too, the inconstant nature of man, and bound him with the strictest charges. I am entirely willing to abide by the Bible. Let the state abide by it too, and give to women the legal power to save themselves. There is no danger that they will abuse it. They will even use it only to correct the most fatal abuse.

But what, then, becomes of the marriage vows? Shall all their solemnity vanish as a thread of tow when it toucheth the fire? No; but I would have the marriage vows themselves vanish. They are heathenish. They are a relic of barbarism. I have never studied into their origin, but there is internal evidence that women had neither part nor lot in framing them. The whole matter is one of those masculinities with which society has been saddled for generations,—one of the bungling makeshifts to which men resort when they are left to themselves, and have but a vague notion of what it is that they want, and no notion at all of how they are to get it. Look at it a moment. Here is the whole world lying before man, waiting for him to enter in and take possession. Woman desires nothing so much as that he should be monarch of all he surveys. She acknowledges him to be in his own right, she implores him to be by his own act, king. The greatest blessing that can fall upon her is his coronation. It is only when the king is come to his own that woman can enter into her lawful inheritance. So long as he keeps his crown in abeyance, so long as he tramples his prerogatives under foot, she too misses the purple and the throne. What does he do? Instead of wearing his dignities, and discharging his duties, he goes clad in rags, he dwells with beggars, he deals in baubles, and depends for allegiance upon a word! With all his power depending solely upon himself, with love and life awaiting only his worthiness, with a devotion that knows no measure standing ready and eager to bless him, all the dew of youth, all the faith of innocence, all the boundless trust of tenderness, all the grace and charm and resource of an infinitely daring and enduring affection,—he turns away from it all and claims the coarseness of a promise! He does not see the invincible strength of that subtile, impalpable bond which God has ordained, but trusts his fate to a clumsy yet flimsy cord which himself has woven, which his eyes can see and his hands handle, and in which therefore he can believe, no matter though it parts at the first strain.

Does it? Did a person ever change his course out of respect to his marriage vows? I do not mean his marriage or the marriage ceremony, but simply the promises: to love, honor, and cherish on the one side; to love, honor, and obey on the other. Did a man's promise ever fetter his tongue from uttering the harsh word? Did a woman's promise ever induce her to heed her husband's wishes? I trow not. The honor and love which a husband or wife do not spontaneously render, they will seldom render for a vow. If the vital spark of heavenly flame remains, the promise is of no use. If it is gone out, the promise is of no power. A solemn declaration of facts, a solemn assertion, calling upon God and man for witness, would, it seems to me, be equally efficient, and much more moral, than the present form of promise. Power over the future is not given to any of us, but we can all bear witness of the present. The history of this war goes to show that oaths of any sort are of but little use,—mere wisps of straw when the current sets against them,—and that Christ meant what he said when he said, "Swear not at all." But, however the case may stand regarding facts, there can be but one opinion regarding feelings. To swear to preserve an emotion or an affection is to assume a burden

222

which neither our fathers nor we are able to bear. And to take an oath which one has no power to keep, has a tendency to weaken in men's minds the obligation of oaths. If there must be swearing, we should act on Paley's hint, and promise to love as long as possible, and then to make the best of the bargain.

That part of the marriage contract which relates to obedience deserves a separate attention. What is meant by a wife's obedience? Shall an adult person of ordinary intelligence forego the use of her own judgment and adopt the conclusions of another person's? Is that what is meant?

To the law and to the testimony again. In the beginning nothing is said of obedience or lordship. There is no subordination of man to woman or woman to man. They are simply one flesh. God created man in his own image; male and female created he them. And God blessed *them*, and said unto *them*, have dominion, &c. Eve was to have dominion precisely like Adam, so far as we can see. But in the fall she forfeited it, and the curse came: "Thy desire shall be to thy husband, and he shall rule over thee." When the king was shorn of his power, the queen was dethroned. That settles the question, does it not? Not at all. God so loved the world, that, when the fulness of the time was come, he sent forth his Son, made of a woman, made under the law, to redeem them that were under the law. Christ hath redeemed us from the curse of the law, being made a curse for us. So then, brethren, we are not children of bondwomen, but of free women!

If you do not believe the Bible, the curse is of no account. If you do believe the Bible, the curse is taken away. Now then where are you?

But St. Paul is brought in here with great effect by the defenders of the old *régime*. St. Paul, living under the new dispensation, became its exponent, reduced it to a system, and must be considered authority regarding its meaning and design. The curse had been as completely taken away then as now, yet he says: "Wives, submit yourselves unto your own husbands, as unto the Lord. For the husband is the head of the wife, even as Christ is the head of the church.... Therefore as the church is subject unto Christ, so let the wives be to their own husbands in everything." Can anything be stronger or more explicit? Nothing. But if you take St. Paul, take the whole of him. Accepting for wives the injunction of submission, accept it also for yourselves; for in the preceding verses he says, "Be filled with the spirit, *submitting yourselves one to another* in the fear of God." The same word is used to indicate the relations proper between husband and wife and between friend and friend. If, then, according to St. Paul, the wife must absolutely obey her husband, her husband must just as absolutely obey his wife, and both must obey their next-door neighbor.

Observe also the manner of the control and the submission,—"as unto the Lord." The husband is the head of the wife, even as Christ is the head of the church. The wife is to be subject to the husband, as the church is subject to Christ. Why, this is just what I want. Not a wife in Christendom but would rejoice to recognize her husband to be her head as Christ is the head of the church. Only let husbands follow their model, and there would be no more question of obedience. Quote St. Paul against me? St. Paul is my standard-bearer! If you had only obeyed St. Paul, I should not be fighting at all. The world would go on so smoothly and lovingly that I should never be required to stir up its impure mind by way of remembrance, but should be occupied in writing the loveliest little idyls that ever were thought of. It is the flagrant disregard and violation of Paul's teachings that brings me unto you with a rod instead of in love and the spirit of meekness. I want no higher standard than was set up by Paul.

Men reason very well so long as they confine their reasoning to pure mathematics, but when they attempt to apply their logic to practical life, they are at fault. They find it difficult to make allowance for friction. They do not observe, and they do not know what to do with their observations when they have made them. Consequently, though their arguments look very well, they do not stand the test of experiment. Nothing can be more charming than this implicit trust which men so love and laud, this unhesitating submission of the fond wife,—the "God is thy law, thou mine" of Milton (which most men evidently believe is to be found in all the Four Gospels and most of the Epistles). Yet its only practical justification would be the infallibility of men. But in actual life men are not infallible. They are just as likely to be wrong as women. The only obedience practicable or desirable is the adoption of the wisest course after consultation. Practically, there is seldom much trouble about this matter; but there is none the less for all the theories and all the vows of obedience. Yet we have it from good authority, that it is better not to vow than to vow and not pay.

When I see the strenuousness with which man has ever enjoined upon woman respect for his position and submission to his will, the persistence with which he has maintained his superiority and her subordination, the compensatory and unreasonable, inconsequent homage which he awards to those who acquiesce in his claims, I seem to be reading a new version of an old story. Man takes woman up into an exceeding high mountain, and shows her what seems to her dazzled eyes all the kingdoms of the world, and the glory of them, and says unto her, "All these things will I give thee, if thou wilt fall down and worship me." But as it was in the beginning, is now, and ever shall be,—"Thou shalt worship the Lord thy God, and him only shalt thou serve." For many generations the world has reaped a bitter harvest from worshipping and serving the creature more than the Creator. Eve's desire was to the man, and he ruled over her consequently, and she brought forth a murderer. The virgin-mother rejoiced primarily in God, and that Holy Thing which was born of her was called the Son of God. For six thousand years the works of the flesh have been manifest, which are these: adultery, fornication, uncleanness, lasciviousness, idolatry, witchcraft, hatred, variance, emulations, wrath, strife, seditions, heresies, envyings, murders, drunkenness, revellings, and such like. But the fruit of the Spirit is love, joy, peace, long-suffering, gentleness, goodness, faith, meekness, temperance.

When women begin to talk of right, men begin to talk of courtesy. They are very willing that women should be angels, but they are not willing that they should be naturally-developed women. They like to pay compliments, but they like not to award dues. One great article of their belief is, that

"A woman ripens like a peach,

In the cheeks chiefly,"

and the rod perpetually held over any deeper ripening is the not always unspoken threat of a forfeiture of masculine deference. From those who want what they have not shall be taken away that which they have. Very well, take it away. No thoughtful woman desires any homage that can be given or withheld at pleasure. The only reverence, the only respect, which has any value, is that which springs from the depths of the heart spontaneously. If the politeness which men show to women, and for which American men are famous, does not spring from their own sense of fitness, if it is a kind of barter, a reward of merit, let us dispense with it altogether. Sometimes I almost fear that it is so. Sometimes I am half inclined to believe that men are kind and courteous chiefly to those who are independent of them. In a railroad-car, not long since, I saw a woman, hard-featured, coarse-complexioned, ignorant, rude, and boisterous, engaged in an altercation with the conductor regarding her fare. The dozen men in the vicinity leaned forward or looked around with intent eyes, and—must I say, smiling? no—grinning faces, and saluted each fresh outburst of violence with laughter. Could a true courtesy have found amusement, or anything but pain, in such an exhibition? The woman was most unwomanly, but she was a woman. That should be enough, on your principles. She was a human being. That is enough, on mine.

In "Our Old Home," Hawthorne—O the late sorrow of that beloved name!—has most tenderly told the story of Delia Bacon. When her book was published, we are informed, "it fell with a dead thump at the feet of the public, and has never been picked up. A few persons turned over one or two of the leaves, as it lay there, and essayed to kick the volume deeper into the mud.... From the scholars and critics in her own country, indeed, Miss Bacon might have looked for a worthier appreciation." But, "If any American ever wrote a word in her behalf, Miss Bacon never knew it, nor did I. Our journalists at once republished some of the most brutal vituperations of the English press, thus pelting their poor countrywoman with stolen mud, without even waiting to know whether the ignominy was deserved. And they never have known it to this day, nor ever will."

Is this courtesy? Is this the lofty manhood which women are to bow down and worship? To such as these is it that women are to say, "What thou bid'st, unargued I obey"? Men may promise all the kingdoms of the earth and the glory of them, and women may make never so persistent efforts to bow down and enter into possession; but the worship will never be heartsome, nor the title ever secure. Never will the human mind, whether of man or woman, rest in that which is not excellent. So long as men are unworthy of fealty, they may forever grasp, but they cannot retain it. Their empire will be turbulent and their claim disputed. They will have a secure hold on woman's respect only so far as character commands it. Feudalism was better than barbarism, and the nineteenth is an advance on the fifteenth century. But the inmost germ of chivalry has not yet flowered into perfect blossom. By the restiveness of woman under the tutelage of man may he measure his own short-comings. It is not necessary that men should be renowned, but they should be great. Fame is a matter of gifts, but character is always at command. Not every man can be a philosopher, poet, or president, but every man can be gentle, reverent, unselfish, upright, magnanimous, pure. In field and wood and prairie, standing behind the counter, bending over lapstone or anvil, day-book, ledger, or graver, a man may fashion himself on the true heroic model, and so

"Move onward, leading up the golden
year;

For unto him who works, and feels he
works,

The same grand year is ever at the doors."

In that grand year courtesy shall be recognized as the growth of the soul and not of circumstance. A man shall bear himself towards a woman, not according to what she is, but to what himself is. He shall dispense the kindnesses of travel, assembly, and all manner of association, not only to the good and the gentle, but also to the froward; and he will do it, not because he thinks it best or right, but because he cannot do otherwise, without working inward violence upon himself. If a woman show herself rude or unthinking, or if in any way she transgresses the laws of taste, propriety, or morality, he shall not, therefore, consider himself at liberty to utter coarse jests or coarse rebuke, to cast free looks, or disport himself with laughter. It shall not be possible for him to do so; but he shall rather feel in his own heart the thrill and in his own blood the tingle of degradation, and gravely and sadly will he

"Pay the reverence of old days

To her dead fame;

Walk backward with averted gaze,

And hide the shame."

Nor shall his deference be confined to woman, but man to man shall do that which is seemly. For all poverty, loneliness, helplessness, repulsiveness, and every form of weakness and misfortune, especially for those worst misfortunes that come from one's own imprudence or misdoing, he shall have sympathy and help. Then, indeed, "shall all men's good be each man's rule." Then between man and woman shall be no mine and thine, but Maud Muller's dream shall be fulfilled, and joy is duty and love is law.

Much of our classification of qualities into masculine and feminine, all assignment of superiority or inferiority to one or other of the sexes, seems to me to be founded on a false conception.[5] No virtue, scarcely a quality, is the prerogative of man or woman, but manly and womanly together make the perfect being. A man who has not in his soul the essence of womanhood, is an unmanly man. A woman who has not the essence of manhood, is an unwomanly woman. It is woman in man,— gentleness, guilelessness, truth, permeating strength and valor, that gives to man his charm: it is man in woman,—courage, firmness, fibre, underlying grace and beauty, that give to woman her fascination. A brutal man, a weak woman, is as fatally defective as a coward or an Amazon. God made man in his own image; God made man male and female. God, then, is in himself type of both male and female, and only in proportion as all men are womanly and all women manly, does each become susceptible of the love and worthy of the respect of the other. Neither is the man superior to the woman, nor the woman to the man, but they twain are one flesh.

XIV.

OUBTLESS there are many men who will say: To what purpose is all this? What new development has arisen to necessitate a new outcry? The world is getting on very well. People marry and are given in marriage; buy, sell, and get gain. There is a good deal of wickedness and suffering, but less of both than formerly, and both are evidently diminishing. Earth is not heaven, and in the world we shall always have tribulation, men and women both, but neither men nor women make any particular complaint, and on the whole it may reasonably be inferred that they are getting on comfortably. Pray let well enough alone.

But your well enough cannot be let alone, because it is not well enough. Nothing is well enough so long as it can be bettered. The world is not getting on comfortably, however comfortable you may be. Mounted in your car of Juggernaut, you may find the prospect pleasing, the motion exhilarating, and the journey agreeable, but your *Io triumphe* has but a discordant twang to those whom you are so pleasantly crushing under your chariot-wheels. Your vision is not trustworthy. Through I know not what process a judicial blindness seems to come upon people, so that those ways seem good whose end is death. True, the world is advancing, but with a motion which, compared with that which it might attain, is retrogression. Whose fiat has decreed, "Thus fast shalt thou go, and no faster"? Why is it that we only creep, when we might run and not be weary, might mount up with wings as eagles? Why do we dwell, with toil and tears, in the Valley of the Shadow of Death, when the voice from heaven centuries ago bade us come up higher? We have for our inheritance the elements of all things good and great and to be desired; but we lack the clear vision and the cunning hand to construct from them the Paradise that every family might be, in spite of the sin that despoiled the first; so we continue to dwell without Paradise, and very far off. Men and women are at variance with themselves and with one another. Power and passion run to waste. Positions are inverted, relations confused, and light obscured. The sanctuary of the Lord is built up with untempered mortar, and jewels of gold are degraded to a swine's snout.

Underneath all wars and convulsions, underneath all forms of government and all social institutions, it seems to me that the relations between man and woman are the granite formation upon which the whole world rests. Society will be elevated only just so fast and so far as these relations become what God intended them to be. Monarchies, republics, democracies, may have their benefits and their partisans, but the family is the foundation of country. I said "it seems to me" so. I have been charged with being sometimes too positive in my opinions. It may have been a youthful fault, but I long since corrected it. I should now suggest rather than affirm the equality between the angles of a triangle and two right angles. I am open to conviction on the subject of the multiplication-table; but on this point my feet are fixed, and, as my Puritan ancestors were wont to

sing, somewhat nasally perhaps, but with hand on
sword,—

"Let mountains from their seats be hurled

Down to the deep, and buried there,

Convulsions shake the solid world,

My faith shall never yield to fear."

All other influences are fitful and fragmentary: the
home influence alone is steady and sufficient, and
the home influence depends upon the relations
between father and mother. Unless there is on both
sides respect first, and then love, such love as brings
an all-embracing sympathy, and so an outer and
inner harmony,—harmony between life and its laws
and harmony between heart and heart,—the child's
head will be pillowed upon discord, his cradle will
be rocked by restlessness, and his character can
hardly fail to be unsymmetrical. We have all seen the
wickedness of man, that it is great in the earth; but
why should it not be, when he is conceived in sin
and shapen in iniquity; when his plastic soul is
moulded amid jarring elements, and the voices that
fall upon his infant ear—voices that should be
modulated only to tenderness and love, and all the
sweet and endearing qualities—are sharpened by
coldness, embittered by disappointment, shrill
through unremitting toil and rough with sordid
ambitions? I only wonder that children bred up in
such uncongenial homes come to be so much men
and women as they are. No outbreak of treachery or
turpitude astonishes me, when I remember the
discordant circumstances into the midst of which the
baby-soul was born. The only astonishment is, that
every soul tends so strongly towards its original type
as to have even an outer seeming of virtue. I wonder
that, when the twig is so ruthlessly and persistently

bent, the tree should reach up ever so crookedly towards heaven. Kind Nature takes her poor warped little ones, and with gentle, imperceptible hand touches them to a grace and softness which we have no right to expect, but to never that divine grace, that ineffable sweetness, of which the human soul is capable, and to which in its highest moods it ever yearns. O, if this one truth could be imprinted upon this age,—the one truth that the regeneration of the world is to come through love,—what hope could one not see for the future! God so loved the world that he gave his only begotten Son, and henceforth there is no more offering for sin. It only remains for us to enter into the holiest by this new and living way which he hath consecrated for us. The offering of Divine love is complete. Let human love come in to do its part, and the human soul shall be sanctified from its birth. When clamor and wrath and evil-speaking and evil-feeling are banished from the household hearth, murder and plunder and lust will fly from the public ways. When the child is the child of mutual love and trust and reverence and wisdom, he will never belie his parentage.

We give to the dead their honors,—meet homage for the dust that shrined a soul. All passion is hushed, all pettiness vanishes in the presence of the dread mystery. But there is a mystery more dread, a mystery to which death is but as the sunshine for clearness,—the only sunshine which lights up its hidden labyrinths. It is the inexplicable secret of life. Fear not before the power which kills the body, but is not able to kill the soul. Stand in awe before that Power which can evoke both soul and body from nothingness into everlasting life. Death does but mark the accomplishment of one stage in a journey, with whose inception we had nothing to do. It is but a necessary change of carriage at some relay-house, —an involuntary and inevitable event in which we are but interested spectators or passive participants. But whether the Spirit shall set out on its journey at all, and what shall be the manner of its going, what its sustenance by the way, and what the light upon its path,—these are matters for concern; for these involve the weightiest responsibilities which man can bear. To fashion an infinite soul and send it forth upon an infinite career,—infinite susceptibilities laid open to the touch of infinite sorrow,—oh! to him who has ever faced the facts of being,—not death, not death, but this irrevocable gift of life, is the one solemnity, the awful sacrament!

You will say that you believe all this now, but you do not believe it. You agree to it in a certain sentimental Pickwickian sense, but you do not hold it as a living truth. You will assent to all that is said of the importance of the family, and then go straightway and give your chief time, thought, ingenuity, to your farms and your merchandise. What men really believe in is making money, not making true men and women. They believe that the greatness of a nation consists in its much land and gold and machinery and ability to browbeat another nation, not in the incorruptibility of its citizens. Wealth and fame, purple and fine linen and sumptuous fare, brute force of intellect, position, and power, one or another or all forms of self-indulgence,—these, not purity, love, content, aspiration, and hearty good-will, they take to constitute blessedness. What a man gives his life to, what he will attend to with his own eyes and mind, and will not trust to any other person, that he believes in. Any amount of fulsome adulation may be poured out upon the womanly in nature, but one particle of true reverence, one single award of rightful freedom, is worth it all. Surely, if you could but see how the land is as the garden of Eden before you, and around you a desolate wilderness, you would suffer yourselves to be charmed into its ways of pleasantness and its paths of peace. You do not know the beautiful capacities which this earth, this very sin-stained, death-struck earth, bears in its redeemed bosom. Where sin abounds to sorrow, grace may much more abound to peace. Through the wonder of the Divine redemption there is possible for us a new heaven and a new earth, wherein righteousness shall dwell, and always and everywhere righteousness and peace kiss each other. You sing the praises of woman, but you do not begin to dream of the loveliness, the blessedness, the beneficence of which she is capable. You extol her in song and story, but with your life you will not suffer women to be womanly. You are so evil, and you decree so much evil, that, alas! a woman wakes to conscious life, and is not free to follow the bent of her nature; she must expend all her energies in clearing a breathing-space. O, you do a fearful wrong in this, and you endure a fearful wrong. For do you think the work is for woman alone? Do you think there is any such thing as a "woman question" that is not also a man question? Do you not know, that

"Laws of changeless justice bind

　Oppressor with oppressed,

And, close as sin and suffering joined,

　We march to fate abreast"?

The first shock of penalty for transgression falls upon woman, but sure and swift as the lightning it passes on to man. Every measure that keeps woman down keeps man down. Every jot taken from woman's joy is so much taken from man. All his wrong-thinking and wrong-doing that bears so heavily upon her bears down upon himself with equal weight. Action and reaction are not only inevitable, but constant. Every small or great improvement in woman's condition elevates society, and society is only men and women. If men persist in alternate or in combined scorn and flattery, and will not do justly, the sorrow as well as the shame is theirs, and both are instantaneous.

We are told of the Persian bird Juftak, which has only one wing. On the wingless side the male has a hook and the female a ring, and when fastened together, and only when fastened together, can they fly. The human race is that Persian, bird, the Juftak. When man and woman unite, they may soar skyward, scorners of the ground, but so long as man refuses God's help proffered in woman, he and she must alike grub on the earth. If he will have her minister only to the wants of his lower nature, his higher nature as well as hers shall be forever pinioned.

You may possibly suspect that I have sometimes insinuated a greater moral obliquity on the part of man than on that of woman; and, indeed, I believe you are right. But the greater obliquity which I attribute to him is the result of his training, not an attribute of his nature. I once held the contrary opinion, but it is not tenable. Man is made in the image of God, and one part of God cannot be better than another. If men were not capable of being nobler than their ordinary life exhibits them, I should think this war an especial providence of God in other respects than are usually mentioned. But look at the developments which this very war has made. Is fortitude in pain, as many have asserted, a womanly attribute? But what fortitude under pain has been shown by our soldiers on the battle-field and in hospital! Torn with ghastly wounds, tortured with thirst, weak from loss of blood and lack of food, untended and unconsoled; or wasting away in the crowded hospital week after week and month after month, longing for home while dying for country; or scarred, maimed, and disabled for life; yet uttering no word of complaint, breathing no murmur of impatience, making a sport of pain, grateful for every word and touch and look and thought of tenderness, when a nation's tenderness is their just due, and glad all through that they have been able to fight for the beloved land,—is fortitude indeed only a womanly virtue? Or is it that gentleness and self-sacrifice are pure womanly, as is so often maintained? Look through the same battle-fields and hospitals; see men waiting upon men with the indescribable gentleness of compassion and pure sympathy; see them risking life to save a wounded comrade; see them passing day and night from cot to cot, to bathe the fevered brow, to moisten the parched lip, to soothe the restless mind, to receive the last message of love, and speed the parting soul. See the wounded man bidding the surgeon pass him by to heal the sorer hurts of his neighbor, or putting the canteen from his own lips to the paler lips beside him, till you shall take every soldier to be a Sidney. Rough men they may be or polished, rudely or delicately nurtured, trained to every accomplishment or only born into the world, but everywhere you shall look on such high heroic gentleness and thoughtfulness and patience and self-abnegation as make the courage of onset seem in comparison but a low, brute virtue. O blood-red blossoms of war, with your heart of fire, deeper than glow and crimson you unfold the white lilies of Christ!

Who shall show us any good that cannot be predicated of the nature which, stunted and twisted from the beginning, can yet bring forth such heavenly fruit? If God can work in man so to will and to do, is it for woman to stand aside and say, "I am holier than thou"?

But though the exigencies of war make more obvious the fine possibilities of men, it does not need a continent in deadly strife to indicate their existence. There are sacred hours in every life when that which is of the earth is held in abeyance and celestial influences reign. No man, perhaps, has ever lived who has not had his better moments,— moments when the spirit of God moved upon the turbid waters of his soul and brought light out of darkness and beauty from chaos: silent moments it may be, and solitary, or hallowed with a companionship dearer even than solitude; moments when helplessness, loveliness, innocence, or suffering thrilled him to the depths with pity and tenderness, with indignation or with adoration. Have you never seen the sweetest ties existing between father and daughter, or brother and younger sister, when the wife has been removed by death, or, through some fatal fault, is no mother to her child? What love, what devotion, what watchful care, what sympathy, what strength of attachment! The little unmothered daughter calls out all the motherhood in the great, brawny man, and they walk hand in hand, blest with a great content. "'Tis the old sweet mythos,"—the infant nourished at the father's breast.

· Every-day occurrences reveal in men traits of disinterestedness, consideration, all Christian virtues and graces. My heart misgives me when I think of it all,—their loving-kindness, their forbearance, their unstinted service, their integrity; and of the not sufficiently unfrequent instances in which women, by fretfulness, folly, or selfishness, irritate and alienate the noble heart which they ought to prize above rubies. I have not hitherto made a single irrelevant remark, and I will therefore indulge in the luxury of one now. It is this: Considering how few good husbands there are in the world, and how many good women there are who would have been to them a crown of glory and a royal diadem, had the coronation but been effected, but who, instead, are losing all their pure gems down the dark, unfathomed caves of some bad man's heart,— considering this, I account that woman to whom has been allotted a good husband, and who can do no better than spoil him and his happiness by her own misbehavior, guilty, if not of the unpardonable sin, at least of the unpardonable stupidity. If it were relevant, I could easily make out a long list of charges against women, and of excellences to be set down to the credit of men. But women have been stoned to death, or at least to coma, with charges already; and when you would extricate a wagon from a slough, you put your shoulder first and heaviest to the wheel that is deepest in the mud,—especially if the other wheel would hardly be in at all, unless this one had pulled it in! I can understand and have great consideration towards those men who, gentle, faithful, and true themselves, possibly disheartened by long companionship with a capricious, tyrannical woman, should fail to acquiesce with any heartiness in the truth of the views which I have advanced. Their experience is of long-suffering men and long-afflicting women, and they can hardly be expected to entertain with enthusiasm a statement which has perhaps no bearing upon their position. Still, when facts meet facts, the argument is always on the side of the heaviest battalions. It is the rule that generalizes, exceptions only modify.

There is another circumstance which makes strongly against any assertion of man's necessary moral inferiority to woman. The manly ideal is often one to which no woman takes exception. In poetry and romance, men, as well as women, paint heroes; and I hold that no one can project from his imagination a better character than he is himself capable of attaining. He can be all that he can portray. The stream through his pen can rise no higher than the fountain in his heart, and out of the heart are the issues of life which he may keep as pure and clear as poesy. It was no woman's hand which limned the grand, sad face of that "good king," who

"Was first of all the kings who drew

The knighthood-errant of this realm and all

The realms together under me, their Head,

In that fair order of my Table Round,

A glorious company, the flower of men,

To serve as model for the mighty world,

And be the fair beginning of a time.

I made them lay their hands in mine and swear

To reverence the King, as if he were

Their conscience, and their conscience as their King,

To break the heathen and uphold the Christ,

To ride abroad redressing human wrongs,

To speak no slander, no, nor listen to it,

To lead sweet lives in purest chastity,

To love one maiden only, cleave to her,

And worship her by years of noble deeds,

Until they won her; for indeed I knew

Of no more subtle master under heaven

Than is the maiden passion for a maid,

Not only to keep down the base in man,

But teach high thought, and amiable
words

And courtliness, and the desire of fame,

And love of truth, and all that makes a
man."

Another fact must also be allowed. Individual men are often better than their principles. Men who will, in cold blood, avow sentiments really atrocious, will, in the presence of a commanding female influence, straighten up to its requirements and carry themselves tolerably well; but with their lips they will all the while deny the power which their lives obey. Many a man who rails at strong-minded women, female education, and petticoat government, who professes to believe only in stocking-mending, love, and cookery, will be utterly, though unconsciously, plastic to the hand of a truly strong-minded, educated, and controlling woman. He does not know it; power in its highest action works ever imperceptibly. Nevertheless, it is there, and he follows it. His wrong opinions help to strengthen the citadel of evil, but himself is less bad than he seems. This ought to be remembered when inquisition is made.

It would be easy to multiply evidence, but it is not necessary. Enough has been produced to show that men have evinced the highest not only of those qualities which belong to their own sex, but those which are usually considered the prerogative of the other. And what men have done man may do. Life can be as lovely as its best moods. *In vino veritas,* said Roman philosophy, and builded better than it knew. In the wine of love is the truth of life. As pure, as thoughtful, as disinterested, as helpful, as manly as is the lover can the husband be. What the poet sings, that the man should live. A race that has attained a temporary exaltation can attain a permanent exaltation. If one man has bent to the stern decree of duty, knowing

"All

Life needs for life is possible to will,"

all men can compass self-control. I am filled with indignation when I see the low standard accepted for man's due measurement. Well may he exclaim, in sad, despairing reproach,—

"Men have burnt my house,

Maligned my motives,—but not one, I swear,

Has wronged my soul as this Aurora has,"

or this Romney or Sir Blaise, who forbids me access to the holy place, denies me power to lead a saintly life. Why, it is because men can be good that we reproach them. It is because we do see in them hints of dormant excellences that we consider it worth while to keep them in a state of agitation. If they must be as bad as their badnesses, there is only one verdict: He is joined to idols; let him alone. But, beloved, I am persuaded better things of you, and things that accompany salvation, though I thus speak. What has been is of no fatal import. What has been only shows the track of error; now we may follow the footsteps of truth. The old world is a world masculinized; a world of rugged, brawny, male muscularity, but slightly and partially softened by feminine touch. Man was satisfied that woman in the beginning should be taken out of him, and he has ever since been trying to grope his way alone,—with what success ages of blunder and blood bear terrible witness. Now, seeing that his *defeminization* has failed, let him compass the spiritual restoration of her who was physically separated from him, that the twain may become one perfect being, and reassume supreme dominion. The power lies ready to his hand. Eve was never wholly torn away. Deep within every heart lies the slumbering Princess still. A hundred years and many another hundred have gone by, and round her palace-wall, round her star-broidered coverlet, her gold-fringed pillow, and her jet-black hair, the hedge has woven its ivies and woodbine, thorns and mistletoes. Burr and brake and brier, close-matted, seem to refuse approach, and even to deny existence, but ever and anon above their surly barricade gleams in some evening sun the topmost palace spires, and we know that the fated Fairy Prince shall come, and, guided by the magic music in his heart, shall find that quiet chamber; reverently, on bended knee, shall touch the tranced lips, and— lo! thought and time are born again, and it is a new world which was the old.

Men, notwithstanding their high privilege, remain in their low estate,—partly because they are not enlightened out of it. They do evil, not knowing what they do. Like all despots, they have dealt more in adulation than in truth. They have heard from women the voice of flattery, the cry of entreaty, the wail of helpless pain, the impotent watchword of

244

insurrection; but they have had small opportunity to benefit by the careful analysis of character, the accurate delineation and just rebuke of faults, and the calm, judicious, affectionate counsel which comes from a wise and faithful friend—like me! Women may stand before them, sweet, trusting creatures, "just as high as their hearts," to be schooled into devotion and amiable submission. They may float demi-goddesses in some incomprehensible ether above the clouds, and receive incense and adoration. But for the ministering angel to turn into an accusing angel, for the lectured to rise and lay down the law to lecturers, is a thing which was never dreamt of in Horatio's philosophy.

> "A man
>
> May call a white-browed girl Dian,
>
> But likes not to be turned upon
>
> And nicknamed young Endymion."

Nor, indeed, is it any more grateful to Dian than to Endymion. To confront man on his throne with the stern, dispassionate charge, "Thou art inexcusable, O man, whosoever thou art, that judgest; for wherein thou judgest another, thou condemnest thyself; and thinkest thou this, O man, that thou shalt escape the judgment of God?" seems to woman so formidable a thing, that very few have had the courage to attempt it. Many are so overborne with toil, disappointment, and faintness, that they have no heart for it. It is easier to suffer than to attempt remedy. They feel, in the lowest depths of their consciousness,

> "What all their weeping will not let them say,
>
> And yet what women cannot say at all
>
> But weeping bitterly."

But they remain silent, and the case goes by default. There is, besides, a dread of personal consequences. Popular judgment is very much given to attributing general statements to private experience. If a woman is married, her adverse opinions are likely to be charged with implying conjugal discontent. If she is not married, they spring from failure and envy, and, shrinking from such opprobrium, the few women who see talk the matter over among themselves, and that is the end of it. There is also a natural reluctance to suggest that which men should do or be spontaneously, and there is a deeper reluctance, instinctive, indefinite, inexplicable.

The result is, that men go on in sin, seemingly unconscious that it is sin. They have been pursuing one course all their life, meeting obstacles, enduring fatigue, losing patience, but incapable of perceiving that they are in the wrong path until the fact is pointed out to them. They do not even understand the nomenclature of the science of right living. Speak of cherishing a departed friend, and they will descant on the absurdity of going about moaning and weeping all your days. They attach no meaning to life-long tenderness but life-long namby-pambyism, something excusable in youth and "courting," but savoring strongly of weakness of character after the honeymoon has waned. Put before them the general allegation of selfishness, indifference, cruelty, and they will deny it with vehemence. Of course. Without such denial they could have no excuse. Moral ignorance alone saves them from utter condemnation. If they sinned wittingly,—if they said, "Yes, I am cold and hard and hateful to my wife, neglectful of my children, I give grudgingly money barely sufficient for the necessities of life, or

I provide for my wife every luxury, but have no sympathy or companionship for her,"—if men said or could say this, even to themselves, they would be —not men, but demons. They are not demons, but men, capable of generosity, devotion, and self-sacrifice. If they knew that they were cruel, outrageous, intolerable in their most intimate relations, they would at once cease to be so, and begin to become everything that could be desired. More than this, I have so great faith in the noble possibilities of men, I believe they have so strong an inward bias towards holiness, that they will welcome the friendly hand which sets their iniquities before them. They will hear the sad story with amazement, and say one to another: "Who can understand his errors? A brutish man knoweth not; neither doth a fool understand this. We have sinned with our fathers, we have committed iniquity, we have done wickedly. So foolish was I and ignorant; I was as a beast. But now I will behave myself wisely in a perfect way. I will walk within my house with a perfect heart." And, when men shall have grown good, there will be no further complaint of women. To Lavater's list of impossible good women, Blake, the "mad painter," appends, "Let the men do their duty, and the women will be such wonders: the female life lives from the life of the male." There are exceptions, but in the mass women are not independent of received opinions, nor strong enough to front prejudice and mould society, or where they cannot mould it, to guide their own lives in its very spite. Therefore opinion needs to be right, prejudice removed, and society renovated; and men must do it. Women are generally said to make society. It is not so. Men make women, and men and women together make society. Men are the rocky stratum, women the soil which covers it. Men determine the outline, the level, the general character; women give the curves, the bloom, the grace. Rear your hills and lay your valleys, and the land shall speedily flow with milk and honey; but if you will upheave mountains and spread deserts, you may expect scant herbage on the one and but scattered oases on the other.

I cannot, of course, pronounce that it is absolutely impossible for woman to attain a truer life without man's co-operation. The Most High ruleth in the kingdom of men and giveth it to whomsoever he will. What revolution may await us in the future no one knows. Fired by what impulse woman may throw off the stupor which has enthralled her so long, array herself in her beautiful garments and mount upward to the heavenly heights, whose air alone her spirit pants to breathe, whose paths alone her feet are framed to tread, I do not know. Yet blessed as is that day, come when and how it will, I would it were ushered in by a peaceful dawn. Better that woman should take her place alone, moved by an ineffable disdain, than that she should remain forever in her low estate. Better still that man and woman should go together, he bringing his sturdy strength to shorten, she lending her manifold grace to lighten, the path that leads up thither; and both, following the still, small voice of love, shall find no roughness, shall feel no grief, shall fear no evil, but shall walk softly till the end come, and shall rest in the peace of the beloved.

L'ENVOI.

SWEET my friend, hastening with happy steps to your marriage-morn, O my poet, singing under your hawthorn-tree the song that never can grow old, am I then a bird of evil omen? Does it thunder towards the left as I pass by? Be not so credulous. I take no lustre from the golden-bright day that lies half-hidden under the mild haze of September: but I would that fair day's light should shine as the brightness of the firmament for ever and ever. I breathe no blight upon the hawthorn, no discord to the song; but I would the bloom of the one and the melody of the other might never die away. Dream, O maiden! your pleasant dreams; sing, O poet! your happy songs; but while the flush of the sunrise is yet ruddy on your brows, think it not strange that I leave your sweet light and go down to them who are sitting in the region and shadow of death.

Have *I* written this book? It is but the voice of a thousand aching hearts. Ten thousand dreary lives are wrought into its pages. It is the sorrow of just such hearts as yours, the disappointment of just such hopes, that have found a record here. The gloom that gathers on these leaves is gloom that hangs over paths just as fair as yours in their glad beginning. I feast my eyes on the beautiful temple of your promise, and I pray that you may go no more out of it forever; but I cannot forget that all my life I have

seen highway and byway strewn with the fragments
of temples which in their majesty of completeness
must have been just as marvellous as yours. And
being fully persuaded in my own mind that there is a
way whereby the wondrous edifice may be made as
enduring as it is brilliant, shall I not proclaim it
throughout all the land, unto all the inhabitants
thereof, that the trumpet of the jubilee may sound?
You shall not make the darkness your pavilion,
because the world is hung with gloom; but neither
shall you reckon it offence, if I cannot wholly rejoice
in your light for thinking of the great multitudes who
are sitting in a darkness which may be felt. To-day is
lost, but it is not too late for the morrow. Wasted life
can never be restored;—

"Though every summer green the plain,

This harvest cannot bloom again."

Only beyond the grave can a new life spring into
beauty, and the death of this be swallowed up in
victory. But for the lives that have not yet been
lavished, for the "poor little maidens" of great-
hearted Dr. Luther, for gentle Magdalenchen, fiery
young Lenore, merry Beatrice, skipping along their
separate paths, each to her unknown womanhood, or
walking already through its shadowy ways,—how
earnestly for them do we covet the best gift! But if
they fail of this, shall not one show them how to live
worthily without it? Shall not one bid them see how
poor and false and mean is everything which offers
itself instead; how sad were the exchange of an ideal
good for a base reality; how fatal the disaster when
the sacred torch pales before a grosser flame? So
through these summer days, my little maid, when all
sweet summer sounds but echo to you the music of
one low voice, add to the happy thought within your
heart this happiest thought of all: There shall come a

day when the same sky that bends in blessing above your head shall bend,—no cloud to darken, but only to adorn, no fogs to hide, but only mist-wreaths to deck its blue,—soft, serene, and beautiful, above an earth purified by the same love which makes to you all things pure. Through that new atmosphere, my poet, the tuneful voices of your song shall go, wakening all the woods to melody, summoning shy response from the ever-charmed hills, ringing out over the listening waters, giving and gathering sweetness wherever a human heart throbs; till earth, all a-quiver with the harmony, shall lift from the dust her long-neglected lyre, sweep once more to her place among the stars, and raise again her happy voice in the unforgotten music of the spheres.